THE
MIDWIFE'S DILEMMA

Books by Delia Parr

AT HOME IN TRINITY

The Midwife's Tale
The Midwife's Choice
The Midwife's Dilemma

HEARTS ALONG THE RIVER

Hearts Awakening
Love's First Bloom
Hidden Affections

CANDLEWOOD TRILOGY

A Hearth in Candlewood
Refining Emma
Where Love Dwells

THE MIDWIFE'S DILEMMA

DELIA PARR

BETHANYHOUSE
a division of Baker Publishing Group
Minneapolis, Minnesota

© 2016 by Mary Lechleidner

Published by Bethany House Publishers
11400 Hampshire Avenue South
Bloomington, Minnesota 55438
www.bethanyhouse.com

Bethany House Publishers is a division of
Baker Publishing Group, Grand Rapids, Michigan

Printed in the United States of America

ISBN 978-0-7642-1735-7

Library of Congress Control Number: 2015956728

This is a work of historical reconstruction; the appearances of certain historical figures are therefore inevitable. All other characters, however, are products of the author's imagination, and any resemblance to actual persons, living or dead, is coincidental.

Cover design by Dan Thornberg, Design Source Creative Services

Author is represented by Linda Kruger

16 17 18 19 20 21 22   7 6 5 4 3 2 1

*Dedicated to my children and their spouses
and most especially my seven grandchildren,
Caden, Ana, Camryn, Sofia, Crew, Jack, and Luke.*

You are all my everything.

Acknowledgments

As the AT HOME IN TRINITY trilogy comes to an end, there are many people I need to recognize and thank. Within my family, my sister Carol Beth, RN, has been by my side as cheerleader and editor from beginning to end. My children—Matt, Brett, and Liz—have inspired me and blessed me with seven precious grandchildren.

I am so very grateful to my three editors: Jennifer Enderlin (St. Martin's Press) and Sarah and David Long (Bethany House) who shared their vision and expertise with me so generously and so wisely. My agent, Linda Kruger, is a sister-in-faith who never let me doubt myself or give up when the going got tough. The team at Bethany House is unbelievably talented and committed to their authors. Bless you all!

And finally, with great humility, I thank my Creator and my God for the talent He has given to me and pray I have used it to bring all honor and glory to Him.

1

JUNE 1831

Barely after first light, duty called for midwife Martha Cade once again.

This time, however, she had left her birthing stool at home, along with her bag of simples filled with remedies to ease the suffering of the women and children who depended on her. She was not riding her faithful mount, Grace, either. Instead, she was afoot and making her way ever so slowly through the woods at the north end of town, carrying a covered basket.

She paused for just a moment to lift the lid on the woven basket and take a quick peek inside. Her tiny yellow warbler named Bird chirped the moment their eyes met. "We're almost at the clearing above the falls, where there's no one to notice us," she said, then quickly dropped the lid back into place before resuming their journey. Somehow she had never given the poor creature a proper name, but she was still determined to hold true to the promise she had made last fall to set Bird free once his broken wing had healed properly.

She just did not want anyone in Trinity to watch her.

With trees swaying gently on either side of her, she resumed a slow pace on the worn dirt path to keep from jostling the tiny bird overmuch. After a harsh winter, some of the trees were still wearing buds on their branches and struggling to catch up to summer, while stands of evergreens proudly displayed an ever-constant curtain of deep green. Spring violets were just blooming, adding a hint of color to a forest floor of pine needles and decaying leaves. Even the birds had arrived later than usual, giving Martha even more time to prepare Bird to return to where he belonged.

Her thoughts were as muddled as the forest that surrounded her, and she lifted the basket with both hands and clutched it against her chest as she walked. Life without Bird would certainly be less stressful, considering he escaped from his cage in her room at will, but she had grown attached to the mischievous little creature. He was good company, lifted her spirits with melodious song, and listened to her pour out her troubles to him when she had no one else, other than God.

Once the path ended in rocky, hard-packed earth at the base of a steep incline, she stopped and blinked back tears. Until two weeks ago, this is where she would have dismounted and tethered Grace. But the horse that had carried Martha so faithfully to those who needed her, regardless of the weather or the miles they had to travel, was gone now, claimed by an illness so suddenly that Martha hadn't had the opportunity to say good-bye.

Her chest tightened, and she closed her eyes as she took slow, measured breaths. Once fiercely independent, Martha now had to depend on fathers-to-be and husbands to fetch her to and from their homes to deliver a new babe or tend to their sick wives and children. She also had to walk everywhere in and around Trinity instead of riding, an added bonus to her constitution on days like today. After delivering Belinda French of a fine, healthy son just after midnight, Martha had arrived home at dawn. She'd headed right out with Bird because she feared if she stopped to rest, she might not get up until tomorrow.

She had no desire to waste any of the energy she did have on self-pity and again offered a silent prayer thanking God for the blessing that Grace had been. She also asked Him to consider blessing her with a new mount, particularly since she had no funds at her disposal to purchase one.

After taking a deep breath, she grabbed hold of the basket with one hand and lifted her skirts with the other. She was more than a bit winded by the time she climbed up the incline and stepped into the sun-drenched clearing just beyond the woods that provided a backdrop to Crying Falls and the town that lay below.

The clearing above the falls was ideal because it was so isolated and well away from townspeople's spying eyes—not an easy task in a town as small as Trinity. She'd claimed this place as her own oasis, a place where she could escape the confines of home and duty to help Bird gain enough strength to be able to fly away and survive on his own. The serenity of nature she found here also made it easier to open her heart and pray.

Soon she was surrounded by the pungent aroma of pine and the gentle scent of new flowers. Noting the comforting sound of the water rushing over rocks to cascade below, she set the basket down. Once she had Bird perched on her shoulder, she stepped just far enough into the clearing to get a good view of the town below. Unbidden tears blurred her vision.

She was tired to the bone, but she was heartsick and lonely, too. Distressed by a growing estrangement with her daughter,

11

Victoria, she also missed Fern and Ivy Lynn, sisters who had temporarily closed the confectionery where Martha now made her home with her daughter. With Thomas Dillon acting as their escort, the sisters had traveled east last January to settle a matter critical to maintaining the reputation they had earned as lifelong spinsters who were generous and loving to a fault.

Her heart skipped a beat just thinking about Thomas, but almost immediately it began to pound with worry for all of them. They were four months overdue in returning, and she had not heard from any of them since February.

Anxious to pray, she closed her eyes and steepled her hands together. She poured out her troubles before asking God to help her. "Please help me to use the gifts you have given me wisely and to answer my calling as a midwife without complaining about all the work I've been asked to do lately. Help me with Victoria, and watch over my friends and bring them all safely home to Trinity. Amen."

When Bird chirped, as if offering his own amen, Martha opened her eyes and chuckled. "I'm rather certain the good Lord heard your prayers, too," she teased, and then she walked directly to the copse of trees where Bird had first taken wing again just a few days ago after a long convalescence. "Ready?"

When she offered the bird her hand, he hopped onto her finger, where he sat for a few moments before he flew to the very same branch of the very same sapling they had been using for the past few weeks. He puffed out his chest and ruffled his feathers a bit before taking flight again, landing in a neighboring tree.

"Look at how far you fly!" she cried, even though he had not traveled more than a few feet. After several more efforts, which still kept him well within her reach, Bird returned to the very same branch where he had started and looked down at her. She smiled and waved her hand, silently encouraging him to continue to practice his flying, but he ignored her.

Concerned that he was apparently exhausted by the little flying he had done, she sighed and held out her hand to him. When Bird held very still, neither hopping onto her finger nor flying off, she smiled. "Having you fly off and live on your own again might seem terribly natural to both of us, but maybe you're not quite strong enough to be on your own quite yet. We can try again in a few days," she crooned.

He hopped right onto her finger, and she did not have to coax him back into the basket.

Both disappointed and relieved that Bird would be going back home to the confectionery with her, at least for a few more days, she checked the position of the sun. "Most folks will be out and about by the time we get back," she cautioned. "I'll let you know when it's time to be quiet again. Until then, I wouldn't mind a bit of a melody."

Bird, however, held silent and still, which only reaffirmed her suspicion that he had tuckered himself out and was not quite ready to leave her yet. She had only taken a few steps when a familiar flash of light from the top of one of the trees below made her blood simmer. Powered by indignation, she charged forward, holding the basket against her as she tore down the incline and through the patch of rocks. She managed to reach the base of a very tall tree just as Will dropped to the ground, but she was clearly out of breath, and Bird was squawking a protest.

Grinning, the boy flapped his arms. "'Look at how far you fly!'" he mimicked. "You sure are one silly lady."

She snatched the spyglass from his hand and scowled at the now nine-year-old boy her friend Samuel had adopted some months back. "And you're a terribly rude young man. Haven't

I warned you about spying on folks with this thing? And why aren't you in school?"

The rascal tried but failed to grab the spyglass back. "I weren't spyin'. I was practicin' using the spyglass, and you just popped right into my view. Besides, you ain't *folks*. You're . . . you're almost family."

Though her heartstrings tugged in response, she knew him well enough to see his flattery as nothing more than an attempt to distract her from being annoyed with him in hopes of escaping punishment. She slid the spyglass into her pocket, pleased that only a hint of the handle stuck out so he could not easily grab it back. "And what about school?" she asked, barely able to keep a smile at bay.

He grinned again. "Last day is tomorrow, but school don't start this early." He squinted at the sky overhead. "I'd say that it's nearin' seven thirty."

She reached into the other pocket in her gown to check the watch her grandmother had carried when responding to her duties as the very first midwife in Trinity, and Martha nodded when she saw that it was fifteen minutes before eight. "You're getting better. You're only off by a quarter hour. Does Samuel know you're out and about, snooping in the woods?"

"He's the one who sent me," Will insisted and brushed a lock of hair out of his eyes. "He said you'd probably be out with that dumb bird today and might need a bit of company walkin' back home if it finally flew away for good."

"So you *were* spying on me," she argued and pursed her lips. How Samuel knew what she had been up to was still a mystery, but she was moved by his concern for her. Completely blind and just as obstinate and independent, the retired seaman still argued that he could find his way through the woods surrounding the isolated cabin where he lived with Will, although she doubted he would ever be able to venture very far beyond that on his own.

Now that his old seafaring friend Fancy had joined the oddest and most reclusive household in the area as a caretaker and cook, however, she had the distinct feeling Samuel might be getting some help in venturing out.

Will studied her for a moment before he held out his hand. "I can walk you home. You look really sad. I think that's 'cause that bird of yours can't fly off, but Mr. Samuel says you're still missin' that dumb, ugly old horse of yours. I don't know why you'd be missin' it so much that you'd end up cryin', but Samuel says girls are like that."

"Like what?" she asked as she shifted the basket to the crook of her arm before grasping hold of his hand.

"Weepy and silly. But mostly, he says they're so unpredictable a man can't be sure of anything a girl might say or do."

She chuckled. The hero worship in the boy's eyes and the tone of his voice was unmistakable. And quite remarkable, considering Will had been a New York City orphan who had been lured west as one of Reverend Hampton's academy boys. The alleged minister had even fooled Martha before revealing himself as a fraud and the leader of a group of orphans he had trained at the so-called academy to steal for him from the folks in and around Trinity last year.

"Girls aren't nearly as hard to understand as Samuel suggests, if you take the time to really talk to them," she suggested. "What does Fancy have to say on the matter?" she prompted.

A voice coming from somewhere straight ahead replied, "I told the boy that girls are a complete and total mystery, but they're right sweet to look at."

Grinning, Fancy stepped into view from behind a tree and into a patch of sunlight. Gaudy jewels that studded the length of each of his ears sparkled in a rainbow of colors, and she noted that one of the jeweled earrings was missing since she had seen him last. Somewhere past sixty years of age, he was a good twenty years older than Martha, and his heavily lined face testified to the many sun-drenched years he had spent at sea.

He was a mere slip of a man, with the top of his head scarcely reaching Martha's shoulder, and since she was not an overly tall woman, Fancy could only be about five feet tall. She was also not quite as plump as she had been before Fern and Ivy had closed the confectionery and left, but she clearly outweighed Fancy, and her hair was still mostly brown, instead of completely gray like the few wisps remaining on his head.

He held up his hand as they approached. "Before you start yakkin', I wasn't spying on you. Samuel sent me to keep an eye on young William here," he offered. He noted the spyglass barely sticking out of her pocket and cocked his head.

Martha shrugged. "I'm keeping the spyglass for a spell."

Will groaned and dropped hold of her hand. "You're keepin' it? For how long?"

"Until you prove to me that you've done well in school this term and you can promise that you won't spy on me or any of the townspeople again. You're only to use that spyglass when you're out hunting with Mr. Fancy. Understood?"

He groaned again.

"Sounds fair to me," Fancy cautioned. "I don't think Samuel will argue with Widow Cade, either." When Will grumbled something under his breath, he cocked his ear. "What's that you said?"

"I-I said, 'Yes, ma'am. Er-er . . . yes, sir. It's fair enough."

"Good," Martha said, then stifled a yawn. "I don't have to rush back home. Let's head back to the cabin together, shall we? I've a mind to pay Samuel a quick visit and remind him how important it is for him to have someone with him when he ventures outside."

Fancy walked along beside them. "Maybe you should come for a visit later."

"Why? Is Samuel not feeling well?"

"He's out practicin' himself. Close to the lake," Will blurted as he tugged on her arm.

Fancy scowled.

Martha halted mid-stride. "He's out in the woods? By himself? Why in heaven's name did you let him—"

Fancy interrupted her with a rather loud snort. "You know he can't stay cooped up in that cabin forever, 'specially now that warm weather's finally here." He gestured for Martha to continue walking. "He's gettin' real good at followin' the trail we set up for him so he can get to the lake by hisself to do some fishin'. If he don't come back, I know right where to look for him."

Martha held her own counsel as they skirted a puddle of mud. Although Fancy seemed convinced that he was perfectly capable of watching over Samuel, she asked God to watch over him, too.

When they were back on a dry part of the path again, Fancy gave her a smile. "Would you want to come for supper tonight? I've been hankerin' to cook up some squirrel stew, assumin' this young man will help me catch and skin a few after school today."

"I'd really love to come, but I haven't seen my own bed since the night before last. I'm afraid once I do, I just might sleep straight through till morning, which is why I came straight here with Bird," she admitted.

"Come if you can. There'll be plenty," Fancy said as they reached the fork in the path where they would part ways.

"I'll try," she promised and started alone down the path that led through the woods to the cemetery on the eastern side of town. "Time to be quiet now," she cautioned, but Bird had not uttered a peep for a good long while and was probably asleep.

By the time she crossed through the cemetery, she was too tired and too hungry to pay any attention to the progress the builder was making on the new brick church. The last she had noticed, he had still been working on the foundation.

The thought of the cot waiting for her in her room in the newly renovated confectionery spurred her onward. She was also tempted by thoughts of the basket of food she had brought back with her from the groaning party, a feast she had shared with all the women who had stayed with Belinda during her labor and helped Martha during the birthing.

An even better thought prompted her to take the food and eat it in bed, lest she fall asleep at the table eating it. She paused for a moment to catch her breath and checked her watch again. It was nearly nine o'clock. At this hour, Victoria was probably still at Aunt Hilda's, where she usually slept whenever Martha was called away overnight while the Lynn sisters were gone.

Until they returned, Victoria's daily routine would not change whether Martha was home or not. She helped Aunt Hilda and her husband with their chores in the morning. After dinner, she spent her afternoons working a bit for Dr. McMillan in his office before spending a few hours writing her poems and stories in his study. In late afternoon, she would check on Aunt Hilda again.

All of which meant Victoria would not be there to witness Martha's utterly silly plan to have breakfast in bed and sleep away the day.

But Martha found she could not face eating a thing or finding a wink of rest until she took care of a difficult task she had been deliberately avoiding for the past two weeks.

18

2

With tears welling anew, Martha entered the stable behind Dr. McMillan's house, where she used to keep Grace. Rather than rush through her task, she took her time, hoping she might give Grace the final farewell she deserved.

She passed by the other two horses stabled there and kept one eye open for Leech, the nasty stable cat who preferred horses to humans, but he had disappeared the day Grace died. She could see no sign he had returned, but when she set the basket down, she made sure the lid was latched good and tight just in case he made an appearance and decided Bird would make a tasty meal.

With Bird properly settled, she gathered up the leather tackle she no longer needed for Grace. Confident that God would provide another horse for her, one way or another, she decided to place everything in the loft next to the saddle already stored there and prayed for the patience to wait.

With the reins looped over her shoulder to prevent her from tripping, she climbed up the ladder to the loft as best she could without stepping on her skirts. The heat in the loft was already growing unbearable, and she managed to plop down on the saddle before a band of grief tightened around her chest and her tears overflowed.

Unable to even choke out the mare's name, she clutched at the reins and dissolved into tears. She had never had the desire or the courage to think about continuing her work as a midwife without Grace. Now that she was gone, the reality of losing her was far worse than she'd imagined.

Her heart ached as one memory after another flashed through her mind's eye—those early first days when she and Grace butted heads; how Grace mastered her responsibility to carry the birthing stool, Martha's bag of simples, and a travel bag; the times they'd traveled nearly fifty miles, which meant staying away for weeks at a time; and finally, Grace as a mature mount, more loyal and trustworthy than most folks she knew, a confidant and a friend.

When her tears were spent, Martha was able to find her voice again. "A gift, that's what you were, Grace. A true gift sent by God to carry me safely to help all those women and children. I'll miss you forever," she whispered.

Anxious to get home, she was about to get to her feet when she heard a very familiar pair of voices coming from somewhere below.

She froze in place, unable to move a muscle.

Before she could even form the idea that she should make her presence known, she heard a giggle and a manly groan, followed by sounds that made her heart nearly stop.

Kissing. The young couple was kissing.

And this was not just any couple.

This was her daughter and Dr. McMillan.

And they were *kissing*!

Martha bolted upright, bumped her head on one of the rafters, and nearly lost her footing. Reeling from the shock, she grabbed hold of one of the support beams to keep from falling as disbelief surged through her body. She looked down, in the direction of the sounds she was hearing, and saw a flash of lavender skirts.

They were nearly right below her!

Obviously they had no idea she was up in the loft, which gave Martha a bittersweet advantage. When she caught a glimpse of the basket sitting in Grace's stall with Bird inside, her heart pounded against the wall of her chest. Praying that Bird would not burst into chatter and give away her presence, she gripped the beam so hard she could almost feel splinters getting ready to pierce her hand if she tightened her hold.

She paused for several thudding heartbeats to get steady enough on her feet to charge down the ladder and demand an explanation from her difficult eighteen-year-old daughter. Martha also needed to confront the young doctor, whom she'd been helping to understand that her remedies and methods were often more beneficial to the women and children she served than his more modern methods and packaged medicines.

Before she could do either, she heard him say words that anchored her feet to the ground and nearly made her heart stop.

"I don't understand why you won't let me talk to your mother to ask for her blessing so we can marry."

Victoria sighed. "She isn't even home. I've been spending most of my time at Aunt Hilda's lately because my mother is hardly *ever* home. And even when she is, she's so busy with her duties, she couldn't possibly have any notion that we've grown so fond of each other. I simply don't see why you're so intent on rushing the matter."

The sound of another kiss sent Martha's pulse racing and the fingers on her one hand curling into a fist.

"I want to marry you, Victoria, and I don't want to wait much longer," he said. "If there's anything I've learned from losing Claudine, it's that this life is far too short and uncertain to waste any of the time we could be spending together as husband and wife."

The rustling of Victoria's skirts made it sound as if she had leaned into his arms, no doubt moved by his reference to the death of his young wife. "I'd marry you tomorrow if I could, but you know my mother. She's bound to tradition. She needs time to adjust to change and new ideas."

"That may be true, but—"

"She's barely accepted the fact that some of her work as a midwife is being done by you or doctors like you. She's only recently begun to work with you instead of against you, and there's no telling how long that will last. If you can just wait a few weeks, I can try to prepare her for the idea that I'm ready to be married before I tell her that the man I want to marry is you."

As they began to walk away, their voices dipped to whispers that Martha could not hear. Her relationship with Victoria had never been easy, particularly since her daughter had shown no interest in becoming a midwife, dashing Martha's hopes that she might one day replace her. But she had been devastated last year when Victoria had run away with a visiting theater troupe. She had spent several unsuccessful months trying to find her daughter before returning home to Trinity, unaware that Victoria had found safe refuge with a prominent young couple in New York City, where she was able to pursue her natural talent for writing.

During the months that Victoria had been gone, Martha had relied on prayer to sustain her and her work to keep her busy.

She also used that time to reflect not on Victoria's faults, but on her many qualities, one of which was her honesty.

Despite how hurt she was now by Victoria's description of her, she had to admit that her daughter was not entirely wrong about some of what she had said. Martha's life had always been rooted in tradition, which made raising a more modern-thinking, independent daughter a challenge.

With her emotions under better control, Martha was still reluctant to say or do anything that might create a deeper chasm between the two of them. She needed to wait until her mind was not befuddled from lack of sleep and her body was not exhausted. More important, she also needed time to pray on the matter. Truly, truly pray.

She bowed her head and silently beseeched her heavenly Father's wisdom. When she finally felt the grace of His peace, she climbed down from the loft and made certain the young couple was gone before she hurried out of the stable with Bird.

Sweating profusely and hungry for both nourishment and her bed, she crossed the covered bridge that spanned Dillon's Stream and separated East and West Main Street. Before she left the protection of the covered bridge on the other side, she peeked out to make sure she could slip across the street and back home without being seen by anyone, especially Anne Sweet.

Anne and her husband, George, had returned to Trinity when George resigned his position as a state legislator. Anne's brother, Thomas Dillon, had resigned as mayor shortly before leaving to escort Fern and Ivy out east, and George had temporarily assumed the duties of mayor until being formally elected.

Despite the quickening of her heart, Martha set aside any and all thoughts of Thomas for the second time that day. Their relationship was far too complicated and unsettled at the moment for her tired brain to fully comprehend. Instead, she scanned the length of the planked sidewalk across the street, looking for Anne. She did not have the energy to match wits with her, either.

With little else to occupy her time, Anne spent most of her time shopping and visiting around town as Trinity's unofficial busybody. A nonstop chatterbox with a nose for gossip, she did not have any malicious intentions, as far as Martha could tell, but she would often piece together bits of gossip and leap to conclusions that were usually wrong, if not totally outrageous.

Fortunately, Anne was not in sight, but with all the activity up and down West Main Street, it was hard to dismiss the reality that change was coming to this once-sleepy town. To the south, teams of men were already at work deepening Dillon's Stream. Others were building up the berm on what would soon be Dillon's Canal, a venture funded by private investments that would link Trinity to larger cities and markets in a statewide system of canals, forever changing Trinity and the folks who called it home.

Martha looked to the opposite end of town. Against the backdrop of the sound of shovels scraping at the earth and hammers forcing nails into wooden frames behind her, the whine of the saws at the mill drew her attention to buildings under construction. Several new businesses had appeared in the past few months. In addition to the first bank in town, a new boardinghouse provided lodging for many of the new workers, and a newspaper expected to produce its first issue in early fall.

"Change is inevitable, I suppose," she grumbled, forcing aside thoughts of Victoria's plan to marry. Instead she focused on her daughter's comments about her role as a midwife. Doctors in most of the eastern cities, including Philadelphia and New York, had already started assuming what had always been a midwife's calling—caring for sick women and children and helping mothers bring new babes into the world. With the trend rapidly spreading westward, and especially with Dr. McMillan here now, Martha knew her role as midwife here in Trinity would diminish. It might even disappear completely in her lifetime.

But a midwife's calling was *her* calling.

And it was *her* life.

Yet at forty-three, she had to admit that after following her calling practically nonstop for the past ten years, her dwindling physical stamina, as well as her lack of a horse, now made her question how long she could continue as a midwife.

Or just as important, how long she *wanted* to continue.

She had been vacillating for months, especially after Thomas Dillon had proposed to her just before he left. She had tentatively accepted his proposal, which forced her to really think about how she wanted to live out the rest of her days.

But in truth, she was so tired she was giddy at this point, and she did not want to think about Thomas or her calling right now. She did not want to think about Victoria or Dr. McMillan, either. All she really wanted to think about was putting Bird back into his cage, storing Will's spyglass in a safe place, and getting out of the gown she had worn for the past three days. After climbing into bed, she intended to devour the basket of food she had brought back with her from the groaning party and spend the rest of the day catching up on all the sleep she had missed.

The rest of her troubles and all of her duties as a mother, as a midwife, and as Bird's protector would have to wait.

3

If this was a dream, it was the absolute best dream she'd had in many months.

Martha kept her eyes firmly shut and held perfectly still in her cot for fear of bringing this sweet dream to an abrupt and disappointing end. The fact that she had eaten the entire basket of goodies from the groaning party before taking to her bed was irrelevant.

The aroma of cinnamon and honey was so strong, her mouth began to water. She could almost taste one of Fern's strudels. Or was it one of her kuchens or one of Ivy's pies? When she risked taking a deeper breath, she detected just a hint of molasses that inspired visions of thick molasses cookies that were so vivid her sweet tooth begged to be satisfied.

But when her stomach growled, she realized that unless she ended this dream right here and right now, she would spend every day until those two sisters returned craving their sweet treats beyond all reason—and every night praying for forgiveness for coveting them. Resigned to that sad reality, she sighed and then forced herself to open her eyes and sit up.

She had pulled back the drapes to let in the warm summer air before she'd crawled into bed. In all truth, the air had turned much cooler while she slept, and the afternoon light coming into the room was dimmed by an overcast sky. Dismissing the muted voices she heard as nothing more than last-minute shoppers passing by on their way home, she took a good long stretch and let go of the silly notion that one of the voices she'd heard had been Ivy's. But when she drew several deep breaths to clear her head, her heart leaped with pure bliss, then leaped again.

She *did* smell cinnamon and honey and molasses and . . . and it *was* Ivy's voice she heard. And Fern's, too. And they weren't outside at all—they were right downstairs in the kitchen. "They're home! They're finally home!" she cried, and her heart whispered back, *Maybe Thomas is, too.*

She quickly set that thought aside and slipped a fresh gown on. When she brushed her hair, she remembered the bump on her head a bit too late, but she had no doubt the bump would disappear faster than the memory of Victoria's escapade would.

Across from her cot, Bird was in his cage, walking back and forth on his perch, apparently as anxious for a few crumbs of a sweet treat as she was. When he began chirping at her, she chuckled. "You'll have a treat tonight. I promise." She then fixed her hair in a simple knot at the nape of her neck like she usually wore and slipped out the door.

Martha rushed down the staircase, and the lower she got, the stronger the sweet aromas became, overwhelming the smell of raw wood that had permeated the shop after the recent renovations the sisters had ordered before leaving on the trip. Even hungrier to reunite with her friends and to fuel her lonely spirit than she was for sweets, she opened the door at the bottom of

27

the staircase only to discover she had used the wrong staircase. Instead of being in the kitchen in the back, she was standing in the shop at the front of the building.

Rather than waste time and retrace her steps, she practically ran through the expanded shop area, past the new display tables that were still waiting to be filled with all sorts of sweet treats again. When she reached the new swinging door that opened up into the kitchen, she shoved it open. She did not realize she had hit the door too hard until it slammed against an inner wall and swung back again, so fast that the door would have hit her square in the face if she had not grabbed hold of it. Thoroughly embarrassed when she heard several screams of fright, she eased the door open this time and stepped into the kitchen wearing a sheepish grin.

Before she could offer a word of apology, Fern and Ivy came right over to her and embraced her from both sides.

Ivy furrowed her brow. "Martha! You're awake."

Martha gave each of them a hug filled with months of longing. "I'm so sorry I frightened you both."

"It's not your fault," Ivy insisted, slipping her arm around Martha's waist. "I've been having trouble with that silly swinging door ever since we got back."

Tempted to remind the two women that they were four months overdue, Martha simply opened her arms and urged Fern to do the same so all three of them could share one giant hug together. "I've missed you both something terrible," she said and urged them closer still.

"And we've missed you, too, haven't we, Fern?" Ivy offered before she eased back and gave Martha a hard look. "You look peaked."

"And a tad thinner, as well," Fern added, stepping back to join her sister. "Not to worry. There's a cinnamon strudel in the oven that I made just for you."

"And I made a small batch of molasses cookies and a couple loaves of anadama bread, which has a good portion of molasses in it, too," Ivy added.

Martha chuckled and shook her head. Without the two sisters here for the past few months to tempt her daily with their sweet confections, she may have lost a bit of her girth, but Fern and Ivy still looked as plump and round as the scrumptious sweets they baked each week. "I hate to admit it, but I've actually had a dream or two about anything and everything you bake."

Fern laughed for a moment, her blue eyes twinkling, but then her expression quickly sobered. "There's so much to tell you. Most of which can wait until later. I know you probably want nothing more than a bite to eat, but before you do, we have two very special people we want you to meet." She glanced toward the far end of the kitchen to a new alcove with a window facing the side alley.

Martha's eyes followed her friend's glance, and her heartbeat quickened when she saw two women standing there. Complete strangers to Martha, one woman appeared to be slightly younger than she was, perhaps in her late thirties. She held hands with the other woman who, on second glance, appeared to be a girl who had only just reached womanhood. The woman's gaze seemed a bit haunted, as if concerned about meeting Martha, but the young woman wore a smile that was almost too genuine.

Fern quickly introduced Martha to Widow Jane Trew and her daughter, Cassie. In stature, Jane was built more like Martha's brother, James, who was also uncommonly tall and reed thin. Her posture, however, hinted at a strength that belied her frame. Her blond hair was mixed with white, and she wore it parted down the middle and joined at the back in a single braid that hung over her shoulder. Her complexion was equally pale, but her light blue eyes offered a steady gaze that met Martha's and held it.

"I've heard a great deal about you, Widow Cade. It's an honor to finally meet you," Jane offered.

"Call me Martha, please," she replied, curious to know if the two sisters had brought houseguests back with them and how long they might be staying, or if Jane and her daughter were simply traveling companions they had met along the way home. She looked directly at the younger woman and smiled. "And you must be Cassie."

The young woman edged just a bit closer to her mother. "Yes, ma'am," she murmured and lowered her head.

"Cassie's a bit shy at first, but she'll warm up once she gets to know you," Jane offered and slipped her hand free to put her arm around her daughter's shoulders.

Unlike her mother, Cassie was short and round all over. She had her mother's pale features, but she had a sprinkling of freckles across her chubby cheeks, just like Martha did. With a short, upturned nose and her hair in pigtails, she had a childish look that did not match her womanly curves.

Martha was stymied at guessing the girl's age. Curious to know how old she was for sure, she smiled at Cassie again. "My daughter, Victoria, should be home shortly. She's eighteen, and I know she'll be happy to meet a young woman close in age like you are."

When Cassie looked up and smiled at her mother, her eyes were filled with the innocence of a girl much younger. "I'm nineteen, aren't I, Mother?"

"Yes, my dear, and a very fine young lady, too," Jane said with a gentle but protective edge to her voice.

Cassie beamed. "And I can work really, really hard. I like licorice root; do you?"

"Indeed I do," Martha offered. Cassie might physically be an adult, but her mind appeared to be a good bit younger, which meant that, unlike Victoria, Cassie had few options in her future and Jane had responsibilities as a mother that would probably never end.

"But there's no licorice root until after dinner and no work today. Not for either of you," Fern insisted, then turned to Martha to explain. "With all the renovations that were made while we were gone to expand the confectionery, we realized that we'd be needing more help. We met Jane and her daughter in Pennsylvania, and we knew right away that they were just the ones we were looking for, didn't we, Ivy?"

"We did. Right off," Ivy replied, nodding her agreement, as well. "We convinced them both to join our household, which is a story we'll share with you later."

Caught by total surprise, Martha still managed a smile. "I hope you'll be as happy here as my daughter and I are."

Jane returned her smile and held her daughter tight. "Thank you. I hope we will be."

"Jane, why don't you and Cassie let me show you both up-stairs so you can get yourselves settled in the sitting room, at least temporarily. Tomorrow we'll decide how we're going to rearrange things so you two have a proper bedroom. Ivy, per-haps you might want to give a thought to supper. Try to make it a little special so Jane and Cassie don't change their minds about wanting to live here with us, and maybe you and Martha can keep watch over the oven until I get back. There's still one more strudel in there, and I don't want it to burn," Fern said, then shooed Jane and her daughter toward the staircase that Martha had intended to use earlier.

While the three of them took to the stairs, Martha tried to silence the questions that hammered at her brain. Exactly how

31

did Fern and Ivy meet Jane and her daughter? Did they have experience as household help, or were they simply two more people like Martha and Victoria who needed a home? Further yet, had Fern and Ivy actually resolved the problem that had led them east to keep the truth about their past hidden?

Closer to her own heart, Martha wondered if Thomas had escorted them home. But Victoria blew into the kitchen that very moment, like a sudden gust of wind. She went straight to her mother and gave her a hearty hug. "When I was here earlier to welcome everyone home again, I checked on you, but you were sleeping. I had a feeling that once there was something scrumptious baking, you'd be down here waiting to devour it the moment it came out of the oven. I figured I'd probably get to see you when I stopped back to pick up the strudel Miss Fern promised to make for Aunt Hilda," she teased.

Martha pressed a kiss to her daughter's forehead. "I've missed you," she said and wondered if her daughter had been too busy spending time with Dr. McMillan to miss her at all.

"I'm glad you're home, but if it's all right, I'd like to spend another night or two at Aunt Hilda's. There's a lot of heavy cleaning to do, and I'd really like to help her."

Rather than suggest that Victoria would have had even more time to help Aunt Hilda if she had spent less time with Dr. McMillan, Martha nodded. "It's perfectly fine, but what about your work at Dr. McMillan's?" she asked, offering her daughter an opportunity to mention her new relationship with the doctor.

Victoria shrugged before whirling away to pick up the basket sitting on the table. "He'll hardly notice I'm not there. Is this the strudel for Aunt Hilda?"

"It is, and we packed up some molasses cookies, too," Ivy offered. "Everything's still a bit warm, so carry it carefully."

"I will. I'll see you all in a few days," she offered, leaving just as abruptly as she had arrived.

Although Martha was disappointed not to have Victoria home for another night or two, she accepted the opportunity to have more time to decide what she was going to do about the affection that had apparently developed between Victoria and Dr. McMillan—affection her daughter did not appear to be in any hurry to admit.

At the moment, Martha was anxious to learn all the details of the journey Fern and Ivy had undertaken in order to resolve, once and for all, the secrets of the past that had forced them to live in fear and move from one small town to another for the past ten years. Since they had brought additional household help back with them and Fern had said they were home for good, Martha could only assume that they had indeed accomplished the purpose of their journey.

The only question Martha had at this point was a simple one that no doubt had a very complicated answer: How had they managed to do it?

4

 "hile I check to see if there's anything we can use to make a proper supper, why don't you set the table?" Ivy suggested and headed to the larder.

Happy to have something productive to do, if only to focus on something other than all the questions she had, Martha smiled. "Soup is always good, and it'll be done in no time. There's enough ham left on the bone from yesterday's dinner in there and a decent-sized basket of early peas Mr. French gave me as part of a reward just last night." She quickly told her about delivering the newest little French late last night. "With your anadama bread, ham-and-pea soup would make a special meal. Especially since we have Fern's cinnamon strudel baking in the oven for dessert," she teased.

Ivy, who was already poking around the larder, grabbed something and turned about wearing a hint of a frown. Holding the basket of peas and a small ham bone in front of her, she shrugged. "I can bake just about everything. I can manage making most things for our meals, as well, but I'm not much good at making soup."

When she held up the ham bone, her frown deepened. "I don't think we can do much with the little ham that's left on this bone—"

"But there's more than enough ham, and I'm good at making soup. Between the two of us, we should be able to make quick work of shelling these peas if we do it together," Martha countered, pleased that the corners of Ivy's lips were beginning to form a smile.

Changing directions, Martha donned a work apron before she took two bowls from the cupboard, a large one to hold the empty pods and a smaller one for the sweet peas inside. "I'll help you, but I need to take a few minutes first to rescue as much ham from that bone as I can and make a good broth. Once that's started on the cookstove, I'll help you shell the peas. How does that sound?"

Ivy smiled and started in on the peas. "It sounds as if my sister is going to be very proud of the first meal we serve to Jane and young Cassie."

"I think you're right," Martha replied. She took the large pot from atop the cookstove, sat down opposite Ivy, then found a paring knife and started carving off every bit of ham she could, as well as a bit of fat that would help flavor the soup.

Although she was bursting with curiosity, she did not want to broach the subject of the sisters' mission before Fern returned. Instead, she asked about the newest members of the household. "If you don't mind me asking, how are Jane and Cassie going to help out here in the confectionery?"

"Actually, we settled the matter with Jane before she accepted a position with us," Ivy replied and tossed an empty pod in the larger bowl. "She'll take over most of the household chores, cleaning and cooking and laundry and such, and she'll have Cassie help her. With all the renovations finished now, Fern expects we'll be baking almost double what we did before we left."

Martha set down her knife and cocked her head. "Double? That would mean you'll be taking on an awful lot of work for yourselves, even with Jane and Cassie here to help out. Are you sure it won't be too much?" Guilt tugged at her conscience, reminding her that she had been called away so often after moving in here that she had not been able to help them as much as she should have.

Ivy shrugged and popped a few peas out of a pod so quickly they hopped all over the top of the table. "In all truth, I think Fern's being a bit unrealistic, but she needs to see that for herself. Unless there are thirty or forty hours to a day, which I suppose might be the case in the fairy-tale world Fern lives in these days, it won't take more than a couple of weeks for Fern to realize that for herself."

Martha chuckled and turned the bone upside down to get at a bit of ham. "I'm afraid to admit this, but I sometimes wish I could live in that world with Fern, especially lately. Some days there just aren't enough hours."

"And once in a while, some days have too many," Ivy noted as she reached around the table to gather up the peas that had escaped.

"Now that you're back, I'll ask Victoria to help out more than she did before you left, and I'll make a better effort at helping you, too," Martha promised, although between Victoria's hidden hopes to marry and Martha's own unsettled future, she was reluctant to share any thoughts of how long they would each continue to live there because she had no idea herself.

Ivy reached one hand over the table and stilled Martha's

hand. "You look so tired, dearie. Have you found anyone who might be interested in taking over your duties?"

Martha swallowed hard before letting out a long sigh. "Not yet, but I'm still hoping to find someone interested in developing her skills as a midwife. It's a lot harder than I thought it would be. Being summoned out so often makes it hard for me to be as helpful to you as I'd like to be."

Ivy gently squeezed Martha's hand. "You have important duties as our midwife here in Trinity and for folks who live miles and miles away. We knew that your duties would always come first when we invited you to come live with us, as they must."

Martha held firm. "Even so, I'd feel better if we could revisit the arrangements we made when I first moved in with Victoria. Instead of putting the full value of my rewards on my account, I'm going to tell Wesley Sweet to put half on yours."

Wearing a frown again, Ivy continued with the peas. "As far as I'm concerned, that idea is wholly unnecessary and completely unacceptable. And, I might add, my sister will like your idea even less than I do."

Martha scooped out the marrow from the center of the bone, then dropped it and the bone itself into the pot. She went to the sink and filled the pot half full with water. "Unless you can see my point of view—"

"Am I interrupting a squabble between the two of you?"

Caught by surprise, since she had not heard Fern return to the kitchen, Martha nearly dropped the pot.

Ivy piped up before Martha could say a word. "Not at all. Martha and I were just having a discussion," she insisted and quickly summarized Martha's offer.

"Don't be ridiculous. If you do any such thing, I'll march straight down to the general store and make Wesley put whatever the amount is back on your account," Fern quipped.

"I think we need to discuss this further," Martha insisted before setting the pot on top of the cookstove to bring it to a simmer.

"Since Jane and Cassie are going to rest upstairs for a while, why don't we spend our time talking about Thomas, instead? I suspect you'd prefer news of him, rather than continue a discussion that will provoke my sister and me into an argument you're destined to lose anyway," Fern stated. She nudged Martha aside, opened the oven door to check on her strudel, and promptly closed it. "Just about ready," she announced before making her way to the cupboard for a couple of heavy cloths she would soon need to take the strudel out of the oven.

At the mention of Thomas's name, Martha's heart started beating just a little faster, and she tried to keep her voice steady. "Thomas returned with you, I assume."

"He did. We couldn't have accomplished what we did without his help," Fern assured her before returning and taking the bubbly cinnamon strudel out of the oven. "I really must apologize for keeping him away for so long. He made us promise to let him know the moment you got back. Dear man that he is, he missed you, but he held fast to his promise to help me in my mission."

"*Our* mission," Ivy reminded her. She grabbed a large tin plate and walked over to Fern.

Smiling, Fern eased the strudel from the baking pan to the plate with a spatula. While Ivy returned to finish the last handful of peas, Martha took her seat again, and when the sisters joined her, Fern placed the sweet treat right in front of her.

"Don't cut off more than a little slice. That's our dessert after supper," Ivy cautioned.

Fern nodded. "And you best let it cool a couple of minutes, or you'll burn your mouth."

"It might be worth it," Martha teased. She cut off a thin

wedge from one steaming end and dropped it onto the plate Ivy had placed in front of her. Despite how badly her mouth was watering, Martha decided to let the strudel cool, along with her burning desire to get answers to her many questions about Thomas.

"I can only imagine how difficult it was to travel as far as you did, especially since it was winter when you left," Martha stated, hoping that introducing the topic might lead right to the heart of her most pressing question.

Ivy sighed, then rose and dumped the empty pods into a slop bucket. "Not as difficult as untangling the legal quagmire we found waiting for us in Philadelphia, even after we found Mr. Pennington. Fortunately, Thomas is a lawyer, so his help was invaluable. He even helped us sell off the pieces of family jewelry Fern had taken when she escaped from her bully of a husband instead of returning them—which you know is why we went to Philadelphia in the first place. Thank heavens everything is settled now."

Martha's mouth dropped open. "You sold the jewelry instead of returning it? I thought your husband had been searching for you for nearly fifteen years to get the Pennington family jewelry back."

"He had wanted it *all* back, even the pieces I still have that he had given to me as gifts, but he wanted to find me and punish me for leaving him even more," Fern whispered. Still sitting at the end of the table, she took one of Martha's hands, then reached across the table to take one of Ivy's hands, as well. "We discovered many things about Mr. Pennington while I was gone. According to what we were able to learn, he wasn't even my husband anymore. He divorced me several years ago."

She paused for a moment to swipe away a tear. "As scandalous as it is to admit, I'm a divorced woman. In Philadelphia, at least, I think *divorcée* is the term they use now." She shuddered, as if the scandalous label were too much to bear.

Ivy snorted. "What he did to you was awful. He should have just let the two of you live apart. To most folks hereabouts, or in the city for that matter, it's not proper to be divorced at all, so it really doesn't matter what term you use."

Fern's cheeks turned the same bright shade of pink as the blossoms on mountain laurel. "Which is why I don't want anyone in Trinity to know about the divorce or that I'd become a runaway wife because he nearly killed me. I took some of the family jewelry completely by accident when I left. I only intended to take the jewelry that he gave me each time he begged for forgiveness after beating me."

Ivy shook her head. "You don't have to worry about any of those things anymore, and you don't need to even consider yourself a divorced woman."

The more the sisters bantered back and forth, almost completely ignoring Martha, the more confused she became. But when they started arguing the difference between a divorced woman's status and reputation as opposed to a widow's, she broke her silence. "Since I know almost nothing about your experiences in Philadelphia, this conversation is confusing. I think you've drifted into matters that aren't really relevant," she suggested.

Startled into silence, both sisters stared at her, as if they had both just realized that she was sitting there.

"But it's entirely relevant," Fern argued. "God be just and merciful, Mr. Pennington died a little over a year ago."

"He's dead?" Martha blurted, shocked by the one possibility she had not even considered when the sisters had left to find him.

"Yes, he is," Ivy replied. "So in my opinion, which is wholly different from Thomas's legal point of view and my sister's, she's earned the right to be called a widow and respected as such," Ivy argued.

"Maybe we should slow down a bit and explain to Martha exactly what we learned as we learned it," Fern offered.

Ivy shrugged and got to her feet. "It's mostly your tale. Tell it as you want. I'll just fill in if you forget something important. But first, I'm going to set some water to boil so we can all have some tea."

Still reeling from the news they had just shared with her, Martha decided now would be the right time to sample her piece of cinnamon strudel so that her mouth would be full and she would not be tempted to interrupt either one of them again.

5

Ivy had just finished bringing the teakettle to the table when there was a knock at the back door. "I'm up," she said, waving Martha back to her seat. She headed down the long hall to reach the door that opened to the side alley and returned right after Martha finished filling their cups.

"That was just Rosalind Andrews. She was hoping to find Dr. McMillan here, but she left in a huff when I told her he hadn't been here at all today."

Martha had no intention of telling any of the women, even if one was his housekeeper, that the doctor was probably out somewhere with Victoria. She preferred to keep that information to herself.

Ivy sat down, took a sip of tea, and quickly set it down. "Too hot," she noted and glanced at her sister, who looked like she was growing more and more anxious to tell Martha about their mission. Or was she having second thoughts about divulging anything?

Martha caught Fern's gaze and held it. "I don't want you to feel obligated to tell me anything—"

"Martha, dear, I want to tell you," she said, taking Martha's hand in her own. Speaking slowly, as if deliberately choosing every word, Fern told Martha the tale of their journey that was as incredible as it was sad.

By the time Fern finished, Martha's head was spinning, and they were all battling tears. No one had even touched the tea. "Let me be certain that I understand everything," Martha said. "Several years ago, shortly after he divorced you, Mr. Pennington suffered a very severe stroke that left him completely paralyzed and unable to speak more than gibberish."

"Correct."

"And later, his lawyer took advantage of the situation to steal Mr. Pennington's fortune and disappear? Surely there must have been someone who could have seen what was happening and stopped him."

"Who would stop him? We didn't have any children," Fern reminded her, "and he didn't have any living relatives, either."

Ivy snorted. "That man's temper always drove away whatever friends he made in short order. When he was too ill to protect his fortune, no one else cared what happened to him or his money, except for that horrid lawyer."

Martha had the sense that Fern blamed herself, at least in part, for not being there to prevent what had happened, and she squeezed her hand in silent support. "So over the course of a year or so, as you understand, this Mr. Ashford hired caregivers to care for Mr. Pennington at home while he concocted a nefarious plan, which he was ready to implement once he purchased a remote cottage in the Pennsylvania countryside miles from anything else."

When both women nodded to confirm her understanding,

she continued. "Jane answered the advertisement Mr. Ashford placed in a Philadelphia newspaper for a caregiver for Mr. Pennington, and she got the position, as well as permission to bring Cassie with her. He gave her wages in advance and left barely enough for them to survive on for the coming year, claiming the doctors assured him that the sick man would probably not even survive that long. After reassuring her that she was free to keep the year's wages and leave once Mr. Pennington did die, even if that turned out to be only a matter of months, he simply disappeared, taking Mr. Pennington's fortune with him. Do I have that right?" Martha was surprised in part that Mr. Ashford had gone to so much trouble and not just abandoned poor Mr. Pennington. She also wondered why Jane would want such a remote position when there must have been ones in the city.

"Exactly right," Fern said. "At least that's what we were able to piece together. That's only half the story, I suppose, but I'd rather not bore you with endless tales of how difficult it was or how long it took to find enough information just to locate Mr. Pennington. All I want to add is that I think we traipsed over most of the roads crisscrossing the eastern half of Pennsylvania and back in our search, only to discover that he had died a few months before. He'd lasted nearly twice as long as the doctors predicted."

Ivy finally added a comment of her own. "As far as Jane knows, the man she had been caring for was our distant relative. We didn't see any reason to tell her any more than that."

Fern nodded. "What a blessing that I never did return the jewelry. If I had, that thief of a lawyer would have gotten that, too," Fern noted. "The other blessing is Jane. We both took to her right away, didn't we, Ivy?" she asked, adding a bit of cream to her tea and pronouncing it just the right temperature to drink.

While Martha added two dollops of honey to her tea, Ivy

took a sip of her own, which prompted Fern to continue her tale. "The poor woman didn't have much by way of references to give us, but the very fact that she'd stayed with that very sick man long after her wages had run out provided all the reference we needed. In point of fact, when we found her, she was desperate to leave. She just didn't have the funds."

Yet another knock came at the back door, harsher this time, and made Ivy scowl. "If that's Rosalind again, I have a mind to tell her that it's not our business to keep track of the doctor," she grumbled and hurried to answer the door when the knock echoed again.

She returned moments later, her expression worried. "There's a Mr. Crowder at the door. He's come to fetch you. Apparently his daughter is ill. I tried to tell him you were too exhausted to go with him right now, but when he said he would get Dr. McMillan instead, I had a mind to tell him the doctor wasn't around but thought I'd better let you talk to him."

"I know who he is," Martha said and got to her feet. "Just after you left, he moved his family here from somewhere near Sunrise to the old Bradford farm. If you'll tell him I'll be right there, I'll go upstairs and grab my bag. And ask him to wait for me. Otherwise, I don't have any way to get all the way out to his farm."

Accustomed to the futility of arguing with Martha when it came to answering a call to duty, Ivy simply nodded and left to deliver Martha's message. Fern shrugged her shoulders and started to package up another piece of strudel for her, along with a biscuit she slit open and stuffed with cheese, a habit the sisters had developed whenever Martha was called away from a meal.

For her part, Martha snatched a bit of crust from the strudel and hurried upstairs by way of the back staircase to retrieve her bag of simples, adding a few different remedies to take with her. After giving the crust to Bird, she returned to the kitchen, where she found Ivy holding her bonnet and cape ready for her.

"You'll need these if Mr. Crowder brings you back after the sun goes down. Why aren't you riding out there with Grace? Is your horse ill?"

Martha took a deep breath. "Grace died very suddenly two weeks ago," she managed and tied her bonnet into place. She accepted the sack of foodstuffs from Fern in one hand and her cape with the other before leaving without saying anything more.

She hurried to the back door as fast as she could. At the moment, however, her weary body did not move as fast as she liked, and a twinge in the small of her back reminded her that it was time to let someone else answer the call to tend to the women and children of Trinity.

Hopefully that meant someone other than Dr. McMillan, who was likely paying far too much attention at the moment to one young woman in particular—her daughter.

❦

Once in a month of Sundays, if that often, Martha answered a call to duty only to discover a complaint that only time and nature itself would be able to cure.

Today turned out to be one of those days, which meant Martha could do little for sixteen-year-old, unmarried Missy Crowder, who did not even realize she was carrying a babe until Martha told her. Missy and her parents, naturally, were shocked. Poor Missy and her mother wailed together, but her father announced that after he delivered Martha back home, he was heading straight back to Sunrise to fetch the young father-to-be and their minister to marry them at once.

As they started back to Trinity, the chill in the air matched the mood of the man who sat next to Martha on the wagon seat. The ride back to town with him was bound to be terribly awkward, and she missed Grace more than ever, wishing she could have returned to Trinity on her own. If she was totally honest with herself, however, she would have to admit that she was so tired right now that she might have fallen asleep in the saddle.

Not that she would have had to worry. Grace had been a wretched-looking horse, but her spirit and her devotion to Martha had been amazing. She sensed Martha's moods better than most humans did, and if Martha had fallen asleep in the saddle, which had happened once or twice, Grace would have stopped and gently jostled her awake.

With a very sullen and silent man at the reins and no hope of conversation to keep her awake, she had to force herself to keep her eyes open. But when she spied an all-too-familiar buggy pull out from behind a stand of trees up ahead, her heartbeat slowed to a dull thud.

Looking as bedraggled and exhausted as she knew she was, meeting anyone at the moment was the very last thing she wanted to do, but she absolutely, positively had no desire to see the man at the reins of that buggy.

"Not now," she whispered. "Please not now."

Mr. Crowder lifted the reins and used them to point ahead. "Do you know who that is that's heading toward us?"

"Yes," she said. "I do."

His expression hardened. "There's no time for idle conversation."

"I know," she replied, quite certain that Mr. Crowder would be pleased when he learned in a few minutes that he would be well on his way without her. She shook the dust from her skirts and slipped off her bonnet just enough to smooth her hair before tying her bonnet back into place again. But she was helpless to keep her heart from racing and pounding against the wall of her chest when he slowed the wagon to a halt, waiting for the buggy to close the last few yards between them.

Yes, she very definitely knew the man who was drawing ever closer to her.

He was the only man who had managed to steal her heart, not once but twice. He also had the very annoying ability to know what she was thinking, even before she did, and he could charm a blush to her cheeks with a simple glance.

6

"Thomas."

Martha whispered his name as he stopped his buggy alongside the wagon. The moment he locked his determined eyes with hers, she immediately knew that their meeting like this was definitely not a coincidence.

His soft gray eyes simmered with such deep want and affection that her heart beat even faster. When he set the brake and removed his hat, she noted with some dismay that he had yet to sport a single gray hair. With patrician features and ebony hair, he was more handsome in her eyes than any man had a right to be. A full head taller than she was, he was nearly as trim and fit as he had been when he first proposed to her twenty-five years ago, and now he was twice as charming as he had been then. His smile made her so weak in the knees she was glad she was sitting down.

"I suspected you'd be heading back on this road," he said before he climbed down from his seat in the buggy. After quickly introducing himself to Mr. Crowder, Thomas easily convinced the man to let him take her home. Given the man's urgent mission, Martha could hardly argue against the idea.

With her fate decided, Martha resigned herself to the inevitable. The only saving grace to her situation, if she could find any at all, was that she and Thomas would have time alone together to discuss a number of issues that had awaited his return to be resolved. Unfortunately, she had not yet resolved those issues in her own mind and knew he would not be pleased.

While Thomas quickly transferred her things from the wagon to the buggy, Mr. Crowder helped her down from her seat to the ground. "We expect your discretion," he said, and his words were very firm despite how quietly he voiced them.

She stiffened at being reminded of any of her duties. "Understood."

He tipped his hat when Thomas reached Martha's side. "Much obliged to you both," he said, then climbed back aboard his wagon and pulled away.

Thomas took Martha's hand and turned her about until they were facing one another with mere inches between them. When he tilted up her chin, his simmering gaze darkened with concern. "I was hoping Fern and Ivy had exaggerated, but I can see for myself they didn't describe by half how exhausted you are. They told me about Grace, too, which is why I decided to fetch you home myself. I'm sorry. I know how much you relied on her. We can talk about replacing her later, but you can borrow one of my horses in the meantime." Without missing a beat, he swooped her up and into his arms.

"Thomas Dillon! Whatever do you think you're doing?"

He chuckled, carried her a few steps, and lifted her into the buggy. "I'm taking care of my future wife."

"I'm not so exhausted that I can't walk on my own two feet, and I'm not your future wife. If you'll recall, I never *fully* accepted your proposal, and we both agreed to keep our relationship secret until and if I did. And replacing Grace is my problem, not yours."

He ignored her words as he tucked a thick blanket around her shoulders and offered her another smile that left her exasperated. "And as I recall, you said yes to my proposal, assuming I'd agree to any number of conditions you were going to think about while I was away."

She huffed and readjusted the blanket so it was a bit less snug. "Well, you certainly allowed ample time to do that, considering you were gone four months longer than you originally said you would be."

He leaned forward, held on to the side of the buggy with both hands, and cocked his head. "I wrote and told you that we'd all been delayed."

"You did, but that was early in February. I hadn't heard from any of you since then, and I didn't know what to think. All I could do was pray that nothing awful happened to keep you all from returning."

He pressed a kiss to the back of her hand. "I'm sorry if we caused you any worry, but if you had any doubt about my intentions, then I'll make them very clear right now." He lowered his face so close to hers she could feel his breath on her face.

She almost forgot to breathe.

"I love you, Martha Cade. I want you to be my wife, and I promise to agree, unequivocally, to any and all conditions you might have," he whispered before he pressed a gentle, soul-stirring kiss to her lips.

Stunned by his words and too exhausted to protest, she instinctively kissed him back—and carefully noted this moment as one to cherish. Later, after she rested, she would need to discuss all the concerns she had about marrying him, and when she did, she would make very certain to remind him of the promise he had just made to her.

He broke their kiss with a chuckle and climbed aboard, claimed his seat close to her, and clicked the reins. "Now that we have properly settled that issue, I should warn you that I have several other very important matters I need to disclose and discuss with you. I doubt you'll find them very problematic, but it's probably best if we save discussing them until you've gotten a solid night's rest."

She fought to catch her breath and moistened her lips. "I'm not certain that kiss was proper at all, but your assumption that I wouldn't find any of your matters to be problematic borders on arrogance, if not conceit."

"Then I apologize for my assumption, but I'll make no apology for kissing you, especially in light of the very pleasant manner in which you kissed me back. We're betrothed. It's highly proper for us to share a kiss now and again, especially when there's no one about to observe us," he teased, then wrapped his arm around her. "Before you fall asleep and topple out of the buggy, lean on me and rest. I'll make certain you keep to your seat."

Rather than argue with the man, she did exactly what he suggested and was nearly asleep before she even felt the buggy roll forward.

When Martha woke up, the clouds had lifted and the sun was making a valiant effort to warm the earth before slipping below the horizon. She had to blink her eyes several times and shake her head to rid herself of the last remnants of sleep before she became fully aware of her surroundings.

She eased away from Thomas and sat up straight, but it took

a moment before she realized they were no longer in the buggy. Instead, they were sitting on the ground atop a blanket, and the buggy was parked several feet away. Resting next to her was a well-worn basket she recognized from the confectionery, and the aromas coming out of the basket were intoxicating.

When she peeked into the basket and saw the veritable feast packed inside, she groaned so loud they might have heard her miles away in town. "Oh, how I love those two sisters."

Thomas laughed. "They're rather fond of you, too, and they refused to let me fetch you home unless I promised to see that you ate properly first."

"I always eat when I'm called out to duty, though not always this well," she quipped, but she neglected to mention that all she had managed to eat since the morning was the food Fern had packed for her, and she had polished that off before she had even arrived at the Crowder farm.

As she set the goodies out onto the blanket, she remembered the winter picnic she had shared with Thomas in the lakeside cabin, which he had restored in anticipation of her agreeing to marry him and move out into the countryside with him.

She did not doubt for a heartbeat that he had planned this picnic, too, and it was a true feast. In addition to hunks of ham and cheese and several biscuits, there were half a dozen molasses cookies, a small tin of salty pretzels, a pair of sugar-crusted fritters, and a jug of water.

She reached back into the basket for a tin plate and a napkin and handed both to Thomas, which he promptly filled with biscuits he then sliced and filled with ham. In turn, she snatched one of the fritters and polished it off in two bites. She licked the sugar from her fingers before setting a couple of molasses cookies onto her plate.

When Thomas started to laugh, she added one more cookie.

"I do believe I've earned the right to eat dessert first today," she offered, making it clear by the tone of her voice that she was not apologizing one iota.

"I'm not suggesting you haven't. All I'm saying is that having dessert before dinner is one of your more endearing habits I've discovered over the years."

She huffed. "What you mean is that I'm predictable."

"Exactly," he replied and turned his attention to devouring his biscuit and quickly filling another one with cheese.

Annoyed by his response, she looked more closely at him. When she noted the thin, jagged scar on the web of flesh between his thumb and forefinger, a battle scar he had suffered last year when he had rescued Will from drowning, she recalled the boy's claim that all females were unpredictable. Maybe it was time she made herself a bit unpredictable in the hope that she could nip at some of his confidence.

She smiled at him. "You seem to relish making fun of my little habits," she retorted playfully, although she accepted the fact that he was far more skilled at flirtatious banter than she was or ever could be.

"Sad to say, I'm at a disadvantage in that regard since I have so many more foibles than you do," he protested and snatched a molasses cookie from her plate.

Martha polished off the last of her fritter. "Perhaps that's a topic we'll save for a discussion another day, since I have more important questions about the time you were away. And about why you couldn't write to explain the reason you were delayed or how long you might be instead of leaving me to worry about all of you," she added.

He set his cookie down on his plate, and his expression sobered. "I traveled with Fern and Ivy as their escort and friend, but I was also their lawyer. I still am, and while I can talk about some things, there are others I can't discuss with you at all because I can't break the confidentiality I owe to them."

Reluctantly, she nodded. As a midwife, she also shared a sacred trust with her patients, and there were times when it was awkward, if not incredibly hard, to maintain that trust. She had never once divulged any of the private information she was privy to during the course of her work in too many households to count, and she was proud of the respect she had earned as a result.

He let out a long breath. "What I can tell you is that Fern and Ivy have nothing to worry about now."

"They told me as much, although we hadn't quite finished our conversation when I was summoned out to the Crowder farm. They will no doubt explain the rest as they see fit, but I'm still confused as to why none of you could write anything after the single post you sent to let me know that you'd be delayed a short while before coming home."

He took her hand. "I'm sorry, but all I can tell you now is that we spent a great deal of time in Philadelphia, but we also had to travel to Harrisburg and a fair number of smaller towns before we even located Mr. Pennington. Between the bad weather, the abominable roads, and the need to file any number of legal petitions just to keep those two sisters from doing anything illegal, there were actually days when I wasn't even certain of the name of the inn or even the town where we were staying."

"It sounds exhausting," she admitted, feeling downright foolish and completely selfish for expecting Thomas or the two sisters to write to her when they obviously had so much to do.

Turning her hand, she entwined her fingers with his and tightened her hold. "You're a good man, Thomas. A good friend. And a good lawyer. And I suspect you might make an awfully good husband. Now that you're home again, we can take our time and sort through our concerns properly," she said as bittersweet memories came to the forefront of her mind.

Nearly twenty-five years ago, she had had second thoughts about marrying him and had ended their courtship, which had inspired more than a bit of gossip at the time. She had married John Cade instead, and in turn, Thomas had married someone else, too. Eventually, each of them had experienced the pain of losing a spouse. They had only recently rediscovered the affection that had initially brought them together.

Thomas sighed, as if he were thinking about the past, too. "I've already told you that I won't object to anything you want or need me to do to get you to fully accept my proposal. Can't you do the same for me?"

7

ould she?

When Martha did not answer him right away and averted her eyes, Thomas sighed and got to his feet. "I need to tend to the horse. Perhaps you can give me your answer when I get back. If not, your silence will be answer enough."

Her heart begged her to say yes, that she could accept his proposal unequivocally, but she had to think long and hard before she gave him an answer. She glanced up and watched him as he carried the jug of water over to the horse, but she quickly looked down again when her heart started racing and threatened to keep her from thinking about anything other than loving him and desperately wanting him as her husband.

Their circumstances, however, could not be more different. As a widower with two grown children and substantial means, Thomas had no one depending on him, which meant that he had nothing to consider more than what he wanted to do. A lawyer by training, he had always enjoyed his status and inherited wealth as the son of the founder of Trinity, and he had spent his life using his talents and energy for the benefit of the town and the people who lived there.

She sighed and worried the napkin on her lap. She, too, held a revered status in town that was important to her. Once widowed, however, the meager rewards she earned had not been enough to support herself and her two children, and she depended on others for a home. After a fire last year claimed the one she had made with her brother, she had been fortunate to have found a home with Fern and Ivy.

Granted, she hadn't had to worry about supporting her son, Oliver, for the past ten years. At fourteen he had moved to Boston to live with his grandfather, Graham Cade, to claim the future his father had rejected. Under his grandfather's tutelage, he had finished his education and now practiced law in his grandfather's firm. He made every effort to return home for a visit once a year or so, but he had yet to come this year.

Her relationship with Oliver was not as strong or as deep as it would have been if he had never left, but she suspected a son's inclination to become independent of his mother was as natural as it was necessary. In recent years, however, she occasionally turned to her son for advice, especially where Victoria was concerned, although he did not fully comprehend the very difficult relationship a mother had with a daughter as opposed to a son.

Victoria, however, had only just turned eighteen, and Martha had an obligation to provide for her. Her relationship with her daughter was still contentious at times and was bound to get even more so once she confronted Victoria about her behavior with Dr. McMillan and her hopes to marry him.

Martha nibbled at another cookie, found it tasteless, and set it aside. However different their circumstances might be, she and Thomas had one very important thing in common: a desire to change the way they lived their lives.

Thomas no longer found satisfaction in his civic responsibilities to Trinity, and he was also weary of traveling for weeks at a time to monitor inherited family investments that were as far west as Clarion, some thirty miles away, and as far east as several major seaboard cities, namely Philadelphia and New York.

For Martha, the demands of responding to constant calls in all types of weather and at all times of the day or night were taking a toll on her. The yearnings for the comfort of a husband, a home of her own, and a more ordinary life had grown stronger over the past year, and she was struggling to rediscover the peace and contentment she had once enjoyed in the life she believed God had chosen for her.

Instead, Thomas had come back into her life and offered her the opportunity to satisfy the yearnings of both their hearts.

When she heard him returning to the blanket, she took a deep breath. She had been confused about what to do for months now, but with Thomas by her side again, all doubt and confusion about how she would respond to his question slipped away. And she knew that she was ready to give up her calling. Ready to truly love again. Ready for the companionship of a husband and a home of her own. Ready to do all the things she had been too busy to do while tending to everyone else.

But before she could seriously contemplate ending her days as a midwife, she had one final duty that had to be met. She was just afraid that Thomas would not give her the time she needed to meet that responsibility.

When he finally sat down next to her, she reached out and took his hand with her own. "I can accept your proposal, unequivocally, with the exception of one issue that would force me to say no and turn you away."

His eyes deepened with an understanding that she knew stemmed from the past. "Your work as a midwife," he stated in a flat tone of voice. He shook his head before he looked away from her to stare into the distance.

"But it's different this time—"

"No," he argued. "It's exactly the same issue that kept us from marrying all those years ago when you were training with your grandmother to replace her. I wanted you to stop, and you refused."

He slipped his hand free. "Before I left, I thought we'd both agreed that we were equally tired of the constant interruptions in our lives, and that now that we were a little older, we wanted to make changes that would make both of us happier. That's why I resigned as mayor and traveled east with Fern and Ivy, planning to dissolve my investments there. I'd hoped by now you'd be able to tell me that you were ready to let someone else take up your calling. Apparently I was wrong." His shoulders slumped ever so slightly.

She placed her hand on his arm. "Please stop and listen to what I have to say without interrupting me. I *am* ready to let someone else take over as midwife."

When he looked back at her, his eyes were wide with disbelief but shaded with hope.

"Are you certain, absolutely certain you are?"

"Yes, I'm absolutely certain," she insisted, "but I can't leave the women and children who depend on me without anyone to help them other than Dr. McMillan. I have a duty to find a competent woman who is willing to take my place. All I ask is that you give me the time I need to find her."

He lifted a brow and started to smile. "More time. That's all you want? More time?"

She smiled. "Yes."

His smile drooped just a tad. "How much time do you think you'll need?"

"I'm afraid I can't tell you that," she admitted. "I haven't been very successful so far after talking to several women I know who are very experienced with helping me during births or with all sorts of illnesses, but there are a good number I still need to approach. If one of them is interested, I don't think it would take more than five or six months before she'd be ready to take over as midwife, although she might still need me occasionally for difficult cases."

"And if none of them are interested? What then?"

She swallowed hard. "If one of the younger women has a true desire to become a midwife but has little birthing experience, then it will take much longer. At least a year, and even after that, for perhaps another year, I'd feel obligated to work very closely with her, which means I can't promise to marry you until you can agree to wait for me . . . for however long it takes."

His expression hardened. "And if I agree to wait, you can promise you'll marry me and not change your mind?"

"I won't change my mind, but I still want to keep our plans to ourselves."

His smile returned. It was a little tentative, but it was there. "Then if you're very, very sure that this is what you need to do, then I can agree to wait, although I must tell you that I'll be impatient at times," he warned.

She nodded, reluctant to admit that she might become impatient, too.

"And after you've gotten some proper rest, we'll talk about picking out another horse for you. Obviously, you're going to need one."

She shook her head. "I've already told you. That's my responsibility, and I'll take care of finding another horse, just as I'll take care of finding someone to replace me."

"Which makes me curious about something," he said. "Since

you're so determined to keep our plans to marry a secret, won't folks find it odd that you're actively trying to find someone to replace you?"

"Not at all," she insisted. "It's been common knowledge for some time now that Victoria has no interest in taking up my work. I've approached several women in the past year to consider taking my place when I'm no longer willing or able to continue, and several others more recently while you were away, but only in very general terms. If none of them are interested, I'll be discreet, but I'll waste no time before I approach others. If I'm not as successful right away as I hope to be and it ends up that we don't marry for another year or two, it doesn't make much sense to announce now that we're betrothed, would it?"

"No, I suppose not," he admitted, "but in all fairness, I do have a few matters to discuss with you that might give you pause and invite you to reconsider accepting my proposal."

"I trust you won't ask me to agree to anything I'd find wholly unacceptable, especially now after you've been so willing to compromise with me."

He brightened. "In truth, there are two matters, although one is little more than highly inconvenient for both of us. I was so busy helping Fern and Ivy that I never got beyond Philadelphia to fully dissolve my investments in New York City. I'd like to stay here at home for a few weeks before I undertake another journey east, but I don't expect that I'll be gone for more than a few weeks this time, a month at the very most. I may have to go to Clarion in the meantime on a family matter, which wouldn't take me away for more than a few days, but I'm not exactly certain of that yet."

Although she was disappointed by the prospect of his leaving again, she was too buoyed by his willingness to wait for her to find her own replacement to be cross with him. The fact that they would have time together before he headed back East again also helped to ease her dismay. "Is that all?"

When her stomach growled, he laughed. "That's all for now. We can discuss the other matter later, since it's a bit complicated, but we do need to finish this picnic and get you back to Trinity before dark."

She grinned and snatched the half-eaten cookie from her plate. This time, she found it full of flavor.

He handed her another. "I don't suppose you'd consider the idea that when I leave for New York that you'd go with me so we could look for a midwife there and bring her back with us, would you? Of course, that would mean we'd have to marry first since it wouldn't be proper for us to travel together otherwise."

Martha pushed the cookie he was offering away. "Certainly not. Unlike Fern, who seems to think it's perfectly fine to hire a stranger without any solid references, I won't do that. I'll find someone I know and trust who'll make a good midwife right here, and you'll have to live with your promise to wait until I do. Unless you're already changing your mind," she added with a scowl.

He offered her a crooked smile. "I didn't think you'd agree, but you can't fault a man for asking."

"Perhaps not." She smiled.

"Then agree, at least, to spend a day with me. Not tomorrow or even the next day. You need to rest. But one day soon," he said.

When he leaned close to kiss her, she leaned closer and whispered, "Yes."

She knew the dangers of his kisses and that he knew she found them almost impossible to resist, which meant she really could not wait too long before thinking of ways to avoid them. One way, she supposed, was to make herself just a little less predictable.

She just needed this one last kiss before she tried.

8

Martha didn't awake the next day until midafternoon.

When she spied Bird perched on top of his cage instead of inside, she sighed. He had escaped once again. Since she had also forgotten to put the cover on the cage last night, she must have slept straight through his morning serenade.

After dragging herself out of bed, she filled his food bowl with a fresh supply of seeds. The instant he hopped inside the cage to eat, she closed the door, hoping for a little peace to say her prayers and dress for the day.

Half an hour later, with Thomas's invitation to spend a day with him the day after tomorrow wrapped around her heart of hopes, she descended the back staircase in the confectionery. She felt more refreshed and just plain happier than she had been for many, many months. The aroma of a heavenly stew awaited her. Famished to the point she was a bit light-headed, she held on to the railing for fear she might take a tumble and add yet another bump to her head.

For the first time in months, Martha realized she felt a renewed spirit within. Her talk with Thomas gave her direction, and with a firm hold on her faith and a level of grit and pluck she had not been able to summon for a long time, she felt ready to face the future and its challenges.

Since it had been too late by the time Thomas had brought her home last night for Martha to go out to Aunt Hilda's to confront Victoria about her behavior with Dr. McMillan, she would need every resource at her command today, because she was determined to see her daughter, right after she'd had something to eat.

She paused at the bottom of the steps, but Ivy was the only one in the kitchen. The moment Ivy looked over her shoulder from her place at the sink to see who was entering the room, she smiled.

"Awake at last, I see," Ivy teased before she turned her attention back to the pan she had been scouring. "I'm afraid you slept right through breakfast and missed dinner, too, but there's a teapot on the table and a plate of chicken stew for you in the oven. Let me know if the tea has turned as cool as the air today. I can heat up some more water in no time." She set down the pan she had been cleaning and dried off her hands. "I've a mind to join you for a cup myself."

"I'm sure it's fine. Thank you." Martha retrieved the plate of stew from the oven and sat down.

Ivy took a place at the table across from her. "Those dirty pans can wait."

Concerned by the exhaustion that creased Ivy's features, Martha filled both of their teacups. "Maybe you should take a few days to rest up and let Jane take care of the kitchen like you said she was going to."

Ivy sighed and passed her a small jug of honey. "We were all so exhausted, we were abed before you came home and never even heard you come upstairs. I trust you were able to help Mr. Crowder's daughter?"

"Yes, I believe I did," Martha replied. As she added two dollops of honey to her tea, she felt certain that by now Missy was a married woman.

"Victoria came by this morning hoping to see you. We told her you'd been called right back out again last night and were still asleep, so she decided to leave you to rest."

Martha swallowed the lump in her throat. She attempted to eat some of the chicken stew, but she was so disappointed that she'd missed seeing Victoria, she barely tasted a thing.

When she heard a bit of a commotion, which sounded like furniture being pushed about, she glanced down the hall to the door to the new storage room. "Is there someone working in there?"

Ivy's sky-blue eyes filled, oddly enough, with tears. "That would be my sister. She's got Jane and Cassie with her, too. After you left yesterday, Fern hired a couple of men to move all the furniture down from the sitting room upstairs to the room we planned to use for more storage down here. They carried up a couple of other pieces for Jane and her daughter to use in their new bedroom."

She paused and blinked back her tears. "There wasn't enough daylight left to do more than shove everything in the rooms, which by rights should have had a good cleaning first. I told Fern there wasn't any need to get all that cleaning and rearranging done today, but she's got it in her head that Jane and her daughter will be sleeping upstairs tonight in a proper bedroom, just like the rest of us."

Martha understood all too well how important it was to

have a room to call your own when you were living in someone else's home. She was not surprised that Fern understood that, too, and dismissed Ivy's grumbling as nothing more than pure exhaustion speaking. She took one last bite of her stew and got to her feet. "I've had more rest than anyone, for a change, so if you'll excuse me, I'll see what I can do to help them."

Ivy sniffled. "Would you? I'd like to help, too, but—"

"But you have a kitchen to tidy, which is work enough, so I'll send Cassie in to help you." Martha walked around the table to press a kiss to the top of Ivy's head and grabbed a work apron before she headed toward a few hours of physical work that she hoped just might keep her mind off of Victoria—and the very handsome man Martha suspected was determined to make her his wife sooner rather than later.

Martha wiped the perspiration from her brow with the back of her hand. Even after cleaning and arranging the new downstairs sitting room, she still had a good bit of energy left, along with solid respect for Jane, who had been working nonstop just as hard as Martha had been. She was just a bit overwarm.

Anxious to get all of the furniture back into place now that they had finished cleaning it, she studied the room and weighed Jane's suggestion. "I think you're right. If you put both of the beds on that far wall, the rug should fit right in between them. That way, come winter, neither one of you will have to tolerate cold floorboards the moment you get out of bed."

Jane handed her a fresh handkerchief she pulled out of her work apron and smiled as she wiped her own brow with another. "Having a rug at all is a luxury for us," she admitted, "but you've done enough work for today. Why don't you head downstairs and see how Miss Fern and Miss Ivy are doing and send Cassie up? She can help me unroll the rug and set it into place."

Martha chuckled. "Right about now, I suspect Fern and Ivy are doing rather well. The last time I went downstairs to fetch some water for us, they were getting ready to take Cassie for a walk around Trinity so she would have a better sense of where she was living now. I suspect they probably included a stop at the general store to get a larger tin of licorice root while they were out and about, so I'm afraid you're stuck with me."

Jane's eyes widened and she shook her head. "Those two women are just too good to be true. I've actually had to pinch myself, just to be sure I haven't been sucked into a fairy tale with not one but two fairy godmothers."

Martha tucked the handkerchief into her apron pocket. "You're not alone. I feel the same way about them, and so do most of the folks in town. But from what I've learned from the two of them so far, the sick man you were caring for long after your wages ran out might have felt the same way about you. I know Fern and Ivy are very grateful that you did," she added as she helped Jane to drag the braided rug.

Huffing a bit by the time they had the rug inside the room, Jane held one end of the rug while Martha positioned the other close to the wall. "I didn't have any way to contact Mr. Ashford, but if I'd left that poor man all alone, he would have died in a matter of days, hungry and thirsty and lying in his own waste. No one deserves to die like that, alone and unloved, regardless of how a life has been spent or wasted," she whispered, as if her choice to stay as his caretaker were so natural and so right, anyone in her position would have made the very same decision as she had.

Martha knew better, however. She dropped her end of the rug down and nodded for Jane to do the same. Once they'd unrolled the rug they had salvaged from storage, Martha was disappointed to see that it was well-worn and needed more than a few stitches to repair places that had separated, creating any number of opportunities for Jane or Cassie to trip.

But when she glanced over at Jane, the woman was smiling as if the rug were brand-new. "It's going to be perfect, especially after I do a bit of mending. Let's see how the beds fit," Jane urged.

Martha followed her back out into the hall and mentally added gratitude as another good quality to Jane's character. Then together they worked to bring in the two beds. The wooden headboards were heavy, the mattresses were bulky and awkward to handle, and by the time they had everything in place, she was in awe of Jane's strength and stamina.

Those qualities were hard to dismiss, mostly because Martha was winded and had a twinge in her back, while Jane had enough extra breath to be humming while she worked. She moved about the room with apparent ease, even though she had already helped to clean and set up the sitting room downstairs while Martha had been sleeping the day away.

"Maybe we should take a minute to rest and plan out the rest of the room before we bring in anything else so we don't have to waste our energy moving things around in here," Martha suggested as she rubbed the small of her back.

Jane cringed. "I'm sorry. I've worked you too hard, haven't I? Why don't you leave the rest to me? There's not much else left out in the hall."

"Only a couple of heavy trunks that even you shouldn't attempt to handle on your own, not to mention a washstand and a pair of side chairs," Martha argued, unwilling to admit she was less of a workhorse than Jane. "Do you always work this hard without stopping?"

Jane paused for a moment before she answered. "Not always. Only when I'm really trying to impress someone."

"Why in heaven's name would you think you had to impress me?"

"Because . . . because I know how important you are to Miss Fern and Miss Ivy and how much they value your opinion. I want you to think highly of me, and I want to reassure you that Miss Fern and Miss Ivy didn't make a mistake hiring me and taking Cassie and me into their household," Jane said quietly.

"Then have mercy and consider your goal met," Martha quipped.

Jane's eyes widened, and almost immediately she reached around to rub the small of her back, too.

Martha grinned. Darn if the woman wasn't human after all. And a good honest woman, too.

Ivy chose that particular moment to walk into the room. "I see you two are making progress," she said as she glanced around. "This is good, but you need to hurry up and finish so you have enough time to really pretty yourself up for supper, Martha. We're having company."

"Company? Since when?" Martha blurted.

"Since Thomas arrived just a few minutes ago asking to speak to you. I didn't think you'd want him to see you looking as dirty as a plow horse at the end of a full day of planting, so I invited him to supper to give him a chance to talk to you then. He'll be here in about an hour." Then Ivy walked right back out of the room, giving Martha no time to argue with her.

"Am I really as dirty as a plow horse?" Martha asked and looked down at her skirts, which were coated with dust and grime.

She was actually caught by surprise when Jane answered her. "Just a bit more than I am, but I think once you wash off all that dirt on your face, you'll look like yourself again. Now scoot. I'll finish up here while you get ready for Thomas. I assume he's someone important to you, isn't he?"

Martha smiled and left the room with Jane's question hanging in the air. There were many things Martha was willing to share with Jane and talk about. Thomas was just not one of them.

Supper was finally over.

The food had been delicious. The company had been more than enjoyable. Martha had even worn her Sunday dress for the occasion. Even so, her stomach was in knots as she walked with Thomas down the hallway when he was ready to leave.

He opened the back door and walked down the two steps before he turned around to bid her good night, his face level with hers and bathed in light from the hallway.

Her heart skipped a beat as his gaze traveled the contours of her face.

"Now that we're finally alone," he said, "I can tell you that you look very fetching tonight, and I'm overly pleased that you agreed to spend the day with me, day after tomorrow."

She was tempted to reply in kind but did not dare give him any encouragement, especially when he climbed back up the bottom step. His nearness made it impossible for her to hold any thought but of loving this man and wanting to be his wife.

Her heart skipped a beat and then another when he climbed a second step higher. "After I delivered you home last night, I thought about the plan we've made for our future together and came up with a better one."

Rooted in place, she swallowed hard. "You did?"

He nodded. "When we spend the day together, I think we should go to see Reverend Welsh to make arrangements for us to get married and go to New York together in a few weeks, just like I suggested. Since you've already made it clear you don't want to look for a midwife in New York, you can double your efforts here when we get back, continue your work as a midwife, and I promise not to get annoyed every time you're summoned away. What do you think about making that our new plan?"

She was surprised that he had not yet discovered Reverend Welsh was not in town and would not be for some time, and when Thomas bent down to kiss her, she placed her hand on his chest firmly enough to make him pause. "I thought we'd agreed that you'd go to New York alone in a few weeks and while you're gone, I'd concentrate all of my free time on finding someone here who wants to replace me," she countered. "And if I did accept this new idea of yours, I suppose you'd find it wholly acceptable that while I'm gone, Dr. McMillan would take over caring for all of the women and children here, wouldn't you?"

He cringed. "I hadn't really thought about that."

She smiled. "That's all right, Thomas. As long as one of us is thinking straight, that's all that matters. But I do feel badly for teasing you," she admitted, hoping she had not deceived him for too long about the one reason they definitely could not marry now.

He cocked a brow. "How so?"

"Reverend Welsh took his wife East for water treatments some time ago, and no one has any idea of when they'll be back. Any plans you might want to make for us to get married and go to New York together are rather pointless without him here, don't you think?"

He leaned forward until his face was so close to her own, his breath fanned her lips and left them tingling. "Believe me, Martha. If you said you'd marry me tonight, I could have a preacher here in a matter of hours, and if you doubt that I'd do exactly that, you don't want to test me," he whispered, then gave her a kiss that lingered just long enough to convince her that he meant every word he said.

He left her standing there wondering if his plan to marry before he went to New York was all that bad of an idea after all.

Until she thought of Victoria.

Concern about her daughter's future eclipsed any she had about her own with Thomas, and she carried those worries back inside with her as Thomas headed to his own home. When she reached the privacy of her room, she dropped to her knees, pressed her forehead to the mattress on her cot, and folded her hands in prayer. "Heavenly Father, You know the troubles of my heart even when I'm too worried or too ashamed to bring them to You, but I'm coming to You now. As much as I long to marry Thomas and devote my energies to finding a woman to replace me, my first responsibility is to my daughter. But I'm uncertain of what I should do with her. She's so young and so vulnerable and so innocent, I feel as if I must protect her as fiercely as I did when she was a young child. Yet even as the urge to protect her remains strong, help me to accept that my guidance must always be second to Yours because she is Your precious daughter, too."

She paused for a moment to gather her thoughts, even though she knew that God understood them already, and continued praying long into the night until she felt the presence of His peace.

By the time she crawled into her bed, it was almost midnight. Her body was weary, but her soul was refreshed. She was confident in what she needed to do when she found a way to talk privately with Victoria in the morning.

And she would, as long as God was by her side to help her in case she faltered or lost her way when she did.

9

Martha was a woman on a mission when she slipped out of the confectionery just after sunrise the next morning.

Armed with her rock-solid faith and a steaming crock of bread pudding she cradled with both hands, she approached Aunt Hilda's cottage just on the outskirts of the southern edge of town. Smoke twirling up from the chimney promised a warm fire that would ease the chill that had roosted in her bones.

She headed down the familiar path that led along the side of the cottage to the kitchen in the back. The closer she got to the back door, the faster her heart was beating. When she finally stood directly in front of the door, she paused to whisper a prayer before tapping lightly on the weathered wood. When no one answered the door, she knocked a little harder.

This time the door cracked open just a bit before it swung wide open, and Victoria stepped back to let her enter. "Mother! Come in. What are you doing up and about this early?"

"I haven't seen you for more than a few minutes since I've

gotten back home," she began. "I thought I'd invite myself to breakfast and bring along something sweet to eat for everyone. Aunt Hilda has many, many talents, but she simply has no knack for baking," she added in a whisper before giving her daughter a quick kiss and handing her the crock of bread pudding.

Hilda Seymour, her eccentric aunt-by-affection, had in fact been the most requested afternurse for miles around until last winter, when she finally gave up staying with new mothers after their deliveries. Now seventy-eight, she still provided new mothers with honey from the beehives she tended with her husband. She also used the honey to make honey wine, which was an essential ingredient in the hot toddies that helped to ease the grumbling pains that often followed a delivery.

Aunt Hilda held an exalted status in Trinity as the last of the original settlers, but she held an equally special place in Martha's heart. In addition to being a close friend of Martha's Grandmother Poore, who had been Trinity's first midwife, Aunt Hilda was her most trusted confidante. She also possessed such deep faith and uncommon good sense that Martha relied on her heavily for advice and comfort.

In all truth, if Aunt Hilda had not been here after Victoria had run away last year and during Fern and Ivy's absence more recently, Martha was not certain how she would have survived with only Grace and Bird to listen to her troubles.

Victoria giggled, breaking Martha's reverie. "The thought of eating any meal without something sweet is simply not in your nature, but if you ask me, I think it's gotten worse since we started living in a confectionery," she teased.

She took a whiff of the bread pudding before she placed it on the table, which had already been set with three places, and turned back to her mother. "You don't have to whisper. Aunt Hilda and Uncle Richard have been up for a while."

Once Martha hung up her cape and bonnet, she looked around the small kitchen. With a long rectangular wooden table in the center and a pair of rocking chairs in front of the fire, there was little room for anything more than a cookstove, a corner cupboard, and a sink with a pump for the water. "Where are they now?" she asked as she edged closer to the fire in the hearth.

"They like to have a cup of tea together in their bedroom before they venture out for breakfast. Aunt Hilda just left the kitchen a few minutes ago, so they'll be a while," Victoria replied. After retrieving another plate and a mismatched cup and saucer, she carried everything back to the table to set an extra place for her mother.

Martha brightened. "Then we actually have a few moments to ourselves. Let me take a look at you," Martha suggested.

"You haven't been gone long enough to forget what I look like, have you?" Victoria teased.

"I'm your mother. I could never forget what you look like," Martha insisted. When Victoria left the table again to secure some additional utensils, she studied her daughter more objectively.

At eighteen, Victoria was no longer a child and had blossomed into a very comely young woman with all the right curves in all the right places. With her dark, curly hair pulled back and held in place by a ribbon at the nape of her neck, her hazel eyes dominated her heart-shaped face, and her porcelain complexion was flawless. She was also very loving, incredibly bright, and talented.

No wonder Dr. McMillan was so smitten.

Martha drew a deep breath and took a moment to recall the measure of peace and grace she had received after a long night of prayer. She also held on to the promise she had made to herself to talk to Victoria openly and honestly about the girl's intention to marry Dr. McMillan. "Would you have a cup of tea with me while we wait?"

"I just refilled the kettle, so I'm afraid the water's not hot enough yet. We can sit together in front of the fire, though. You look a bit chilled after walking all the way here. You must really miss Grace."

"Very much," Martha admitted. She sat in one of the rocking chairs and stretched out her legs for a moment before setting the chair into a slow rock to ease the twinges in the small of her back. "I can walk farther now without getting winded, but even though my back doesn't always cooperate, I don't mind walking about town. I just can't walk far enough or fast enough to answer all of my calls on my own, I'm afraid."

Victoria sat in the other chair and started to rock. "Will you be able to get another horse soon?"

"That's not very likely," she admitted and chuckled. "By the time I save up enough to purchase another mare, I'll be too old to ride, so for now, I'm trying to be content relying on other people to take me wherever I have to go." She didn't delve into explaining she would have no need for a horse at all once she gave up her calling and married Thomas.

In fact, she was glad that she and Thomas had both agreed to still keep their plans to get married a secret. Telling her daughter now, when she had no idea of when they might marry, would be tantamount to telling Dr. McMillan. She simply refused to give him any information that would benefit his own practice over her own, which assuaged her guilt for being less than candid with Victoria.

"That's enough talk about me. How have you been faring these past few weeks? Have you had time to do more of your writing?" she asked, again giving her daughter the opportunity to broach the subject that lay heavy on Martha's heart.

Victoria sighed and frowned. "Very little that's any good, I'm afraid. I did write to Mrs. Morgan, though, but I haven't heard back from her yet. I just wanted to find out if anything had been decided about the series of little articles on remedies and sketches that we worked on together in January. The last time she wrote, she said they might not be published until next spring, and I wanted to know if that had been decided or if the original date for this fall would remain." Her gaze settled on the fire.

"Mrs. Morgan's babe was due in late spring. I'm sure she's delivered by now, which means she's probably very busy, so I wouldn't worry too much if you don't hear back from her for a while," Martha offered, but the deep disappointment in Victoria's voice tugged at her heartstrings.

June Morgan and her husband published a very popular women's magazine in New York. Last summer they had taken Victoria into their home after she decided not to continue with the theater troupe that had provided her with a way to escape from Trinity, and for that, Martha would be forever grateful.

June and her husband had also recognized and encouraged Victoria's writing talents. As the magazine's editor, June had offered Victoria a place as her assistant, as well as in their home, but she'd insisted that Victoria first return home to Trinity to see her mother and ask for permission. She had even escorted Victoria home to guarantee her safety.

Martha's reunion with her runaway daughter had been bittersweet. In the end, she had reluctantly given Victoria permission to accept the Morgans' offer. She had also agreed to share her knowledge of healing remedies with women far beyond Trinity by identifying and sketching plants with healing qualities while Victoria took what Martha knew about them and wrote the verse to accompany the sketches. Having those little articles published, however, was much more important to her daughter than it was to her.

"I'm sorry. I know you're anxious to see our work appear in print, but it will be eventually. And no matter when that happens, nothing can change the fact that we had the opportunity to do something very interesting together." Martha treasured the memories she had stored deep in her heart of a time when she and Victoria had actually grown closer.

"We did, didn't we?" Victoria said.

"If you haven't been doing much writing, how have you been spending your days?" Martha asked, anxious to change the conversation from the past to the present and to give her daughter one last opportunity to introduce the subject of her relationship with Dr. McMillan before she was forced to do so.

Victoria shrugged. "In all truth, I've done quite a bit of writing. It just isn't very good, so I keep writing and rewriting and getting nowhere. Poor Mrs. Andrews. She tiptoes around the study at Dr. McMillan's, where he's set up a place for me to write, as if she's afraid she'll distract me while she's cleaning, when it's my own distractions that keep my poems and stories from developing properly."

With the conversation getting close to the topic Martha wanted to discuss, her pulse began to race. "What kind of distractions?"

Victoria let out a long sigh, but she still kept her gaze focused straight ahead at the fire. "They're not distractions, really. They're more like longings, but I'm not sure you'll understand them," she whispered.

Martha swallowed hard. "But perhaps I will," she managed.

Victoria stopped the rocker and turned in her seat to face Martha. "I don't want you to think I'm ungrateful, because I know how hard it's been for you to provide for us since Father died, but . . . but I want more now. I want a home of my own. I want a family of my own. Most girls my age are either married or betrothed . . . or they want to be."

"Those longings are perfectly normal for a woman of any age," Martha said as the yearnings of her daughter's heart wrapped around her own. "Are you quite certain that Dr. McMillan is the man you want to spend the rest of your life with?"

Victoria's eyes widened, her mouth gaped, and her cheeks turned crimson.

"Don't bother to deny it," Martha said, then quickly admitted to eavesdropping on the young couple at the stable behind Dr. McMillan's home. "I'm not particularly proud of myself for not making my presence known, but I daresay we would all have been quite embarrassed if I had. And, I might add, the two of you have made it very evident that there's good reason why young couples should be properly chaperoned at all times."

Victoria's blush deepened. "I know you're not overly fond of him and that our interest in each other places you in a difficult position. . . . We didn't mean to upset you."

"Fortunately for both of you, I've had some time to think things over. I can't say I wouldn't be happier if you wanted to marry someone else, because I would. But it's not my life, though as your mother, it's my responsibility to make certain that you think this over very, very carefully to be certain that this is the path God wants you to take."

"I know. And I am, but—"

"I must confess that I did have several ideas about what I should do about you and this young man," Martha interrupted, and she was pleased to see that she definitely had Victoria's full attention now. "My first thought was that I could simply refuse to give Dr. McMillan permission to marry you and count on the fact that given his place in the community, he'd be far less inclined to ignore my wishes than you would."

Judging by the flush on Victoria's cheeks, she knew she did not have to go further and remind Victoria of her running away.

"Then I thought that I should ship you off to New York to live with the Morgans, or even to Boston to live with your brother and Grandfather Cade, but I decided that those were fruitless ideas since you'd probably run straight back to Trinity to be with Dr. McMillan."

"Wh-what did you finally decide?" Victoria asked, her eyes brimming with tears.

"In the end, I came up with another idea about what I should do," Martha said, ever so grateful for the time she had had to pray and for God's guidance when she did.

Victoria worried the fingers on both hands. "What do you plan to do?"

"I want to speak to you and your young man together. Tonight. Just the three of us, and when I do, I want the two of you to tell me why you each think that this marriage is what you both want."

Victoria's eyes widened, allowing a single tear to escape. "And if we do, you'll . . . you'll give us your blessing? Truly?"

"I suppose that depends entirely on your answers," Martha admitted. "In the meantime, now that Fern and Ivy are back, I want you living back at the confectionery, where there's plenty of supervision when I'm called away. I also want you to promise me that you won't be spending any time alone with that young man."

"Can I still work in his office a bit and continue to use his study upstairs to write my poems and stories?"

"Only if Mrs. Andrews is there. If she goes to market or leaves for any reason, you leave, too," Martha insisted, and she was confident that her friend would continue to keep an extra close eye on Victoria once Martha spoke to her.

Victoria blinked away the rest of her tears before she nodded. "I promise."

Martha clapped her hands on her thighs. "Good. Now that that's settled, I need a good strong cup of tea."

"The water should be ready by now," Victoria offered, then rose and planted a kiss on Martha's cheek. "Thank you."

"Don't thank me yet," Martha cautioned with a smile. "I still have one more thing I want to ask you to do."

Victoria grinned. "Anything."

"Fix the tea. Then we'll talk about it," Martha suggested, but she was confident that Victoria would not hesitate to grant Martha's last request and wait awhile before marrying. Although she might have to struggle a bit to welcome her daughter's impending betrothal to Dr. McMillan, her daughter's joy was contagious and ignited a happiness in her mother's heart that she could not deny.

But she also knew one thing for certain. She was not going to make the same mistake that her father-in-law had made so many years ago. A prominent and wealthy lawyer in Boston, Graham Cade had disowned his son and only child when he refused to follow in his father's footsteps and instead moved west to follow the life of a plain and simple yeoman farmer. Later, after John had married Martha, his father had never recognized her or their children and continued to refuse any contact with his son or his family.

Until John died.

At the time, Oliver was thirteen and Victoria was only seven. Even then, however, Graham Cade showed virtually no interest in them, except for Oliver. Within a matter of months, he convinced Oliver to join him in Boston, where his grandson was now fulfilling the dreams that he had always had for his son.

It would be hard and it would be challenging, but with God's help, Martha knew that she would let nothing on this earth ever fill her daughter's heart with the pain and grief her husband had carried with him to his grave. Not ever.

Some way, somehow, Martha would have to learn to accept Dr. McMillan not only as her daughter's husband but also as the man who would love and protect her daughter when she was no longer here to do that—assuming Martha could truly come to terms with the notion that it was time to let her daughter go and fully embrace the joy that was pouring out of her daughter's heart and into her own.

10

Reluctant to leave the warmth of the fire, Martha remained in her rocking chair while Victoria poured steaming hot water into a teapot. "I know your writing is important, Victoria, but I want you to continue to spend some time each day helping Aunt Hilda, as well as a few hours helping out at the confectionery."

"I'll help out at home, of course," Victoria replied. "And yes, I'll help Aunt Hilda, too. As a matter of fact, she asked me just the other day if I wouldn't mind helping out a bit more, just for a few weeks."

Alarmed by the thought of how devoted Aunt Hilda and her husband were to those beehives of theirs, Martha planted her feet hard on the floor and stopped the chair from rocking. "They didn't ask you to help with those bees, did they?"

"I don't want anything to do with them. I barely tolerate caring for Bird when you're away, and he doesn't sting like they do. But don't worry. She hasn't even mentioned those bees."

Heavy footsteps drew Martha's attention to the doorway,

where Richard Seymour was just entering the kitchen. Just shy of eighty, he looked much healthier and far stronger than when he'd returned home a year ago. He was still nearly bald, but his once-scraggly white beard was nicely trimmed. The dark blue eyes behind his spectacles were clear and sparkling now, and although his frame was still a bit bowed, he seemed to be a little stronger.

The fact that he was here at all after being gone for thirty years was indeed amazing. Everyone, including Martha, assumed the man had either died or had made a new life for himself elsewhere. Aunt Hilda, on the other hand, had never wavered in her devotion to him, even after burying all four of their children.

When he finally did return and beg for her forgiveness after wasting so many years searching for the fortune he felt he needed to provide for her, she had welcomed him home as if he had only been gone for a fortnight.

To Martha, Aunt Hilda offered a lesson in forgiveness that she would never forget.

Richard paused for a moment when he saw Martha and smiled. "We thought we heard your voice, Martha. Hilda will be right here. Did I hear somebody mention our bees?"

Martha cringed and got up from her rocking chair to greet him properly while Victoria carried the teapot over to the table. "That was me. I was worried that Victoria was helping you with them."

He returned her hug before motioning her to the table. "No worry there. The bees and the hives are gone," he told her as he held out her chair for her.

Surprised, Martha took her seat and noted the look of surprise on Victoria's face, too. She waited until he sat down before addressing him again. "Did the bees die?"

"Nothing like that. Hilda took good care of my bees all those years I was gone, but we decided to sell them to Michael Keyes. Apparently, he'd been after her for some time now to get them."

Martha's heart sank, and she frowned. No more bees meant there would not be any more honey or honey wine from Aunt Hilda, and she knew she wouldn't be the only one disappointed.

Aunt Hilda entered the kitchen. With her thick white braid shaped into a crown atop her head and her dark purple gown, she looked every inch like an aging queen about to join her subjects. She took one look at Martha's frown and gently scolded her husband. "Whatever did you do or say to Martha to upset her?"

Instead of defending himself immediately, he rose, gave her a peck on her cheek and escorted her to her seat at the table. "Just a bit of truth, love. Isn't that right, Martha?"

"He just told me that you've sold all the bees."

Aunt Hilda waved her hand about. "I suspect it's my honey and my honey wine you'll miss more than the bees, Martha, but don't worry. We made a rather impressive trade with Mr. Keyes to make sure you'll have both, and I doubt Wesley Sweet down at the general store could have done any better, either," she noted as Victoria added more wood to the cookstove.

Thomas's nephew was known to drive quite a hard bargain with customers, so Martha asked as she began serving the tea, "What kind of trade?"

"In return for the bees and the hives and all of our equipment, we got a fair bit of coin," Uncle Richard said proudly.

Aunt Hilda grinned. "And I gave Mr. Keyes my recipe for honey wine. I had to do a bit of convincing, but he finally agreed to deliver whatever honey the Lynn sisters need for their larder at the confectionery, and he promised to provide you with all the honey wine you need to help make it easier for all those young women bringing new babes into the world," she said proudly.

Hilda then pulled back the cover on the crock of bread pudding and grinned. "Bless you, Martha," she said before spooning a generous helping onto her husband's plate as well as her own. "Can you hand me your plate?" she asked.

Still a bit stunned by the fact that Michael Keyes now owned all the bees and the hives, Martha didn't realize her aunt had spoken to her until she felt a tap on her hand.

"I asked if you could hand me your plate," Aunt Hilda repeated.

"I'm sorry. I didn't hear you." Martha held out her plate and watched Aunt Hilda fill most of it with bread pudding before motioning for Victoria to join them.

"Those griddle cakes can wait," Aunt Hilda said to Victoria. "Come enjoy this treat while it's still warm."

Victoria wasted no time obeying, and the four of them shared lighthearted conversation all through breakfast and for a good spell beyond. When they finished, Victoria insisted on restoring the kitchen to order and shooed them all out of the room. "I shouldn't be long, Mother. If you can wait for me, we can walk back together. I have a few things to get for Aunt Hilda from the general store."

Pleased that her daughter actually wanted her company, Martha followed Aunt Hilda into the adjoining sitting room. She had not been to the cottage for a spell, and she was surprised to see that the sitting room was in complete disarray. Aunt Hilda had always been such a stickler for keeping her home tidy and clean.

Two faded upholstered chairs, along with several side tables, had been pushed back against the far wall. The knotted rug that usually covered the middle of the floor lay rolled up along the opposite wall, and the exposed floorboards needed a good sweeping and a strong scrub brush.

"Don't look at all this mess. Victoria and I are in the middle of cleaning," Aunt Hilda offered. "You and I can have a visit in my bedroom."

"And I'm off for my constitutional." Uncle Richard grabbed a sweater and a knit cap off of a peg near the front door and took his leave.

Aunt Hilda's eyes remained focused on the door for a few long moments after he was gone. "He's really a wonderful man," she murmured before she led Martha into the bedroom the elderly couple shared.

The door to the second bedroom was open, and Martha had a rare glimpse inside. Instead of holding the four little cots she remembered being there years ago, the room held only two now, and she recognized Victoria's robe lying at the foot of one of them. Otherwise, there were two small travel bags, similar in size to the one Martha used to hold her simples, sitting on top of a trunk. She recognized one bag as the one Aunt Hilda had used when she had been called out as an afternurse and assumed the other belonged to Uncle Richard.

The moment she followed Aunt Hilda into her bedroom, Martha dismissed any curiosity she might have had about the contents of the other bedroom. This room was exactly as she remembered.

The heavy winter drapes were tied back, allowing sunlight to pour through a single window. Directly ahead, a large trunk rested on bare floorboards at the foot of a double bed, and a small washstand to her left held a cracked, flowery basin and a pitcher for water.

She focused her attention, however, on the coverlet on the bed. The quilt was a bit faded now and well-worn, but the beauty of the design and the workmanship required to create the quilt still testified to the unique talent her mother had been given.

"I love this quilt, too," Aunt Hilda said. She sat down on the bed and patted the space next to her. "Your mother had quite a talent for the needle. I think of her every time I make my bed."

Martha sat down and traced some of the stitches with her fingertips. "She used to make cradle quilts that Grandmother Poore would give to the new mothers after delivering their babes, too. Unfortunately, I didn't inherit a bit of her talent."

"Talents are God-given, although we make up our own minds about whether or not we use them," Aunt Hilda cautioned. "Even though we might be related to someone, that doesn't always mean we share the same talents."

"I know," Martha said as more memories brought the past into the present.

Aunt Hilda sighed. "I know how disappointed Sarah was when your mother didn't continue family tradition by becoming a midwife and that you're just as disappointed with your daughter. But you need to remember what a gifted writer Victoria is instead. And remember, too, that God always finds a way to bring us joy, even in the midst of our sorrows and disappointments. In your grandmother's case," she continued, "that was you, Martha. You brought her such joy by following in her footsteps."

"Unfortunately, I don't have a granddaughter to do that for me—not that it matters much anymore," Martha replied, quickly confiding her decision to give up her calling and marry Thomas as soon as she did.

"You'll find someone," Aunt Hilda insisted and put her arm around Martha's shoulder. "Just keep in mind that God likes to surprise us now and again. You might find a new midwife in the most unlikely of places," she said. "Speaking of surprises,

I have one of my own to share with you, but you must promise not to say a word about it, not even to Victoria." Aunt Hilda hugged Martha a little closer. "It seems that my dear darling husband still has a yearning for travel in his soul. He's planning to leave again in a few weeks."

Caught completely off guard, Martha eased out of her aunt's embrace and turned to search her face. Instead of the grief or sorrow she expected to see etched there, or perhaps a stream of silent tears, Aunt Hilda's countenance radiated sheer joy. Her eyes, however, were oddly mischievous. "You're not upset?"

"Not in the least," her aunt insisted. "I can't decide if I'm a bit daft or not, but this time I'm going with him."

Martha gasped. "You're . . . you're leaving?"

Aunt Hilda grinned. "Rather exciting, isn't it?"

"Where are you going?"

A shrug. "Probably west, at least at first. Richard has a few places he wants to show me. After that, we'll discover a few new ones together."

"Are you absolutely certain you want to give up everything you have here in Trinity? How can you be sure that this is what you want to do?"

Aunt Hilda smiled. "Because I trust that God wouldn't put the desire to leave with my husband in my heart and make it possible for me to go if He had other plans for me."

Envious of her aunt's faith, Martha took one of her aunt's hands and held on to the last living link she had to her mother and grandmother. "But you're my rock! What will I do without you?"

Aunt Hilda pressed their hands to Martha's heart. "We'll always be together *here*. Always, sweet Martha. But there's only one place I want to be, and that's with Richard. Wherever he goes, for as long as he lives, I want to be with him and share my life with him. If that's how you feel about Thomas, then stop dawdling and marry that man now, Martha, and make every day you have together really matter."

With her heart pulsing rapidly against her hands, Martha grew even more determined to find a woman to take over her duties as midwife as quickly as possible. Then she'd do exactly as Aunt Hilda suggested: marry Thomas and make every day they spent as husband and wife even better than the day before.

11

The sun hung high in the sky as Martha and Victoria walked back to the center of town and parted ways.

While Victoria continued on to the general store, Martha walked down the alley alongside the confectionery. She could hear voices inside, although the curtains in the new alcove were drawn and blocked her view.

The white horse lightly tethered to a post near the back door, nuzzling a baking pan that must have been returned and left on the back step, however, garnered all of her attention.

In a matter of heartbeats, she considered the reasons the horse would be there. Even if the confectionery had reopened— which it had not—customers entered by the front door, and so did visitors. Deliveries arrived in the alley by wagon, not a single horse, and customers returning baking pans walked down the alley and left them by the back door. Which meant there was only one reason for the horse being there: another call to duty.

Her heart sank. Unless she was needed somewhere very close

for something easy to resolve, she would have to postpone meeting with Victoria and Dr. McMillan tonight.

Martha hurried her steps, paid little more than passing attention to the horse on her way inside, and rushed down the hallway to the kitchen with a prayer on her lips and hope in her heart that there might be another reason for that horse to be there. Instead of finding someone she knew who had come to summon her away, she found Fern and Ivy standing by the door on the opposite side of the room. There was no one else with them who might have come to summon her away.

"We were just talking about you. How was your visit with Victoria and Hilda?" Ivy asked.

Relieved that she had not been called away, Martha quickly removed her cape and bonnet. "They're all very well," she replied and hung her cape and bonnet on a wooden peg on the wall. "Did you know there's a horse tied up in the alley, right outside the kitchen door?"

Fern walked over to the cupboard, retrieved a small bit of paper, and handed it to Martha. "Jane found the horse when she left with Cassie to get a few things from the general store. This was tied to the horse's reins, though she had a bit of a time getting it. I hope you don't mind, but Ivy and I were too curious not to read it. Go ahead. Read it quick before I blab out what it says and ruin everything."

A bit perplexed, Martha wiped her hands on her apron and looked at the note. The paper was badly crinkled, so she straightened it a bit first before she started reading. But the penmanship was so poor, it took her a moment to decipher the words:

Widow Cade, I heard about your horse dyin' so I figured the best reward I could give to settle my debt to you is this mare. Her name is Bella.

Martha read the note twice again before looking up at Ivy, who was beaming. "The horse is for me?"

"That's what the note says. Too bad whoever gave it to you didn't remember to sign the note. Now you won't know for sure who gave it to you, and you can't settle his account in that book of yours."

For half a heartbeat, Martha wondered if Thomas had gotten the horse for her, but she dismissed the thought because he would have given it to her directly. "Even if I could figure out who did this, a horse of any kind is worth far more than anyone owes me," Martha said, but her heart swelled with such joy that her chest actually hurt. "The horse is for me!" she gushed as she rushed out of the kitchen and down the hallway, Ivy and Fern following.

Her pulse was racing and her mind was churning with thoughts of how much easier her life was going to be and how much faster she would be able to reach each of the four women she had in mind as her replacement now that she had a horse of her own again. She opened the back door slowly, half afraid she would find the horse gone, but her fears were unfounded.

Bella was still there, and she was as fine a mare as Martha had ever seen. To her surprise, the horse was still licking at that baking pan, and she nearly chuckled at the idea that this horse had a sweet tooth just like she did.

"Good Bella," she whispered and stepped outside to stand next to the post in front of the horse. Fern and Ivy, however, remained standing side by side in the open doorway. As best as Martha could judge, Bella was only three or four years old. Now that she was really studying the mare, she could see that it was not pure white, but a softer cream color. Her mane and tail were flaxen, but it was the pale, irregular star on her face, just between her eyes, that made her extraordinary in Martha's eyes.

She stroked the mare's face and found brown eyes staring back at her, a bit wary, but definitely interested in the person who was paying such close attention to her. "I don't know you very well right now, Bella, and you don't know me, but I promise to take very, very good care of you. We have a lot to learn about each other, but we're going to have some amazing adventures together," she whispered and leaned forward to nuzzle the horse's face with her own.

She never got close enough. Without warning, Bella hit her square in the chest with her muzzle. Hard. Jolted back, Martha hit her shoulder on the post and landed square on her bottom on the hard-packed dirt.

She heard Ivy and Fern scream and would have screamed herself, but the air had been knocked right out of her lungs and her brain was too scrambled by the jolt she had taken to have any thought but one when she saw the horse lift a foreleg: Get out of Bella's way.

Acting out of pure instinct, she used the heels of her hands and feet to scramble back, well out of the mare's reach, before she was able to stand again.

Even though her fear that Bella had been about to kick her never materialized, she kept her attention focused on Bella to take stock of the situation, more surprised by the mare's odd behavior than anything else.

Despite the fact that her hands were stinging from scraping against the ground, her back and shoulder ached, and she was still trying to draw measured breaths of air, she had nothing more to complain about than a rather large bruise on her pride.

After reassuring Fern and Ivy that she was fine and sending them back inside, Martha took a few moments to wipe the grit and grime from her hands before she brushed off her skirts. She made no attempt, however, to go near the horse to retrieve the baking pan, now covered with dirt.

Unfortunately, Thomas chose that precise moment to appear, and Martha took what solace she could from the fact that he had not actually seen her fall so ignominiously.

He took hold of her elbow as if she were not capable of remaining steady on her own two feet. "I was just passing by when I saw the horse knock you off your feet. Are you all right?"

She slipped her arm away and ignored the growing pain in her shoulder. "I'm fine. Just getting acquainted with my new horse, who doesn't appear to be very open to the idea that she now belongs to me."

He looked back and forth from Martha to Bella and back again twice. "You bought this horse? I thought you said that you—"

"Of course not. If I bought any horse at all, I'd buy a gentle, well-mannered horse like Grace. Unfortunately, someone must have thought that I needed an ill-tempered horse like this one and left her here, along with a note claiming she was my reward," she quipped before she realized she was talking out of anger and not being fair to the horse. "As I recall, Grace wasn't all that gentle when I first claimed her, though, so I should be able to win Bella over, too."

He took a few steps closer to study the horse for a moment before he reached out to scratch behind the mare's ears. When he slid his hands down to stroke her face, the horse gently nuzzled at his chest, leaving Martha grumbling under her breath.

Thomas looked over to Martha and shrugged. "Maybe the mare just prefers men, in which case there's probably little you can do to change her mind." He checked the mare's hindquarters as well as her shoulders with gentle strokes that evoked no response from Bella. "What did you say her name was?"

"It's Bella," she said, still unable to get past the idea that if Thomas was right, God had answered her prayers with a horse that preferred men. Mercy!

He slipped the reins free from the post. "Do you have any idea who left the horse for you?"

"Unfortunately, whoever left the note forgot to sign it."

Thomas laughed. "Or didn't sign it because he was more interested in getting rid of Bella and used the fact the he owed you a reward to justify tethering his problem at your doorstep."

"I don't believe that anyone would do such a thing!"

"Maybe you should," he argued. "But maybe I'm just judging Bella too rashly. Let's see what she does when you take the reins."

The moment Martha had the reins in her hand, Bella reared and tried to yank them away, but Thomas grabbed the reins midway up and held them fast so Martha could let go. "Easy, Bella. You can trust Martha. She can be a bit cranky at times, too, but a dessert or two can usually sweeten her mood. Maybe all you need is a bit of a sweet treat, too."

Martha rolled her eyes but decided not to protest his rather ungallant description of her. "In case you haven't noticed that baking pan lying in the dirt, Bella already had a treat," she argued, mostly to suggest he was wrong to think the horse preferred men. "I think she's just a bit nervous with me because she doesn't know me yet. Or because she wanted more of a treat than a few crumbs stuck to a baking pan."

"In that case," he argued, "I'll hold on to Bella while you slip back inside. There must be some dried apples in the confectionery left from last year's crop. Grab some and let's see what happens when you offer them to her."

She headed inside and returned with a handful of dried apples. Although she was a bit anxious, she piled the dried apples in the palm of her hand, well away from her fingers. Under

97

Thomas's watchful gaze, she held her hand out to Bella very slowly, prepared to yank her hand away the minute the horse made any move to bite her.

To her great relief, the mare daintily nibbled at the dried apples and managed to polish them off as if she and Martha were the best of friends. "See? She likes me better now. She's perfectly happy with me."

"Right now she is, but just a few minutes ago, she tried to yank the reins out of your hand and knocked you off your feet before that," he reminded her. His expression grew somber and his gray eyes darkened with real concern. "I know you need a horse, and it's awfully tempting to think this horse is the answer to your prayers, but the only thing worse than an ill-tempered horse is an unpredictable one. If you can't truly trust the horse to carry you to and from your calls without any kind of incident, then you have no use for her. Just promise me that if she turns out to be as unpredictable in her behavior as I think she will be, you won't hesitate to come to me. If you can't agree to let me buy you a more reliable horse, you can simply borrow one of mine. Can you at least agree to do that for me? Please?"

Thomas's mood had become so serious, Martha almost asked him why—until she remembered that his wife, Sally, had been killed in a riding accident.

Although Bella appeared to be quite content at the moment, and Martha was confident she could win the horse over eventually, she took his words to heart. "I will," she said, "but she's a young horse, Thomas. I really think that if I give her a little time to get used to me, she'll turn out to be quite manageable. I just want to give her a chance before I give her up."

He cocked his head. "How much of a chance?"

"I'll give her a week. Two at the most. After that, if I still can't trust her to behave even a little bit better and it turns out you're right and she truly does prefer men, then I know exactly what I'm going to do," she offered and gave him the biggest smile she could muster. "I'm going to give her to you."

His eyes widened. "Me? Why me? I already have a horse of my own."

She laughed. "You have several horses, in fact, but if it turns out that Bella can be cranky with anyone, man or woman, there isn't anyone I know who could turn an unpredictable horse like this one into a manageable one better than you could, assuming you put your mind to it."

He snorted. "And why is that?"

"Because you can be as stubborn in some of your ways as I am," she retorted. "In the meantime, however, I need to get Bella over to Dr. McMillan's stable. Maybe once she's properly settled into a stall and fed, she'll be a whole lot happier. And along the way, perhaps you can explain how you just happened to be passing by when Bella and I had our first meeting."

Martha was relieved when Bella offered no objection as she led her down the alley, but Thomas was on the other side of the horse holding on to the bridle strap, prepared to take charge should a problem arise that she could not handle.

"I didn't happen to pass by. I was coming to see you."

"Any particular reason?" She noted the heavy wagon traffic on Main Street and got ready to hand the reins over to Thomas if Bella balked.

"I know we'll be spending the day together tomorrow, but my daughter asked me to invite you and Victoria to come to supper the following night so you wouldn't make any plans in the meantime that might prevent you from coming. I believe I heard Dr. McMillan's name mentioned as a guest as well. Eleanor said to tell you that if you can come around seven, you could have a visit with my grandson before he gets put to bed," he suggested, and the pride in his voice was also etched in his features.

"Thank you. We'd love to come. You can tell Eleanor that we'll be there at seven so I can see her little one," she replied, then slowed her steps as they approached the corner of the building.

They waited for several wagons to pass before venturing into the roadway, and a docile Bella seemed oblivious to the noise of the heavy traffic and the racket workers were making along the soon-to-be canal. They crossed the covered bridge and entered the stable without incident, and Martha was feeling altogether happy by the time they finished.

Thomas walked her out of the stable. "I'm picking you up at nine o'clock tomorrow morning, and I'll have everything packed in the buggy so we can have a full day together, just like we discussed," he reminded her.

She gave him her very best and biggest smile. "Assuming I don't get summoned away between now and then, can we make it ten o'clock instead?"

He narrowed his gaze. "Do I want to ask why?"

She shrugged her shoulders. "Probably not, because if you do, you might not like the answer you get."

"If the answer involves that horse of yours, I'm quite certain I won't like it at all."

She looked about to make sure no one would see what she was about to do before she got on tiptoe to whisper in his ear. "Then it's better if you don't ask," she whispered, barely skimming the lobe of his ear with her lips before she scooted off and walked the rest of the way home by herself, equally certain there was not a thing he could say that would make her change her plans to take Bella for a bit of a ride early tomorrow morning.

If all went as well then as she hoped, she would be able to begin a renewed and earnest search for her replacement. Between now and then, however, she had lots of praying to do, most especially before her meeting tonight with Victoria and Dr. McMillan.

12

Martha had never been faced with making a decision about her daughter's future as important as the one she would make tonight.

At eight o'clock that night, steadied by God's grace, she was sitting on the settee in Dr. McMillan's second-floor parlor waiting for one very nervous young couple to rejoin her. Dr. McMillan and Victoria were downstairs in his office, where she had sent them half an hour ago to prepare for this all-important meeting to discuss their possible betrothal. Rosalind Andrews and her husband, who took care of the grounds and the stable after working at the mill all day, had retired to their rooms on the third floor before Martha and Victoria had arrived.

The parlor looked exactly as it had when the late Doc Beyer had lived here, and she still found the dark burgundy color on the walls to be oppressive, even though a pair of oil lamps on the mantel cast a gentle light to the room. Heavy winter curtains still covered the windows that faced Main Street to offer privacy should anyone pass by, but they also made the parlor feel almost claustrophobic.

The pair of footsteps coming down the hall warned of their approach and left her with only enough time to whisper one final prayer, straighten her back, and take a deep breath just before Victoria entered the room with the doctor following right behind her.

Martha held out her hand and motioned for the young couple to sit across from her. As Dr. McMillan held the chair for Victoria to take her seat, Martha realized how much he had changed since his arrival in Trinity, and even more so these last few months.

Although he was shorter than the average man, he was still a bit taller than her petite daughter. She had not noticed it before now, but he had lost his chubby cheeks as well as a paunch more likely to be found on a man considerably older than his twenty-five years. And there was a light in his dark blue eyes when he looked at Victoria that she had never seen before.

Once Victoria was settled in her chair, he walked around to take his seat, and Martha was surprised to see that all the confidence Victoria had shown when she had first agreed to this meeting appeared to be gone. Her face was pale, her cheeks were flushed pink, and she sat stiffly, perched on the edge of her seat.

Dr. McMillan did not look any more at ease than Victoria did. He, too, sat on the edge of his seat and held his back uncommonly rigid and straight. He had apologized earlier, profusely and earnestly, for not approaching Martha months ago to ask for permission to marry Victoria, but he never once blamed his reluctance to do so on Victoria.

Martha locked a firm expression on her face. "Before I say anything else, I need to remind you how deeply disappointed I am in your behavior. What I witnessed by chance at the stable was shocking and thoroughly unacceptable, and I expect both of you to act with proper decorum in the future. Am I understood?"

Properly chastised, the two young people nodded, each wearing a well-deserved blush of shame.

"I only have one question to ask you both before I make my final decision about whether or not I'll give you my blessing to marry. I'd like you to respond first, Victoria," she stated, but qualified her question before she posed it. "I'm going to set aside the idea that you've each fallen in love. Mutual attraction is important, but you each need to tell me why the other would be a good and loving helpmate, should you marry."

Victoria took in a deep breath, let it out slowly, and kept her gaze focused on her mother. "Benjamin may seem to be analytical and single-minded about things, which may lead one to think he's a bit arrogant or even heartless at times, but he's not like that at all," she began, and Martha wondered if Victoria realized she could also be describing her brother. "He cares deeply about what I think and how I feel and . . . and he listens to me when we disagree about something. He isn't above changing his mind after he does, and if he doesn't, he takes the time to explain why," she ventured, offering a quick side glance at the man sitting in the chair next to her.

For a fleeting moment, Martha wished she could say the same thing about Thomas, which left her flustered, and she quickly looked to Dr. McMillan to offer his response.

"Being with Victoria is sometimes like trying to treat a patient who already knows what treatment is in order and disagrees with one I recommend. I used to dismiss that patient's attitude as ill-informed and uneducated, but Victoria is helping me to learn how to be more understanding and more tolerant with people. You've done that for me, too," he added.

Martha accepted his compliment and had to admit to herself

that she found both of their answers to her liking. Indeed, she found it nearly impossible to stop the flow of happiness for her daughter that was filling her heart to the point that it threatened to overthrow and distract her from her mission.

Victoria giggled nervously and her cheeks turned a brighter shade of pink. "May I say something else?"

Curious, Martha nodded her permission.

"In all truth, he has no sense of order at all, especially when it comes to his office. He also has no sense of time, especially when he's reading books or journals about new advances in medicine or the notes you've made for him on remedies, which means he often forgets everything else," she offered and paused to think a bit before she continued. "I find it frustrating at times, but I wouldn't respect him as a doctor if he did anything less, and watching him struggle to do the best he can for his patients has helped me to understand why you're so devoted as a midwife and to realize that you did the best that you could for me and for Oliver, and . . . and that it hasn't been an easy life for you."

Martha swallowed hard. Hearing Victoria give voice to the frustrations she had experienced as the daughter of a midwife—who was often called to duty and who, so many times, put her responsibility to the women and children she treated above her responsibilities as a mother—brought tears to her eyes.

She shifted in her seat and blinked the tears back. "Thank you, Victoria." To her surprise, Dr. McMillan also offered more thoughts of his own.

"Even though Victoria claims that we can talk through whatever disagreements we might have, she can be headstrong and incredibly stubborn, which are traits she no doubt inherited from her mother," he offered and raised a hand to keep Martha silent when she opened her mouth to protest. He slipped his other hand into Victoria's when she scowled at him. "I also happen to admire those qualities to some extent. If God should see fit to call me home, leaving her as a young widow with children, I have the financial means to see that they have no worries in that regard. More important, I know she'll do anything and everything in her power to care for them and to protect them from any threat they might face, just like you've done for her."

This time, Martha was barely able to blink back her tears before they escaped. She could not have scripted answers from either of them that would have touched her more deeply or that would have convinced her that this match would be a good one. Still, she had one final concern. "If I told you both that I wouldn't give you my blessing tonight and that I'd do everything in my power to keep you from marrying, what would you do?"

Victoria paled and blinked back tears, but Dr. McMillan answered immediately, out of turn and without hesitation. "As much as I'd respectfully disagree with you, I'd accept your decision, but I'd have to ask you, again and again, until you understood that I'd love your daughter, provide for her, and protect her every day of my life for as long as I live. In any event, I'd also pray that you'd continue to share your experience and knowledge of remedies with me so I have alternatives if my approach is less than successful. I still haven't given up hope that you might accept some of my treatments as less than diabolical, too."

"I have no problem sharing what I know with you," Martha insisted, though she ignored his efforts to lure her into embracing much of what she had seen in modern medicine. Instead, she looked directly at her daughter. "Victoria? Are you prepared to answer my question?"

Victoria bowed her head for a moment, and when she looked up again, her eyes were clear and she tilted up her chin ever so slightly. "For my part, I'd be sorely disappointed that we'd failed to convince you to give us your blessing. Father never spoke about it with me, but I know how much he lost by choosing a profession different from his father's and marrying you against his father's wishes. I'm my father's daughter as much as I am yours. Eventually, I'll do exactly as he did. He followed his heart," she said. "Please, please don't put me in a position where I have to make the same decision he did."

This time, Martha failed to hold back her tears, and she did not bother to wipe them away. "I was thinking about your father just before you arrived. He'd be very proud of you, and I believe he'd support your desire to spend your life with this young man," she said and glanced at Dr. McMillan before addressing Victoria again. "I won't pretend that this marriage won't pose some difficulties for both of us from time to time, but you have my blessing and my permission to marry, assuming you'll both agree to one more thing."

The young doctor took Victoria's hand and nodded gravely. "What do you want us to do?"

"I want you both to agree to wait awhile before you marry. While I may need some time to consider changes I hope to be making in my own life, especially now that I'm only going to be responsible for myself, it's most important to me to have your brother here when you get married. He hasn't come for a visit yet this year, so I'd like you to write to him with your news and ask him to come home, perhaps at Christmas, and you can be married then. If he can't come until later, I leave it to you to convince him otherwise. Are we agreed?"

Dr. McMillan's grin stretched from ear to ear, but Martha was quite surprised when Victoria flew up from her seat to hug her so hard she had trouble breathing. "Thank you, Mother. Thank you!"

Martha found herself grinning back at both of them, even

more surprised by how easy it was to embrace the happiness for her daughter.

Dr. McMillan stood up, looking a bit helpless as to what to do. Martha urged her daughter back, stood up, and managed to erase her smile and give him a stern look. "I'm entrusting you with a young woman who is very dear and precious to me. Don't disappoint me."

"I won't, ma'am. Not for a moment."

Victoria edged between them and hugged them both to her at the same time. "Does this mean it's really, really official?"

"Not quite," Benjamin said before he took a small object wrapped in pale green velvet from his pocket and handed it to Victoria.

Her fingers shook as she opened it, and her eyes widened when she lifted back the velvet folds, revealing a small gold brooch lined with three small pearls.

"In anticipation of receiving permission to marry my mother, my father designed this brooch and commissioned a jeweler to make it," he explained. "He gave this to my mother when they became betrothed, but no one, other than my mother, has ever worn it before tonight. It would give me great pleasure if you'd wear it as a sign of my affection for you and my intention to make you my wife."

Martha took a step back and watched him pin the brooch to the collar on Victoria's dress. She was caught completely by surprise, however, when he turned and pressed a small wrapped object into her hand. When she furrowed her brows, he opened it for her, only to reveal an identical brooch.

"My father actually had the jeweler make two identical brooches, and he gave this one to my grandmother," he explained. "He asked her to wear it as a sign of his deep respect for her and his pledge to be a good husband to her daughter.

I make the same pledge to you and hope you'll accept it and wear it, just as she did."

Overwhelmed, Martha was utterly speechless and entirely flustered. She had never, ever owned anything quite as lovely or as expensive as a gold brooch before, but it was the sentiment behind his gift and his interest in continuing a family tradition that wrapped around her heart.

"I'll take your silence as a yes," he teased. Chuckling, he pinned the brooch to the collar of her cape. "I took the liberty of asking Miss Ivy to bake something special for us tonight, and I asked Mrs. Andrews to set everything out in my office so you wouldn't see it when you arrived. All we need to do is heat up some water for tea. Shall we go downstairs and celebrate?"

Martha sniffed. "Were you that confident you'd prevail?"

He blushed. "Merely hopeful."

"So hopeful that you included Ivy and Rosalind in your little plot?"

"Neither of them knew what we were going to discuss tonight," he insisted.

Victoria took his arm and grinned. "I daresay they won't be very surprised. Mrs. Andrews won't find out until morning, but I can't wait to tell Miss Fern and Miss Ivy when we get home tonight. I was just wondering . . . When you said that you needed some time to think about making some changes in your life, Mother, one of those changes wouldn't involve the charming and very handsome former mayor who is entirely smitten with you, would it?"

Martha did not know what annoyed her more, the grin on Victoria's face or the smile on Dr. McMillan's.

"I'm going downstairs to see if everything is ready," he said. "I'll meet you both in the office," he suggested, then abruptly left the room with Victoria's question still hanging in the air unanswered.

When Victoria stood there staring at her, Martha felt a hot blush spread across her cheeks and down her throat.

"One of those changes does concern him, doesn't it!" Victoria exclaimed. "Has Mr. Dillon proposed? Of course he has," she quipped, answering her own question. "Did you say yes? You should have said yes. Please tell me you said yes!"

Thoroughly flustered, Martha struggled to find her voice as all of the promises she had made to Thomas and to herself to keep their plans to marry a secret evaporated. "Yes. I said yes, but we're not going to marry for a good while yet for reasons I really don't want to discuss, and if you tell a single soul about our plans, including that young man you're planning to marry, I'll . . . I'll . . ."

Victoria whooped for joy and stole every thought from Martha's head as she pulled her into a crushing embrace. "Finally! It seems like he's loved you almost forever, and I know you love him, too. I'm so happy for you!"

Martha struggled to breathe. "Happy enough to let me take a breath?"

Her daughter set her back and giggled. "Both of us getting married is ridiculously wonderful and exciting, isn't it?"

Oddly enough, Martha found she was tempted to giggle, too, and gave in to the urge before she touched a finger to her lips. "You mustn't say a word. It appears as though we might not be getting married for a while yet, and right now I don't want our plans or anything else to take away from the wonderful news of your betrothal. This is your time, Victoria, not mine, and this has to remain our secret."

Victoria grinned, looped her arm with her mother's, and led her from the room. "A secret it is. Yours, mine, and Mr. Dillon's. I promise. I'm so happy you told me."

Martha blinked back tears. "Me too."

13

Even though Martha knew she had made the right decision to give Victoria her blessing, she hoped she had not made a mistake in telling her daughter about her plans to marry Thomas.

Since her own life was fraught with so many challenges, however, she had little time to give in to second thoughts and had to admit that she and Victoria seemed to be closer now than they had been for years, in part because of the secret they now shared.

The joy of sharing the news of Victoria's betrothal with Ivy and Fern last night had been cut short when Martha had been summoned to help Henny Goodfellow bring her son, Peter James, into this world, but the delivery had been unusually quick and easy. The Goodfellow farm was also only five miles from town, which meant she had been able to return and still get a solid six hours of sleep.

Well rested, Martha was energized by the prospect of taking her first ride with Bella, and for the moment she tucked away the promise she had made to Thomas to allow him to provide another horse, for fear it would undermine her confidence.

She hurried down the staircase and smiled as her split skirt brushed against her legs. She had not worn her riding skirt for several long weeks, but instead of wasting her thoughts on the last time she had ridden Grace, she kept her mind focused on the future. She would have a better handle on whether or not Bella would be part of that future in the next few hours, and the mere possibility that she would be able to search almost anywhere to find a replacement for herself almost put wings to her heart.

She reached the kitchen with a hopeful heart and bid a good morning to Jane, who was at the cookstove browning sausages for breakfast, and young Cassie, who was setting the table. "I'm glad to see that Ivy and Fern are finally taking a morning to sleep in a bit."

Cassie furrowed her brow. "They're not sleeping. They went to the general store to place a big, big order."

"At this hour? It's barely seven o'clock!" she said. Although area farmers often delivered goods to the store at this hour, most customers waited until midmorning to do their shopping.

"Now that we've got our sleeping arrangements settled, they're anxious to reopen the confectionery," Jane explained. "If you're ready for breakfast, the sausages are ready, but I'm afraid I haven't even started the griddle cakes. If you give me a few moments, I'm sure I can—"

"I'm taking Bella out for a ride this morning before I leave for the day a little later. I don't have time to stay for a big breakfast, but I wouldn't mind snatching a few of those sausages to eat on my way to the stable," she suggested, hoping to keep her stomach from rumbling a protest.

Jane grinned. "Miss Ivy and Miss Fern were surprised you

didn't take the horse out yesterday. I'll put a few into a napkin for you to eat now, but I'll set aside a few griddle cakes in case you're hungry when you get back."

The day was already warm enough that Martha decided not to wear a cape, but by the time Martha had tied her bonnet into place, Jane had the sausages all wrapped up and handed them to Martha. "Ride safely."

"Thank you. I will," Martha replied and hoped those words would not come back to haunt her as she closed the distance between the confectionery and the stables behind Dr. McMillan's home. She polished off the last sausage right before she walked into the stable; otherwise, she would have choked the moment she stepped inside. Her heart lurched and she rocked back on her heels. Thomas was standing at the far end of the stable, directly in front of Bella's stall, where her horse was saddled and ready to be ridden.

"What are you doing here?" she blurted.

He held up both of his hands. "I didn't mean to startle you, but did you really think I wouldn't know exactly why you wanted to delay leaving this morning by an hour?"

Annoyed that he had been able to read her mind yet again, she huffed. "No, I suppose I didn't, but I did assume that you'd allow me the right to take Bella out for a ride without finding it necessary to be a . . . a chaperone," she argued, noting his horse was ready to ride in a nearby stall. If this was how protective he would be of her now, would he become completely overprotective once they married and smother the independence she had come to enjoy?

"You don't need a chaperone any more than I do, but even I wouldn't take a horse out to ride alone without being certain that I could trust it," he countered before he set his lips in a firm line.

Mindful of the manner of his wife's death, she kept her words and her tone gentle. "I didn't intend to ride very far or for very long, Thomas. Just enough to see if she'll respond to my commands. I appreciate your concern, I really do—and if it makes you feel better to ride along with me, then all you had to do was tell me so, instead of showing up unbidden and assuming you could force me to let you accompany me."

He dropped his head for a moment and let out a long breath before looking up at her again. "You're right. I should have asked you. I'm sorry."

"I'm sorry, too. I should have let you ask your question yesterday and given you the opportunity to either accept my answer or discuss it with me."

A smile tickled the corner of his lips. "Does that mean you'll really let me come with you?"

She returned his bit of a smile. "Only if you'll let me handle Bella my way and not interfere unless I ask you for help. Agreed?"

"Agreed," he said and stepped back to give her the room she needed to pull up the bar and take hold of Bella's reins.

Murmuring soft words of encouragement, Martha led the horse outside without incident and waited until Thomas had joined her with his own horse before attempting to mount.

Unfortunately, Bella had other ideas. Every time Martha tried to put her foot in the stirrup, the horse backed up, moved sideways, or, in general, made it impossible for Martha to get into the saddle. With her hands burning from repeated harsh tugs on the reins and saddle horn, she realized too late that she had forgotten her riding gloves. More worried about her ability to even get astride than her hands, she finally asked Thomas for help.

The moment he took the reins, Bella settled down, just as

she had done yesterday. To her surprise, Martha was able to get astride on her first attempt, although Bella was clearly not happy about it. "Hold her firm and steady while I mount my horse," Thomas cautioned.

He had barely taken a second step away when Bella made it very clear that she had no intention of letting Martha ride her.

Martha may have had years of riding experience, but she had never, ever been astride a horse that reared high enough to paw the air. When the mare started to buck, it took every ounce of strength Martha had to hold on to the reins and stay in the saddle.

To Martha, it seemed like an eternity, but it was only a matter of seconds before Thomas was able to grab the bridle. He pulled her down to the ground so quickly she did not even realize she was off the horse until her feet hit the ground with a thud that shook every tooth in her mouth.

The stark look of fear on his face was one she would never forget, and when he pulled her hard against his chest, she wrapped her arms around his waist and leaned into his strength so closely she could feel his heart hammering in his chest.

"Are you all right?" he asked, his voice husky with emotion she knew reflected memories of his late wife's accident, too.

With her own heart pounding, she managed to nod against his chest to let him know she was fine, or would be, once she felt strong enough to stand on her own two feet without falling down.

Ever so grateful that she had not let her pride keep her from letting Thomas help her, she stayed within the protection of his arms until her heartbeat finally returned to normal. When she dared to pull away, she saw that Thomas's mount had moved off to munch on a patch of grass. And Bella was right there, too, sampling the grass as if nothing at all had happened.

"I'm afraid you were right. Bella isn't the horse for me. She's docile enough to let me feed her or lead her by the reins at times, but she won't even let me sit long enough to ride her," she admitted.

Thomas wore a rueful smile. "In all truth, I think she just doesn't like women, although I can't say I've ever encountered a horse like that before. But I suppose it's possible if you consider that her previous owner might have been a woman who abused the horse. That could explain why she doesn't balk at all if a man handles her or rides her."

"You sound a little sure of yourself," she said and furrowed her brow as she gave his explanation further thought. When she realized what he must have done before she arrived, she pursed her lips for a moment. "You rode her this morning, didn't you?"

He cringed. "Actually, no. I rode her last night, but just enough to know that she was capable of handling a rider. I really didn't want you on her back until I knew at least that, but if I'd had any idea that she would react so violently to having you in the saddle, I never would have let you near her."

She swallowed hard, slipped her chafed hand into his, and forced herself not to cringe when her palm touched his own. "I'm glad you didn't stop me from trying, and after what just happened, I'm truly glad you were here."

He pressed a kiss to the back of her hand. "Glad enough to let me keep Bella at my stables so I don't have to worry about you giving Bella a second chance?"

"Bella doesn't get a second chance. Not with me, but I'd like to keep her here until I can give her back to whoever gave her to me or find her a new owner, whichever I manage to do first. Burton takes care of Dr. McMillan's horses, and he won't have any trouble caring for her, too," she replied. "Assuming you'll get her back into her stall."

He reluctantly agreed with her and had Bella back in her stall within minutes, while Martha kept a good distance away. She waited for him to lower the bar to keep Bella inside, and she could not help thinking that she had lost the opportunity to use a horse of her own to search beyond the town's limits for her replacement.

Suddenly, before she could even think about accepting Thomas's offer to let her borrow a horse, that cranky stable cat, Leech, appeared out of nowhere, leaping onto the side of the stall before jumping straight onto Bella's back.

Startled, Bella reared up and charged out of the stall, running right past Thomas and Martha and out of the stable.

"Mercy!" she cried, then scowled when Thomas started to laugh. "It's not one bit funny," she snapped and shooed Leech away by stomping her feet and clapping her hands. "Thanks to Leech, I'll never get that horse back in here again." She looked at Thomas and shook her head. "If I have any good fortune coming my way at all, neither of them will come back, but I suspect this is only the beginning of more trouble than I can imagine from those two."

Thomas gathered her up in his arms and pressed her close. "Don't worry. I'll find the horse and keep her at the stable behind my house, which is what I wanted to do in the first place. Of course, you wouldn't have to worry about anything at all if you changed your mind and came with me in a few weeks when I leave for New York."

She resisted the urge to lean into him and rest her head against his chest again. Instead, she stepped back and put her hands on her hips. "You are one very persistent man."

He grinned. "I suspect the very stubborn woman standing in front of me expects no less, and I should hope I never disappoint her."

"I don't believe you will disappoint, although I'd be very happy if you could prove yourself to be not quite so persistent or stubborn when it comes to finding that horse."

"Well then," he offered and cleared his throat, "why don't we both go home and get ready for our day together? I've got a buggy ride planned. May I pick you up at nine, like we originally planned, or would you still prefer to leave at ten?"

"Let's make it ten."

When he did not ask why, she prompted him. "Don't you want to know why?"

"Do you want me to ask?"

She chuckled. "No, I'll just simply tell you that I didn't have more than a few sausages for breakfast and I'm starving. I just want to make sure I have enough time to eat the griddle cakes Jane was going to make for everyone before we go."

After a rather delightful buggy ride out into the countryside, where Martha and Thomas shared a picnic dinner, she directed him to the isolated spot she had claimed as her own, just above the falls.

They spent the early afternoon sitting on a blanket together while she answered his many questions about all that had happened in Trinity while he had been gone. She also made certain there was a good space between the two of them so she would not succumb to the temptation of allowing him to kiss her, for fear she would happily kiss him back, again and again. The ointment she had put on her chafed hands had worked well, which left no explanation for the way her hands continued to tingle, other than the fact that she was longing to hold hands with him—a dangerous longing she was finding more and more difficult to resist.

When there was finally a lull in the conversation, Thomas cleared his throat. "Before you come to dinner tomorrow night and see Eleanor, Micah, and the baby, I wanted to speak to you about something. One of those matters I mentioned the other day that you should know about before we get married."

She raised a brow. "Go on."

"As you recall, when you brought Eleanor and her husband from Clarion to live with me so you could care for her while she was carrying my grandson, Micah's father made it clear to him that he wasn't welcome to return there to practice law with him. At the time, there didn't appear to be much of a future here in Trinity for another lawyer, either, and even with the changes taking place it could be some time before there will be. The inheritance from his mother won't last forever," he informed Martha before taking a long breath. "I've asked Micah to take over my practice, and he's accepted my offer."

She smiled. "I suspected you might do that."

"What I need to tell you," he continued, "is that they'll be living in my house permanently, which shouldn't pose a problem since we'll be moving out to my cabin on Candle Lake once we're married—although all they know right now is that I'll be moving out to the cabin when I get back from New York. I tried to give them the house outright, but they refused and insisted on paying rent, which I neither want nor need. I haven't told them yet that I'm going to set up a trust fund for my grandson with the money they give me, but as my wife, you should know that."

Relieved to know he had not changed his mind about moving out of town after they married, she was also grateful for the opportunity to raise one of her own concerns. "I'm quite content with the arrangements you've made, but I must be honest with you. After living at the cabin with Victoria for four or five weeks last winter, I felt totally isolated from town and my

119

friends here. I was hoping that you and I might come to town on Saturdays and stay over for services on Sunday morning, weather permitting, of course. That way we'd get to see our families on a regular basis, too." She shooed off an insect preparing to land on her nose. "Do you think Eleanor and Micah would mind if we stayed at your house here in town that often?"

He laughed and tugged at another blade of grass. "They wouldn't mind at all, but I'm afraid I might. Living with a small child again is a bit more challenging for me than it was when Harry and Eleanor were little, but I rather like the idea of spending our weekends back in Trinity. You haven't mentioned Victoria, but I assume she'll be living with us."

"Perhaps not." Martha quickly told him about the relationship that had developed between her daughter and Dr. Mc-Millan and their meeting last night when she had given them permission to marry.

"Last night must have been difficult for you, in many ways. It's not easy letting any of our children go, or to accept their choice of a spouse. In Victoria's case, having her choose Dr. McMillan won't be particularly easy for you, will it?"

"No, but she's chosen the right man for her, and we'll just have to make it work. Once I'm no longer practicing as a midwife, however, it won't matter at all, I suppose."

"How much does she know about our own plans?" he asked.

She swallowed hard. "Actually, I told her . . . that is, she suspected we might . . ." She paused to clear her throat. "Victoria is very intuitive, and she can be rather persuasive. I'm afraid I've told her about our hopes to marry, but she's promised to keep it a secret. I hope you're not annoyed with me, since I've been rather insistent about keeping this to ourselves."

He leaned to the side and closed the distance between them. "In all truth, I'm pleased that you told her, and I'm sorely tempted at the moment to kiss you until you change your mind about waiting so long for us to marry," he whispered, his lips dangerously close to her own.

Although it was getting nearly impossible to resist him, she knew that his kisses were far too dangerous, especially when they were alone like this. "I'm sorely tempted to let you, but you'll get only one," she cautioned before pressing a quick kiss to his lips. She then scrambled to her feet and straightened her skirts. "I'm afraid it's getting late. We need to leave right now if we hope to get home for supper and, more important, before dark. Along the way, perhaps we could discuss the idea that I might want to borrow one of your horses. But just now and then."

"There's no need to discuss it. You can borrow one of the horses whenever you want," he replied and reluctantly got to his feet. "And I'm not worried about supper or driving the buggy in the dark, either," he grumbled.

She felt a blush spread across her cheeks. "Neither am I."

14

ortunately, Martha arrived home before dark and just in time for supper.

She had barely sat down when a worried Jonathan Goodfellow appeared at the door, telling her that Nell Carruth, the afternurse who was staying with his wife, had sent him here to fetch Martha back to check on Henny. In a matter of minutes, she had changed into her riding skirt, tied her bonnet in place, and was hurrying down the hall with her bag of simples in her hand and a prayer on her lips.

Before she opened the door, she paused just long enough to put a reassuring smile on her face. Once outside, she was pleased to see that the same old, docile mare he had brought for her earlier would accompany her again. Before she mounted, she ran back inside to remind Victoria of their plans to have supper with Thomas and his family tomorrow night. Since she did not know quite what to expect, she also asked Victoria to offer apologies on the off chance she had not come home by then.

She got back outside just as Mr. Goodfellow finished tying

her bag in place. She accepted his help to get astride before he mounted his own horse, and she continued to pray as she followed him down the alley. Noting the man's troubled features, she waited until they had left the noise of the town behind to try to ease some of his concerns. "It's not all that uncommon for me to be summoned back, especially where first babes are concerned. Your place isn't all that far from town, but it would be really helpful to me if you could repeat exactly what Mrs. Carruth said to tell me before we get there," she said as they passed the new tavern and headed west on Falls Road at a steady pace.

When he looked over at her, the worry that creased his brow also simmered in his eyes. "She said something about Henny losing too much blood. She might have said more, but Henny was so pale and so listless, I was too worried to hear much else. You can help her, right? You won't let anything happen to my Henny, will you?"

"I'll take good care of her," Martha promised and kept up with him when he urged his horse into more of a gallop than a canter. They reached his farm in half the time it had taken on her previous visit. The moment she entered the bedroom in the two-room cabin, she took in the grave concern on Nell's face, turned around, and sent the man back to wait in the other room. She quickly walked past the cradle, where the newborn was sleeping, to reach his mother's bedside.

With her heart beating just a little faster, she stood next to the slight, seventy-something woman who had years of experience as an afternurse, and they both looked down at Henny. Normally the stunning woman with flaming-red hair had a porcelain complexion, but there was nothing normal about the woman's pallor, which now made her appear to be more dead than alive. Just as alarming, her breaths were coming in slow, shallow efforts.

"I've never seen anyone slip so fast," Nell whispered and wrung her hands. "Everything was going so well. Then a couple of hours ago, she started bleeding, and bleeding hard, so I did what I always do. I packed her up good with cloth and got her to drink a toddy with an extra dollop of honey wine and waited a bit, but it didn't seem to help much at all. That's when I sent Mr. Goodfellow to fetch you back."

"You did exactly the right thing." Martha tossed her bonnet aside and washed her hands while Nell gathered up some fresh cloths and a fresh basin of water. Martha's attempts to revive Henny by pressing cool cloths against her face were met with only a few groans.

When she eased away the bedsheet that covered Henny's body, she was horrified to see a pool of fresh blood that warned her she might already be too late. Henny was hemorrhaging, and Martha wasted no time to see if she could determine the reason. Working quickly and silently, she rolled up the sheets from the bottom of the bed until they reached the middle of Henny's chest, keeping her long nightgown in place to protect the woman's modesty.

It did not take Martha long to dismiss the possibility that the woman was hemorrhaging because she had not expelled all of the afterbirth. And with no visible tears caused by little Peter's birth, that only left the likelihood that there were injuries within Henny's womb that were responsible for the bleeding.

Deeply concerned at her ability to stop the bleeding before it was too late to save Henny's life, she drew a deep breath and walked straight out of the room to talk to the harried husband and ask him to do something she had never done before. "Your wife is gravely ill. I'll do everything I can to stop the bleeding, but at this point, every minute counts. We can't afford to wait more than another hour or so to see if my efforts are successful. If they aren't, it might be too late by then to summon Dr. McMillan. I think it would be wise and in your wife's best interests to fetch him now and pray he might have a treatment that will save her if she hasn't improved by the time he gets here."

The color drained from his face. "Is she going to die?"

"Not if we can help it, but the longer we stand here talking, the longer she'll have to wait for me to help her and the longer it will be before Dr. McMillan gets here."

He tore out of the cabin so fast he did not even close the door behind him.

"You must be able to think of something!" Martha exclaimed.

After waiting half the night for Dr. McMillan to arrive, she was frantic. She could not blame him for taking so long, since he had been out on a call when Jonathan Goodfellow arrived at his home and came as soon as he could. She kept her gaze locked with Dr. McMillan's and hoped she kept her voice low, but her heart was pounding in her ears, and she could not be sure if he answered her or not. "Henny is going to die unless you do. In fact, I'm surprised she's lasted this long."

He raked his fingers through his hair. "I've told you. I can't do more than you've already done," he insisted. "As difficult as it might be to admit it, sometimes you just have to accept the fact that you can't save everyone, and neither can I. I fear this is one of those times."

Thankful that they were alone together in the bedroom and Henny was not conscious to hear them, she shook her head. "This is not about me or my opinion of my abilities, and it's not about you, either. It's all about that young woman lying over there who is going to bleed to death, and a newborn babe named Peter James who'll grow up never knowing his mama, unless you can help her. You're the one with the fancy medical degree hanging on your wall and a stack of medical journals on your desk with the latest advances in medicine from here, there, and everywhere. Think, young man, think! There must be something you can do to try to save her."

He looked away. After several long, tension-filled moments, he turned and faced her again. "*The Lancet* is a weekly medical journal in London. I've read a number of articles in it written by Dr. Blundell that might be of help. He's renowned for his work in the field of childbirth, but there isn't anything I've read elsewhere to suggest his method of saving a hemorrhaging woman after she's given birth has been widely accepted in Europe, let alone on this side of the Atlantic."

"Do you think his method will stop the bleeding?"

He grimaced. "Not per se, but according to what I've read, it may give her body the time it needs to heal, which in turn will stop the bleeding. But you have to understand something: I've never done anything like this before. I may not do it right, and even if I do, it may not work at all. Some critics of his method claim that half the time it doesn't."

"Then half the time it does," she argued and turned him about until he faced the door. "Go out there and talk to Mr. Goodfellow. Tell him what you've just told me. If he wants you to go ahead, you owe him and you owe his wife your best efforts. The rest is in God's hands. It always is."

After drawing a deep breath, Dr. McMillan walked out of the room and returned with Henny's husband a few moments later. The doctor looked as grave as she had ever seen him. Judging by the square set of his shoulders, he was ready to proceed, and he put the wooden chair he was carrying next to Henny's bed. With Nell still tending to little Peter in the other room, he told the young husband to take a seat on the chair and roll up one of his shirtsleeves. He put Martha to work clearing the small bedside table, opened his medical bag, and laid out a number of instruments on top of the table the moment she finished.

"I need fresh cloths for bandages and a small basin on the table," he ordered before removing his frock coat and rolling up his shirtsleeves. "Listen very carefully, both of you, because I only have time to explain it once," he cautioned while he washed his hands.

Martha swallowed hard and noted the pale expression on poor Jonathan. What the doctor proposed to do was like nothing she had ever heard of before, and she offered a silent prayer that he would be successful.

He took a deep breath. "Remember. Once I actually start the procedure, I have to work very, very quickly, and I cannot stop."

He began by using a lancet to open the flesh on Henny's arm to reveal a small vein, which is exactly what he would have done if he intended to bleed her. Next, he pressed a cloth to the open wound and had Martha hold it in place. After taking another deep breath, he performed the same procedure on her husband and had the young man hold a cloth against the incision himself.

The doctor was sweating profusely at this point. Martha watched with awe and disbelief when he picked up the metal syringe she had seen him use to suck infection from a wound, removed the cloth covering the incision he had made in Jonathan's arm, and inserted the needle into the vein to withdraw some blood.

"The moment I finish, I need you to remove the cloth from Henny's arm," he said firmly. Seconds later he withdrew the needle, forced out any air from the barrel of the syringe, turned, and inserted the needle directly into Henny's vein to infuse it with her husband's blood. After repeating the procedure once more, he stitched up the incision in both of his patients' arms, secured a bandage around both, and sent the husband away with orders for the man to take a good swig of honey wine and rest.

Dr. McMillan collapsed into the chair and mopped his brow, while Martha sat down on the bed next to Henny and tried to absorb the incredible thought that it was possible to transfer blood from one person to another to save someone's life. She had neither the knowledge nor the skill to even attempt such a thing, and it suddenly occurred to her that after struggling to help this young doctor over the past few months, she had been wrong to consider this man as her professional enemy or to judge all of his methods as wretched.

While it may be the case that midwives were being forced to abandon their work as doctors took over, especially in large eastern cities, here in Trinity, she was in the unique position of having a doctor who was willing to work with her, rather than against her. And if Trinity continued to grow at the current rate, there would be more than enough work to keep both a midwife and a doctor busy.

There was a certain peace about that whole idea now that gave her hope that there was indeed a future here for the midwife who would replace Martha. And she had a whole new respect for the man who claimed her daughter's heart, too.

"I'm very proud of you. You did really well," she said. "How soon will you know if this will work?"

He blew out a long puff of air. "Her color should improve within a few hours at the most. If it does, we can take that as a good sign. If it doesn't . . . then I've failed. Would you have the time to sit and wait with me?"

"I'd be honored," she replied. "Truly honored."

15

By dawn, Henny Goodfellow still had a long road to travel, but by midafternoon, both Dr. McMillan and Martha agreed that Henny was well on her journey back to full health.

Martha stayed with Henny for an hour after the doctor left before heading back to Trinity herself. After convincing the relieved husband that she was quite capable of returning on her own, he agreed to let Martha borrow the same mare and stable her overnight at Dr. McMillan's, where he would retrieve it the following day.

She rode away still bathed in the afterglow of the miracle she had just witnessed. Since she still had a few hours before she needed to be back in town to have supper at Thomas's, she decided to take advantage of having her own mount and detoured some eight miles west to speak with one of the four most likely women to replace her: Charlotte Weyland.

With two of her daughters already grown and married, Charlotte was not Martha's first choice, in part because she lived so far away from town, but she had a good heart and a real talent with laboring women. She had also dismissed any interest in taking over Martha's duties as midwife when Martha mentioned the idea last year, although she had agreed to think it over some more.

As Martha approached the homestead, she held on to the hope that she might change the woman's mind. When she arrived and found Charlotte recovering from devastating burns that left her with little use of her left arm, she never even approached the topic that had brought her here. Instead, she gave the woman a number of remedies to help ease her discomfort and left an hour later with a heavy heart. She prayed for Charlotte all the way back to Trinity.

With no time to waste on chitchat if she saw anyone she knew, she bypassed Main Street completely and took the narrower road that skirted the rear of the properties on the east side of town. She passed the tavern first and noted that the wooden structure was still so new it had yet to be weathered by the elements.

She focused on the packed roadway as memories swirled in her mind and escaped from the recesses of her heart. With her mind's eye, she could still see her brother's tavern, the room he had added for her to share with Victoria, and the gardens just outside her window, where she had cultivated the herbs for the tavern that she also used to make her simples.

She was eternally grateful to God that she had survived the fire that had reduced the tavern to ashes. And for Thomas, who had risked his life to save Grandmother Poore's diary and the box of papers where every birth since the town's founding were recorded, although the daybook she had been keeping for Victoria had been lost forever.

Her daughter had escaped the fire simply because she had not yet returned to Trinity after running away; otherwise, almost everything Martha had ever known or loved at that tavern was now gone, including her brother and his wife, who had moved to Sunrise to be near their three grown daughters and to find work for James.

She glanced back over her shoulder to take another look at the new tavern and sighed. Since Dr. McMillan was one of the investors who now owned the tavern, she made a mental note to ask him if she might temporarily reclaim her old gardens to grow her plants and herbs again, at least until she could find her replacement, who might need the space, as well. She hoped her future son-in-law would agree with her idea, especially since she would promise to provide the tavern kitchen with any herbs they wanted.

Buoyed by the possibility, she spurred the mare to go a little faster and reached the grounds behind Dr. McMillan's house without incident. She dismounted and led the horse toward the stable to stretch her legs a bit. The moment she stepped inside, however, she braced to a halt so quickly the horse actually walked into her. Stumbling forward, she managed to catch herself before she fell, and she glared at young Will, who was sitting on the side of a stall where that insufferable white horse was munching on some straw.

"What do you think you're doing?" Martha asked.

The boy gave her a smirk. "Waitin' for you. I found this dumb horse in the woods out by the lake in that old meadow near our cabin. Looks just like the one Mr. Dillon said you lost, and I wanted to collect the reward he promised to anyone who found it. It's the right horse, isn't it?"

Martha rolled her eyes. "Yes, although I didn't lose that horse. She ran away," she grumbled and took a quick glance around. With no sign that Leech had made his way back, she led the

131

mare she had ridden home into the first stall and got her settled. "Just exactly what kind of reward did Mr. Dillon promise?"

Will jumped down from the stall and handed her a crude and badly wrinkled flier he had stuffed into his pocket. "Two whole dollars. See?"

Her eyes widened. "Where did you get that flier?"

"Mr. Fancy brought it home. He said there were lots of 'em posted around town."

Martha could not imagine why Thomas would post fliers to get Bella back, but she surely intended to ask him tonight. "Two dollars is a good sum of money." Two dollars was also the sum she received for delivering a babe, although she rarely received her rewards in coin.

She was tempted to tell the boy to take Bella over to Thomas's house, but the mare looked content at the moment and Leech must have been scared off, at least for a while. She decided to keep Bella here and talk to Thomas about it when she saw him tonight.

Will grinned. "I bet lotsa folks were lookin' real hard, but I found the horse first."

"Well, I don't have two dollars in coin, so you'll have to see Mr. Dillon about that." She set her bag of simples outside of the stall before removing the saddle.

"I don't want the two dollars. I was hopin' we could make a trade instead."

She set the saddle on the ground and turned to him. "A trade?"

"You get your horse back, and I get my spyglass back. And Mr. Dillon gets to keep his two dollars. Simple as that," he suggested and grinned. "You don't need no spyglass, but you sure do need a horse." He wrinkled his nose. "That old thing you got there don't look like she's good for much anymore, but Bella's real young and kinda pretty, if you like horses," he added.

"Which you don't, I know." She folded the saddle blanket and set it on top of the saddle before she tossed Will a brush. She had completely forgotten about the boy's spyglass, which was safely stored in the trunk at the foot of her cot. "For your information, this old horse is a reliable sweetheart, while that beauty over there with you can be especially disagreeable. Fortunately you haven't discovered that, because she has a particular dislike she reserves for girls, which means I'm not all that interested in getting her back. Give this one a good brushing while I get her some oats. When we're done, we'll talk about that reward."

To her surprise, Will took the brush without argument. Apparently he wanted his reward more than he disliked horses, but when he held back and looked at her with a quizzical expression on his face, she sighed. "Have you ever brushed a horse before?"

He shrugged. "Nope."

After showing him what to do, she stepped away to give him some space and left just long enough to get a feed bag and fill it with oats. She found Will standing next to the horse with a grin on his face and the brush in his hand when she returned and slipped the straps for the feed bag over the horse's head and into place. "Can I get my spyglass now?" he asked.

"I haven't agreed to the trade, have I?"

His grin widened. "No, but you will."

"And what makes you so all-fired sure of yourself?"

"I'm not, but Mr. Samuel says you will and—"

"And Samuel's never wrong, at least in your eyes," she teased, still amazed by the incredible bond shared by the blind seaman and the orphaned boy that God had brought together. "You can go right back to Samuel and tell him that while he's not often wrong, in this particular case, he is. I have no interest in giving you that spyglass in exchange for a horse that I don't particularly like and don't intend to keep. As far as I'm concerned, you're not getting that spyglass until I see your grades for this term. Unless you brought them with you," she added.

"Left 'em behind, but I can get 'em right quick."

She blocked him with her arm when he attempted to charge off. "It's too late in the day for that, and I won't be home by the time you get back anyway. Why don't you come see me tomorrow morning? That should give you time to think about how you're going to convince me you won't use the spyglass for anything more than hunting with Fancy."

He shrugged, but his eyes were twinkling. "If you don't wanna do the trade, I guess I could always let the horse go again. Or maybe I should talk to Mr. Dillon tomorrow, instead of talkin' to you."

She looked down at him sternly. "Mr. Dillon doesn't own Bella. As unfortunate as it may be, I do, and I'm the one who will decide what happens to her. And since I'm having supper with Mr. Dillon tonight, I'll be sure to tell him not to give you a reward of any kind. Now scoot back home before I decide to go along with you and talk to Samuel about this myself."

She double-checked the bar again on Bella's stall to make sure it was properly in place before she followed Will out of the stable. She made sure he was headed toward home before she hurried her way back to the confectionery, said another prayer for Charlotte, and took solace in the fact that she still had three more women left on her list of possible replacements.

Hoping she would have enough time to wash up and dress properly for the occasion, she was halfway down the hallway when Victoria came rushing out of the new sitting room, where the rest of the household was apparently gathered. The girl's cheeks were flushed a deeper shade of pink than Martha had ever seen.

"Thank goodness you're finally home," she gushed. "Jane's

put fresh water upstairs in your room, and she pressed your gown for you. It's lying on your bed, along with a clean petticoat. And don't bother about the brooch. I've already pinned it to your gown. Now please hurry! If we don't leave in half an hour, we're going to be late."

Martha put her arm around her daughter and hugged her close. "And if we're late, even though I'll do my best to rush, I'll apologize and take all the blame. In the meantime, while I'm getting ready, I want you to try to calm yourself. Your cheeks are so flushed, folks tonight might think you painted them," she teased. "Take a few moments to relax, and it wouldn't hurt to put a cool cloth rinsed with rose water on your cheeks while you do. Come upstairs with me. I have a bottle of rose water in my room you can have."

Victoria groaned. "I was so worried you wouldn't be back in time. It's only the most important night of my entire life!"

"Up to this point, perhaps," Martha said. Once she sent Victoria off with a promise that she would do her best to hurry, she managed to wash up, change, and fix her hair in far less time than she expected.

Even so, they were still going to be a little late to supper. She did not think Eleanor or Thomas would mind overmuch, but if his sister was there, Anne would certainly make a point of it.

When Martha reached the bottom of the staircase, Jane was in the kitchen rinsing a cloth at the sink. She turned to look over her shoulder and smiled. "Since you're ready, Victoria won't be needing another fresh cloth, although I was only getting her one to keep her calm. This is a big moment for you, too, isn't it?"

"Indeed it is," Martha replied. Mindful that in all likelihood, Cassie would never marry and Jane would never have a night to share with her daughter like the one Martha would have tonight with Victoria, she said, "I wanted to thank you for helping to

135

get everything ready for me so I could dress much more quickly than if I'd had to do that myself when I got home."

"Since you were called away overnight with poor Mrs. Goodfellow and were gone most of the day, I thought you might need some help in that regard. I didn't get to ask you this morning, but were you able to help Mrs. Goodfellow, I hope?"

"Not entirely," Martha admitted. While she wrapped her cape around her shoulders, she described the rather amazing work that Dr. McMillan had done. "He truly saved that woman's life and reminded me how fortunate I am to be able to work with him here in Trinity. From all I've heard, that wouldn't happen back East, where midwives have had little future for some time now. I think you're from the city originally, aren't you? Am I correct?"

Looking a bit pale, Jane lowered her eyes. "Yes, I believe you are. I-I shouldn't keep you any longer. Victoria's anxious to leave. I'll let her know you're ready," she said quickly, sidestepping Martha's question, and hurried off.

Martha put her bonnet in place and headed toward the sitting room. Anticipating the joy and excitement that awaited both her and Victoria tonight, she tucked away the secret plans she and Thomas were making and set aside any concerns she had about finding a woman to replace her as midwife.

Just for tonight.

16

Martha and Victoria were standing side by side, waiting for someone to answer their knock on Thomas's front door. Martha was not surprised when her daughter asked her the same question for the third time, and she chuckled when she gave her the same answer for the third time.

"Yes, I'm going to announce your betrothal tonight, as long as Dr. McMillan is here, too. And if Anne Sweet found out we were all coming to supper, I suspect she wrangled an invitation for herself and her husband from her brother—which means half the town will know about your betrothal by noon tomorrow."

Victoria giggled. "And the other half will know by the time the sun sets," she whispered, fingering the brooch Martha had added to the underside of her pale blue collar.

If all went according to plan, once Martha announced her daughter's betrothal to Dr. McMillan, he would move the brooch to the top side of Victoria's collar and do the same for Martha, which would give him the opportunity to explain the family significance of the twin brooches. If he were not present because he had been summoned away, however, the brooches were safely out of sight, and the announcement would simply be delayed.

"I hope they're all as excited as everyone back at the confectionery," Victoria said, but before Martha could reassure her daughter that everyone here would be pleased indeed, Thomas opened the door and urged them inside.

"'And the last shall be first,'" he teased as he helped them both to remove their capes and bonnets and store them away on the massive hall tree that filled the formal foyer. "Everyone else is here, but before we join them, I should probably warn you that—"

"Martha! Victoria! Don't let that brother of mine keep you dawdling out here in the hall now that you're finally here," his sister said and rushed toward them with a genteel smile on her face.

"I'm so sorry we're late. I was summoned out of town last night and barely got back to town in time to get here," Martha ventured, noting both the pleased look on her daughter's face and the frown on Thomas's.

Anne waved away Martha's apology, took Martha's arm, and urged her toward the staircase just beyond the sitting room, leaving Thomas no choice but to escort Victoria. "Dr. McMillan has been entertaining us with any number of tales while we were all waiting for you. Eleanor is upstairs feeding that darling little son of hers, so supper was delayed anyway. She said to send you up the moment you arrived." Anne then lowered her voice to a whisper. "Maybe you could tell her that her guests are all quite hungry, so she can speed things up a bit."

Martha was tempted to remind Anne that trying to hurry a suckling babe was a bit like trying to coax a fire from wet firewood, but instead she promised to bring Eleanor downstairs as quickly as she could.

She glanced back at Thomas, noted the flush on his cheeks, and smiled. There was only one woman who frustrated that man more than Martha did, and that was his one and only sister. "We'll be down as soon as we can," she repeated and mounted the stairs.

She went directly to the room where she had helped to bring little Jacob into this world only a few months ago. After knocking very gently, she entered the room when Eleanor called out for her to come in.

She found Thomas's daughter sitting in the rocking chair where she had been rocked as a babe. Despite a very difficult pregnancy, Eleanor was the picture of health again. With her pale ringlets and blue eyes, she was the image of her mother, Sally, whose death two years ago still burdened her daughter's heart.

Little Jacob, named for his great-grandfather, the founder of Trinity, lay propped against her shoulder. "I was hoping you'd get here before he fell asleep," she said, nodding toward the chair. "He still needs a good burping. If you wouldn't mind holding him, I can freshen up a bit before we go downstairs," she suggested and handed the babe over to Martha.

Thrilled by Eleanor's offer, she sat down in the chair, nestled that pudgy little bundle of heaven against her shoulder, and made sure he was on the opposite side of the brooch she wore on the underside of her collar. She leaned her head to the side until she felt his forehead and his breath on her neck. "There's nothing on this earth quite like having a baby to cuddle," she whispered as she started to rock and pat his back.

Eleanor chuckled. "Nothing at all, unless it's the third time you've been up during the night and there are still hours to go until morning. Not that I'm complaining. Losing a few hours of sleep is a small price to pay for the privilege of finally having a little one to call my own," she added as she sat down at the dressing table to redress her hair.

Martha noted the shadow that crossed Eleanor's face and knew the young woman was remembering the other babes she had lost in the early months of pregnancy before finally giving birth to Jacob. "I can see for myself that he's growing and gaining weight just fine," she noted, "but babies seem to have a few days once in a while where they just can't seem to get enough of mama's milk. If it lasts more than another few days, let me know, and I'll bring you something to help him settle that little belly of his down a bit."

"Did Aunt Anne tell you to remind me that I was keeping our guests waiting?"

"In a manner, but Victoria and I were late and kept everyone waiting, so it's more our fault that supper is delayed than yours," Martha replied. Her words were followed by such a loud burp that Martha laughed out loud. "My goodness, I don't think a grown man could burp any louder than that!" she exclaimed, completely disregarding the fact that little Jacob had also dribbled a good bit of milk down the side of her neck and, in turn, drenched the collar of her gown.

"You haven't heard my husband," Eleanor commented before retrieving her son. "This little one will drop right off to sleep if I get him into his cradle," she whispered, then noted the stain on Martha's collar and frowned. "I'm so sorry. I'll help you take care of that in just a minute," she promised. She settled little Jacob down and returned to Martha with a cloth she had dampened with water.

Martha took the cloth, wiped her neck, and blotted the collar of her gown. "It's nothing but a little milk. It's not the first time a little one decided to share a bit of milk with me, and it certainly won't be the last," she insisted, handing the cloth back to Eleanor. "There. All done."

Eleanor took the cloth and furrowed her brow. "Not quite." She pressed the cloth down again on a spot Martha had apparently missed, even as her eyes searched for more. She leaned forward and squinted a bit before setting the cloth aside. "You really must have been rushed to get here tonight. You've pinned your brooch on the wrong side of your collar," she said and quickly switched the brooch to the other side before Martha quite realized what was happening.

"That's such a lovely brooch. I don't believe I've ever seen you wear anything quite as lovely."

"I don't usually wear what little jewelry I have, but I couldn't resist wearing this tonight. Why don't we head downstairs before your aunt comes up here looking for us," Martha suggested and led Eleanor out of the room, confident that no one would notice the brooch she wore before she announced her daughter's betrothal, which she planned to do the very moment they rejoined the others.

The moment she entered the sitting room, just ahead of Eleanor, she felt oddly uncomfortable. To her mind, walking into this room was entering a world totally uncommon to her life.

She looked around and could not decide whether it was the ornate furniture, the abundance of silver lined up on the mantel above the hearth, or the candlelight tickling the striped French wallpaper that left her feeling more uncomfortable and longing for the far simpler surroundings of home. The small group of people who were gathered in the sitting room, however, was far more welcoming, and all conversation ceased the moment she and Eleanor appeared in the doorway of the elaborately staged room.

In addition to Eleanor's husband, Micah, who was standing by the hearth with Thomas, Anne and her husband, George, the current mayor of Trinity, sat in identical upholstered chairs angled toward the sofa. Victoria and Dr. McMillan sat together a very proper distance apart, but it was Thomas's gaze that drew her into the room. Her heart was beating faster with every step she took as she prepared to make an announcement that would no doubt delay supper a bit longer, but she stood and waited until Eleanor had joined her husband before attempting to make her announcement.

Anne, however, rose immediately and motioned for Martha to come inside and take her seat. "Finally. I'll let them know in the kitchen that we're ready to dine," she said, but Martha held up her hand to keep the woman from scurrying out of the room.

"I know you're all anxious for supper, but there's something very important that I'd like to announce first." Martha took a deep breath and squared her shoulders.

Victoria blushed, and so did Dr. McMillan, but Anne rushed right over to Martha, took one look at the gold-and-pearl brooch pinned to her collar, and spun around to face her brother. "Congratulations, Thomas! The brooch suits her well. It's about time you finally had the courage to ask this woman to marry you," she gushed before turning back to Martha. "To my mind, you two should have married years and years ago, but I'm so happy you set things right now. And you'll never have to worry about being homeless again or rushing out at all hours of the day and night, will you, dear Martha? At your age, it must be getting quite difficult for you."

Martha was appalled that Anne would leap to such a conclusion simply because Martha was wearing a piece of jewelry. She did not know if she was merely insulted or annoyed that Anne had ruined Victoria's special moment, when Thomas stepped to her side and faced his sister.

"Once again, I'm afraid you've jumped to a conclusion that's blatantly false. I've never seen that brooch before tonight, and

I daresay that I'll be the one to make the announcement, if and when I ever decide to remarry."

"What I intended to say," Martha interjected before Anne could respond, "is that Dr. McMillan has asked for my permission to marry my daughter, and I've granted it."

Anne blinked hard, again and again, looking from Thomas to Martha before she faced the newly betrothed couple. By the time she did, Dr. McMillan was already on his feet and helping Victoria to stand beside him. Just as they had agreed, he pinned her brooch for all to see and took her hand. "Indeed, I'm honored to say that Miss Victoria Cade has agreed to become my wife, and we're both grateful for her mother's blessing," he said proudly. He then quickly explained the significance of the two brooches the women wore.

Completely avoiding the issue of her obvious blunder, Anne sped over to the young couple, and Thomas led Martha to the hallway just outside the sitting room. "I'm so sorry," he said. "I wish I could say this would be the last time Anne stepped into our lives to ruin something, but—"

"But it won't be," Martha whispered back and offered him a smile. "Don't worry about Victoria and Dr. McMillan. They're far too happy to be upset. Besides, Anne's your sister, which makes her more your problem than mine," she teased. "Once we're married, we'll be living well outside town, so I don't think we'll have to waste too much time worrying about what Anne might do or say, especially where we're concerned."

"Well, before Anne blabs out another bit of news, I need to tell you myself that I'm leaving tomorrow at first light."

Stunned that he was leaving so soon after being home for no more than a few days, Martha simply remained speechless.

17

Beyond disappointed, Martha stared up at him and finally found her voice. "You're leaving for New York already?"

"No. As it turns out, I'm going to Clarion. I believe I mentioned I had a family matter to attend to there."

"You did indeed, although I'm disappointed that you have to leave when you've only been back home for a few days," she admitted. She was reluctant to complain overmuch, especially since his journey there probably involved logistics around his announcement about offering his legal practice to his son-in-law.

"I won't be gone a moment longer than I have to be," he vowed and stole a quick kiss.

With her lips still tingling, she smiled again. "I don't suppose I could ask you for one tiny favor before you go, could I?"

He cocked his head. "Which would be what, exactly?"

"Instead of your usual mount, I was wondering if you might want to take Bella."

He laughed out loud. "Bella? She's run away, remember?"

"Actually, she's back in a stall at Dr. McMillan's, and it was your promise of a two-dollar reward that's responsible. I don't suppose you'd care to tell me why you thought it was a good idea to post fliers around town, when the best thing that could have happened after Bella ran off would have been that no one would have known she belonged to me if they found her."

He cringed. "You found out about the fliers already?"

She frowned.

"Before you get all fussy, I want you to consider this," he cautioned. "What if Bella did some kind of damage after she ran off? I don't know. Maybe she ended up trampling crops or hurting some unsuspecting girl or woman who tried to ride her? Under the law, whoever owns Bella could be held financially responsible."

He raised his hand when she opened her mouth to protest.

"Maybe you're right. Without the fliers, maybe no one would have ever known that Bella belonged to you. But maybe the person who gave you the horse would reveal that she did belong to you now. You'd be hard-pressed to explain why you hadn't stepped forward in the first place to admit it, wouldn't you? And even if no one, other than the two of us, ever found out that you owned Bella, would that mitigate your responsibility as her owner, morally speaking, at the very least?"

She wanted to argue that he was wrong, but she knew in her heart that he was absolutely right. She let out a very long sigh and wished she had realized her responsibility as Bella's owner instead of railing against it. "You're right, of course. I shouldn't hide the fact that she belongs to me, especially if she's done any damage or hurt someone," she admitted.

"If you just tell me who found the mare, I'll take care of the reward."

"Will did. He found that horse somewhere out by Samuel's

cabin and brought her to me. You owe the boy two dollars, and I'd appreciate it if you'd move Bella over to your stable in the morning, just in case Leech decides to reappear."

"Will's the one who actually found Bella?"

"Of course he found Bella! That boy can do most anything if he puts his mind to it."

"Reminds me of someone I happen to love," he teased.

She batted his comment away with a wave of her hand. "Before you leave town, make sure you take down those horrid fliers, and you should speak to Samuel before you give that young man so much money. Since you're going to Clarion, I'd like to ask you to do two things there for me, too," she suggested.

"Anything."

But just before she began to speak, Betsy, one of the maids, came into the hallway.

"Begging your pardon, Mr. Dillon, there's a gentleman at the back door asking to speak to you."

Thomas frowned. "At the back door?"

"Yes, sir. He says it's rather urgent."

Martha smiled. "Go see to your caller. I'll tell you about my requests after supper when you walk me home," she offered and returned to the other guests to share in the excitement over her daughter's betrothal.

She was barely back inside of the sitting room when Anne flew over to her like a famished bird who sighted vulnerable prey. Anne had the same dark hair as her brother, with nary a strand of gray to be seen, but her eyes were a bit darker than his. She was a woman of quite generous proportions, and the great volume of fabric necessary to create her silk gown rustled rather noisily as she crossed the room. "Martha, dear, you are so blessed to have such a fine young man about to become your son-in-law." She paused, looked about, as if making certain no one was close enough to overhear their conversation, and leaned forward a bit. "I simply cannot begin to fathom the troubles this might make for you. You've already lost a few women and their children to Dr. McMillan's care, and there are bound to be more. But perhaps it's all for the best. You'll all be family. And if I'm right about my brother's intentions, I suspect you won't need to worry about supporting yourself for much longer anyway."

"Indeed." Martha refused to be baited into saying anything else, because whatever she said was bound to be repeated tomorrow when Anne made her rounds shopping. She was grateful to have Thomas rejoin them, but her relief was short-lived when she noted her cape in his hands and his grave expression.

He wrapped her cape around her shoulders and gave his sister an order in a sharp tone of voice that only an older brother could use with his sister. "Tell everyone that Martha has been summoned out, then have Eleanor take everyone into the dining room and start the meal. Hopefully we'll be back before you've finished," he said before he led Martha down the hallway.

"Why did you tell Anne the caller was for me? I thought the caller was looking for you," Martha said, hoping against hope that she would not be forced to miss any of this special night with her daughter.

"I'm afraid he wants to speak to both of us, and I wasn't able to convince him otherwise without risking a scene that Anne would have gossipmongers chewing on with great gusto," he explained, then led her through his study and out a side door into the darkness that had fallen.

"What could he possibly want that would involve the two of us?" she asked, before realizing there was only one thing they had in common that would have someone searching them out at this hour: Bella. "So help me, Thomas, if this has anything to do with that horse—"

"I could argue that it's not as bad as it could be, but you'll likely feel otherwise," he said before he took her arm and guided her along the side porch that was lit only by the light pouring from the inside of the house. The porch ended right after they rounded the side of the house, and there Martha saw a rather well-dressed young man standing in the shadows holding the reins to the one and only Bella, who was standing rather docilely beside him.

"I'm Widow Cade. I understand you wanted to speak to me," Martha said, stepping ahead of Thomas as they approached him.

He tipped his hat. "Rob Carroll, ma'am. I'm working for Mr. Grumley at the First Trinity Bank that opened just last week, and I'm staying at Mrs. Reed's boardinghouse."

She nodded and waited for him to continue.

He cleared his throat and held up the reins. "I'd just come home from taking a walk after supper when I found your horse munching away in the vegetable garden Mrs. Reed planted a few weeks back. I'm afraid it's pretty much ruined. She's a might too upset about it to come herself, so I promised her that I'd talk to you and Mr. Dillon for her."

"How is that possible? Will and I had Bella well stabled more than an hour ago," she argued, baffled by the idea that the mare could have escaped and done that much damage in such a short time.

The young man shrugged. "All I know is that I found her there, and Mrs. Reed isn't too pleased about it. I'm thinking that the two-dollar reward from Mr. Dillon would be a start to making her happy again, but Mr. Dillon said that someone else had already found and returned the horse," Rob offered.

"That's true, but you didn't know that, and since Bella apparently escaped yet again, I think you've earned the same reward. Don't you agree, Thomas?"

"I had a feeling you might argue exactly that point and came prepared," Thomas gritted.

He reached into his pocket and handed over several coins to the young man. "I'll be taking down those fliers at first light on my way out of town tomorrow, but in the meantime, you're entitled to the reward. Since Widow Cade is here with other guests for supper, I'd be obliged if you would get Bella settled in my stable before you leave."

"That I can do," he replied and turned his attention back to Martha. "I know there isn't anything you can do for Mrs. Reed as far as her vegetable garden is concerned, but she was wondering if you might stop by to see her tomorrow and help her with a problem she's having with her shoulder, without asking for a reward. As a way of making up for what your horse did," he added.

Martha let out a long sigh. "Of course. Please tell her that I'll stop by in the morning." She had a feeling she would be replanting the woman's garden soon, too.

Grinning, he tipped his hat and led Bella back toward the stable. Once they had both disappeared into the darkness, Martha turned to face Thomas. "An old friend of my grandmother's lives near Clarion. The last I heard, she was still helping out occasionally as an afternurse. She might know of someone I could contact about replacing me. It would reach her faster if you took her a note from me than if I sent it by post, and I have a number of remedies I usually purchase in Clarion that I need. If I write a quick note to her and make up a list of remedies before I leave tonight, will you see that she gets the note and bring the remedies back for me?"

"Of course," he murmured, but when he leaned down to kiss her, she put her finger to his lips. "I'd also like to ask you to rethink my suggestion to use Bella as your mount when you leave tomorrow."

He frowned and pulled his face away. "And if I don't take her?"

She shook her head. "While you're gone, Bella may prove to be one very, very costly horse."

⁂

Later that night, long after Victoria had shared every detail of her special night and the rest of the household was fast asleep, Martha was still awake.

With her room bathed in gentle moonlight, she sat up in her cot with her back against the wall and Bird perched on her shoulder as she glanced around the room. She was surrounded by all that was familiar. The cot she slept on and kept out of habit instead of exchanging it for a proper bed, the birthing stool she stored underneath—as much to protect it as to keep it within reach if she were summoned away during the night—and the quilt, which her mother had stitched together with her own hand, that kept her warm, even on the coldest of winter nights.

She did not have any plants or herbs she used to make her remedies hanging overhead like she'd had in the room she once kept at her brother's tavern, mostly because she did not have a garden anymore. Reminded that poor Mrs. Reed didn't have a garden anymore, either, thanks to Bella, she focused instead on the supply of remedies she still had stored in her room, as well as the remedies Thomas had promised to bring back from Clarion.

She nudged Bird ever so gently with her cheek and smiled when he nudged her back. "All this will be gone once I marry Thomas and we make a home together," she whispered, and she realized that the one thing she expected to miss the most was not in this room at all but existed only in her mind and heart: her independence.

"I wonder if you miss that, too, little one." She promised him that she would make time to take him back up to the falls in the morning to see if he was strong enough now to fly away and survive on his own.

As a widow, she had fended for herself for ten long years, but now all of her longings for the companionship of a husband and a home to call her own again—as well as bidding farewell to financial concerns—would be met once she married Thomas. Then why oh why was she sitting here, in the middle of the night, thinking about the fact that marrying Thomas would also mean learning to compromise again and mean subjecting her will to that of her husband, as custom demanded?

"I'm afraid I'm being very foolish and ungrateful," she murmured before she settled Bird into his cage and dropped the cover over it so he would not wake up at first light with a morning serenade. Once she was lying in bed, Martha tugged her mother's quilt up to her chin, folded her hands, and eventually fell asleep with a fervent prayer on her lips and hope in her heart that God would help her to find a replacement and bring Thomas home safely.

And that she would not mind at all if God could help Bella to disappear from Trinity forever.

18

For the next two weeks, nonstop work was one sure way to make time pass quickly.

After barely five hours of fitful sleep, Martha squinted at the bright light pouring into the room, rolled over, and covered her head with her pillow. The weather outside had already been balmy at dawn, when she had returned from her second call of the night, promising more hot July weather. She prayed fervently for a single day she could call her own.

"Just one day," she whispered, although the prospect of getting the answer to that prayer seemed unlikely. While summer in Trinity was typically marked by any number of maladies, this year was proving to be particularly difficult, as much for her as for Dr. McMillan.

Of course, if she'd had a reliable horse of her own instead of Bella, she would have been able to return on her own every time she was summoned, rather than having to wait for someone to bring her back to town. She was sorely tempted to just borrow one of Thomas's horses to complete her duties, but more often than not, she was called away at odd hours and did not want to trouble his stable hands or rouse them out of bed.

Instead, she tried to be satisfied that Bella had not managed to escape from the stable behind Thomas's house again. She sighed and lifted her pillow to take a peek at the covered birdcage. She had not had a single moment to take Bird out to the falls again or to restore Mrs. Reed's garden, but her biggest regret was not having the opportunity to approach the three women left on her list of possible replacements.

Thomas, as always, was ever in the forefront of her mind, and her longing for him was growing stronger. As of early last evening, he had yet to return from his trip to Clarion, but he had written to her once already to keep her from worrying. Hopeful there was a letter from him waiting for her at the general store, or perhaps a reply from the letter he had delivered to her friend Naomi Benson, she added a prayer that he would be back soon.

By the time she dressed, fed Bird, and went downstairs, it was midday and the kitchen was already insufferably hot. The half-opened window in the alcove allowed sunshine to bathe the room with light, but with no breeze outside at all, it did little to ease the heat in the room.

To her surprise, the kitchen was deserted. She could hear Fern and Ivy's voices and a gaggle of others coming from the shop, and Martha smiled. Half the town had been in and out of the shop ever since the confectionery had reopened a few days ago.

Victoria was spending one last day helping Aunt Hilda, who was planning to leave tomorrow, but there was no sign of Jane or Cassie, which was odd considering the stack of cooking pans and dishes waiting to be scrubbed clean. Still too tired and overwarm to be more than mildly hungry, Martha settled for a cup of tea and a few bites of a honeyed biscuit.

Before deciding how to arrange her chores and errands for

the day, she looked out the window and peeked down the alley, where she saw Cassie walking toward the back door with a small empty basket, and realized the girl must have been behind the building hanging laundry. But she was not alone, and Martha squinted to make certain her eyes were not deceiving her as she studied the skinny little man walking alongside Cassie carrying two larger baskets.

"Fancy?" she murmured, but who else could it be? There wasn't another man in town, let alone within a hundred miles, who would wear half a dozen jewels in each ear like he did.

Cassie spied her and waved. "I'm all finished and ready for my next task, and Mr. Fancy is here to help, too, just as soon as we store away these baskets," she offered in a singsong voice. She headed back inside with the man who had apparently become the girl's self-ordained protector.

Although Fancy had established a close and paternal relationship with Will, Martha made a mental note to speak to Samuel about the man's relationship with Cassie. Perhaps learning more about the old seaman's past, as well as Samuel's opinion, would ease her concerns about Fancy's interest in the girl.

Cassie gave Martha a solid hug the moment she entered the kitchen. "I made sure all three baskets were back on the proper shelf so when it's time to take down the laundry, I'll be able to find them easily."

"You're a good, hardworking girl," Martha replied. Still amazed by the girl's loving and affectionate nature, she hugged her back under Fancy's watchful gaze. "Do you know where your mother might be?"

"Yes, ma'am," Cassie replied while nodding her head. "She left on an errand, but before I left she said that when I finished hanging out the laundry, I was to take a note she tucked into my apron pocket down to Mr. Sweet at the general store. Mr.

Fancy is going with me to help me carry everything back home, aren't you, Mr. Fancy?" she asked, turning to face him with her wide grin.

"Absolutely right. I've got a list of my own to take care of there, too. Is there anything we can bring back for you while we're there, Widow Cade?"

"If you could see if there are any letters waiting for me, I'd be most grateful. You might check for Victoria, too. She's expecting to hear back from her brother. I'll give you a note to let Mr. Sweet know that I've asked you to call for our mail and ask him to put the charge for any postage on my account," she suggested. "Do you know if Mr. Dillon had time to speak to Will before he left a few weeks ago?"

Grinning, Fancy nodded. "He stopped on his way out of town. That two-dollar reward for young William is safely put away in that new bank, though he don't seem too pleased about it. He did ask me to mention his spyglass. Any chance he can get it back?"

"I still haven't seen those grades of his, so tell him I'll try to stop by in the next day or two with the spyglass in hand," she promised, feeling guilty for having been too busy to even give the spyglass a thought.

He nodded and waited while Martha scribbled out her note before he left with Cassie. To make herself useful, she donned a work apron before she tackled the dirty baking pans and dishes stacked by the sink. She pumped water into a basin in the sink and took hold of the baking pan on the top of the pile. Part of a gooey honey bun spun with cinnamon stuck in one corner was too tempting to waste, and she swept it up with two fingers and gobbled it down before scrubbing the pan clean.

Half an hour later, she had cleaned every single pot and pan and stored them away, but she had also devoured tiny remnants of apple strudel, several burnt molasses cookies, half a bran muffin, and pieces of three broken pretzels.

"Dishes next," she said and dumped the dirty water into a large bucket that she could empty out in the alley later. Before she pumped fresh water into the basin, she heard the back door open and close.

She turned around, expecting to see Cassie back, but instead, a barefoot Jane walked gingerly into the kitchen. Her apron and the hem on her work gown were covered with dirt, and most of the hair around her face had escaped from her braid. With her smudged cheeks flushed red, the poor woman looked as if she were about to faint.

"Martha! What are you doing up already?"

Martha ignored the woman's question, hurried to her side, and urged her into one of the chairs at the kitchen table. "Sit right here until I get you some water. What on earth happened to you?"

Jane let out a long sigh. "Nothing that couldn't have been prevented, I'm afraid," she replied before accepting a glass of water and downing it straightaway. "Other than suffering from a couple of blisters from wearing boots that are a tad too big and forgetting to wear a bonnet, I'm just feeling overheated. I really didn't expect to be gone or out in the sun this long."

Martha frowned, refilled the glass with water, and handed her a damp cloth, which the woman immediately pressed to her flushed forehead. "Gone where?" Martha asked once she had both of Jane's feet resting in a footbath.

"I know how hard you've been working, and I wanted to do something to help. Every time I thought to ask for your permission, you'd been called away again," she replied cryptically.

Martha knew at once where Jane had gone to end up covered with so much grime, and she sat down beside her. "You shouldn't have been working at Mrs. Reed's. It's been my obligation to replant the garden that Bella destroyed, not yours," she argued. One of the chores she had planned for the day was to finally start meeting that obligation.

In all truth, she was still surprised that Mrs. Reed had given her permission to use a patch of ground where she could grow the herbs and plants she needed for her simples, as long as she also shared some of that bounty with her.

Jane let out a long sigh and smiled. "You've been so busy lately, it just didn't look like you were going to have any time soon to get to the task yourself, and Mrs. Reed was getting impatient waiting for you. I knew it wouldn't take much time to replant her garden, which I managed to finish the other day, but I thought that if I could get your garden planted, too, then all you'd have to do would be to keep it weeded. You'll probably need to add more, but at least you've got a start," she added. She reached into her apron pocket and pulled out a dirt-stained paper she handed to Martha. "This is what I planted for you today."

Dumbstruck, Martha only had the wherewithal to scan the list of plantings and be amazed. Martha could not have chosen a better selection if she tried, and there were only a few she needed to add. "You chose all these plants yourself?"

"Not entirely," Jane admitted. "Fern and Ivy recommended a few. Your daughter was here the day I was making up the list of what I thought to plant, but she said she didn't really know much about the plants or the remedies you made from them."

Martha pursed her lips. "No, she wouldn't. She's never had the slightest interest in anything I do as a midwife, I'm afraid. Her talents lie elsewhere with pen and paper, not a bag of simples or a birthing stool. I've only recently been able to fully accept that and to look for a woman to replace me."

Still curious to know where Jane had learned so much about plants, she realized she knew very little about the woman's background, other than the fact she had lived in Philadelphia and worked in a number of well-to-do households before taking care of Mr. Pennington. Jane had not shared much more than that. Since Jane deserved to be judged by what she did now as a member of their household and not her past, whatever that might be, Martha posed a question to her that only concerned the present.

"In all truth, Jane, beyond helping a woman to safely deliver her babe, one of the biggest responsibilities any midwife has is to have a full knowledge of herbs and plants and how to make remedies from them so she can help the women and children who depend on her, whether they're ill or teeming with a babe. Since you clearly have knowledge of remedies and how to use them, I wonder if you might consider learning the rest of a midwife's duties. It would probably take a good year or more, but I'd be honored to teach you, and I have no doubt that Fern and Ivy would allow you to stay here with Cassie, just as they did for me and my daughter," she suggested, convinced it would be a true answer to prayer if Jane agreed.

When Jane abruptly broke her gaze and started brushing more dirt from her hands, Martha noticed the woman was trembling. "Whatever woman you choose will be fortunate to be a midwife here in Trinity, but that won't be me. I . . . have absolutely no interest in ever being a midwife," she said in a shaky voice.

Concerned that she had upset the woman, she remembered sharing the story of almost losing Henny Goodman before Dr. McMillan intervened and wondered if that might be one reason why Jane was not interested. She accepted her answer and turned their conversation back to the work Jane had done in their garden. "Then just let me say that the work you did in the garden for me is an absolute blessing. You're an amazingly kind woman. Almost to the point of self-destruction," she teased. "Thank you."

When Jane finally looked up, Martha noted unshed tears glistening in her eyes. "You're welcome."

"I do have a promise I'd like to hold you to, though," Martha cautioned. When Jane raised a brow, Martha started to nod. "The next time you decide to wear those boots of yours, wear an extra pair of socks so you don't get blisters again. And don't go out again without your bonnet."

Jane laughed. "That's a promise!"

"Good!" Martha pronounced and got to her feet. "As for those blisters of yours, I've got just the cure upstairs in my bag. Don't move. I'll be right back," she ordered and hurried upstairs to get an ointment she had made from marigolds. Troubled by Jane's reaction to the offer she'd made to her, Martha had the sense that there was something in her past that had made the woman tremble and be on the verge of tears. Jane, however, had no obligation to explain why the thought of becoming a midwife distressed her.

Martha hurried back to the kitchen, and when she did, the room was abuzz, with most everyone in the household gabbing together like a gaggle of geese. She slipped the ointment into Jane's hands without anyone else taking notice. Fern and Ivy were making a fuss over Jane's poor blistered feet while Cassie and Fancy were laughing together as they unpacked the goods from the general store.

In the midst of all this, Fancy walked over to Martha and quietly slipped yet another blessing for this day into her hand: a letter from Thomas.

19

Martha was elated to have gotten a letter from Thomas, but with so many people now living in the household, privacy was truly a precious commodity.

Anxious to read his letter alone before sharing any news with the others, she left the confectionery ten minutes later. With Bird tucked safely in his basket and her letter stored in her reticule, she started off to the clearing above the falls, where she would have the privacy she craved.

Main Street was the usual beehive of activity, with wagon traffic clogging the roadway and pedestrians shopping along the planked sidewalk, sandwiched in between the noisy canal workers at one end of town and mill workers at the other. She started across the covered bridge to reach the path that would wind through the woods and end up at the clearing, but she paused just inside the far end of the covered bridge to take a good look up and down East Main Street. With no sight of anyone walking about to her left, she looked right and found no sign of anyone seeking treatment at Dr. McMillan's home, either.

Too excited to wait any longer to read her letter, she decided that right there, within the shelter of the covered bridge, would be private enough.

She set the basket down on the ground and took a step beyond it so she could be as close to the light as possible while keeping the basket in the shade. Her hands were shaking as she broke the seal and unfolded the single piece of paper, and her heart raced a little bit faster as she read his short but tender message dated a week ago:

> *My dearest Martha,*
>
> *Although I'm desperate to return to you, my beloved, I must remain in Clarion for another week and possibly longer. I pray you're finding more success in your search for someone to assume your duties as a midwife than I am having here trying to convince Micah's father to end their estrangement. I delivered your letter to Mrs. Benson and had a rather lengthy visit with her. Instead of writing back to you, she asked me to reassure you that, while she had no one she could recommend as a new midwife, she would keep your request in mind.*
>
> *I miss you more and more each day. Once we're together again, I intend to shower you with kisses until you agree we should marry and travel to New York together.*
>
> > *Ever faithful,*
> > *Thomas*

Disappointed by Naomi's response, she shook her head. Persistent man. Only mildly annoyed that he was still trying to get her to go to New York with him as his wife, she intended to remind him when he returned that he needed to be a little more patient. Thankfully, she would not have to wait long to do so.

In the meantime, before she attempted to walk to the falls she needed to have better control of her heart, which had started racing the moment she began to read his letter and had not stopped. Just the thought of the kisses he promised her made her vow to double her efforts to find a new midwife for Trinity.

"This is a rather odd place to be reading your correspondence."

Startled, Martha slapped the letter to her chest before she tipped her chin up to find Thomas standing only a few feet away, directly in front of her, holding the reins to his horse in one hand and his hat in the other. "Mercy, you frightened me half to death!"

"I'm sorry. I thought you'd heard me coming toward you and were ignoring me."

She huffed. "I wasn't ignoring you. I didn't even hear you approaching. And for that matter, I didn't even know you were back from Clarion."

"I came back late last night, but it was too late to let you know," he offered. When he leaned forward to get a peek at the letter she still had pressed against her chest, she hastily folded it up and shoved it into her reticule. He chuckled. "If that's my letter, then that accounts for it."

She tilted up her chin. "Accounts for what?"

His gaze smoldered. "With your absolute inability to be aware of anything other than how much affection you have for me when you're reading my words, which happens to be exactly how I feel about you when I'm penning them to you."

When he took a step closer, as if he were ready to shower her with those kisses he had promised, she put up her hand. "In all truth, I was more troubled by your lack of patience.

Persistence isn't always an admirable quality, either, particularly when it comes to repeatedly asking a woman to change her mind about when she would marry you, when you've already accepted her answer."

"And I might argue that a man who loves a woman as much as I love you is apt to do most anything to change her mind, although one of your kisses might convince me I should apologize."

When he took yet another step closer, she took two steps back, tripped over Bird's basket, and cried out as her skirts twisted about her legs. With her arms flailing and the bird squawking and attempting to get out of the basket, she fought to stay on her feet.

She would have ended up falling if Thomas had not dropped the reins he had been holding and caught her by both arms. The next thing she knew, his horse charged past them, and Thomas went running after it. She watched in horrified fascination until they both turned north toward the confectionery, with any further view blocked by a pair of farm wagons headed down the street and the side of the covered bridge.

"What a disaster," she grumbled. She righted the basket and lifted the lid to check on Bird. He was shaking in a corner. "Poor little thing. You're so scared, I haven't a feather of a hope that I'll get you to fly very much today."

Carrying the basket close to her with both hands, she hurried off to find Thomas, only to find him tethering his mount to the post on the sidewalk right in front of the confectionery.

"I'm sorry to have caused such a ruckus, but at least you found your horse before it got too far," she said.

He gave her a hard look. "I wouldn't have had to go charging after my horse if you hadn't been carrying that confounded bird of yours about town. I thought you'd set it free by now."

Martha stiffened her back. "It's not like I haven't tried. His wing is healed and he can fly pretty well now, but I don't think he's strong enough to fly off and fend for himself in the wild quite yet."

"It's a bird, Martha. Try as I might, I simply can't comprehend why you still have that creature. If you'll just set it free, it'll manage to survive because that's what birds do. They fly. They eat. They survive. And they'll peck at your flesh and draw blood if you get in their way," he snapped, clearly vexed and still troubled by his childhood encounter with some jays that had left him with a few scars on his scalp and an aversion to birds of any kind.

"I'm sorry. If I had expected to meet you or anyone else on the street, I wouldn't have had Bird with me. In point of fact, I was actually on my way up to the clearing above the falls with him to see if he's really strong enough to fly away," she explained, grateful that her apology had eased his frown, although not quite into a smile. "Were you on your way out of town when you found me?" she asked, curious to know if he had intended to stop to tell her he was home before he left again.

"I'm not quite certain where I was headed," he offered and paused for a moment before he continued. "You may as well know. Apparently Bella ran off again the day before yesterday. Since I couldn't find her when I walked around town this morning, I was heading out to see if I could locate her somewhere beyond Trinity before she caused any more trouble. But as it turns out, I don't have to bother now. I know exactly where she is," he said with a twinkle in his eyes.

He took the basket out of her arms and set it on the planked sidewalk. Taking hold of her hand, he marched her straight to the entrance of the alley.

To her surprise, she saw Bella standing at the back door to

the confectionery where she was licking at one of the half-dozen pans that customers had returned there. "Bella may not particularly like you, but she's smart enough to remember where to find the sweets she apparently craves as much as you do," he said, keeping his voice low. "Wait here and stay very still while I walk down to get her. She won't be likely to bolt as long as she doesn't hear you and you aren't anywhere near her."

Unfortunately, when he was only a few feet away from the horse, Ivy opened the back door, yelped when she saw the horse there, and slammed the door. Just as startled, Bella reared her head and knocked all of the pans off the step. When they clattered every which way, Bella charged down the alley, headed straight for them.

Thomas raced back and pulled Martha into his arms and out of harm's way barely in time to avoid the petrified horse, which had kept running and finally disappeared. Pressed between the side of the building and Thomas's chest, Martha could feel her heart pounding against his and held on tight.

Breathing hard to catch his breath, he made no attempt to let her go. Instead, he bent down to whisper in her ear, "If keeping that horse around gives me the opportunity now and again to hold you this close, I may just let you give that mare to me like you offered to do, remember?"

"I remember no such thing," she countered and wriggled out of his embrace.

"I've got a sweet little mare in my stable that you can ride if you'd care to come with me now and help me to look for Bella."

"I can't. I should pick up all those pans and finish the work I have to do in the confectionery," she replied.

"Then promise I can see you later today or tonight, perhaps. I've got those remedies you asked me to get for you in Clarion and matters we still need to discuss. What time would suit you best?"

"Tomorrow would probably be better," she suggested, without letting him know that tonight she had something very difficult to do. She had to say good-bye to Aunt Hilda.

❧

The next morning, while the rest of the household was still fast asleep and darkness blanketed the entire town, Martha slipped out of the confectionery carrying a lantern to light her way. Even though they had said their farewells the night before, Martha could not let Aunt Hilda leave today without one last hug.

She reached Aunt Hilda's home just in time to help pack the last few boxes into the small covered wagon that was now a traveling home for the elderly couple. The interior of the wagon was as homey as Aunt Hilda could make it. Crates loaded with supplies and the few personal belongings Aunt Hilda had wanted to take with them had been tied into place on either side of a makeshift bed that was covered with one of the quilts made by Martha's late mother. A thick pad protected by a layer of oilcloth on top covered the front seat, and Martha hoped her idea to add the pad might help to cushion the ride for the two septuagenarians who were both beaming with anticipation and anxious to depart.

Martha could not imagine setting off for the unknown at any age, but she could not deny Aunt Hilda the right to follow her heart and join her husband on a grand adventure that would surely unleash a storm of gossip once everyone in town discovered what they had done.

Finally, when a glorious sunrise blessed the earth with both warmth and light, they shared one last hug. "Be safe," Martha murmured, unable to say more because she had a lump in her throat and was struggling to keep tears at bay.

"I love you, sweet girl. And remember. There are only three things you need to do in this life: Follow God, follow your heart, and follow your dreams. And if you ever have any doubt about what to do, just trust that He'll guide you to the life He means for you to have," Hilda whispered and squeezed Martha tight before she joined her husband on the wagon seat, where he was waiting for her with reins in hand.

"We both thank you for your help," Uncle Richard said and nodded toward the house. "Since we didn't expect to see you this morning, Hilda left a little note for you on the kitchen table, and we finally found the key to the house," he added with a chuckle. "We never used it, but we sure don't have any need for it now. We left that on the table, too," he offered, then tipped his hat in a final farewell and clicked the reins.

Martha watched through tear-filled eyes until the wagon disappeared from sight. With a heavy heart and spirit, she returned to the little cottage and took some solace from the fact that if they ever wanted to return, their home would be right here waiting for them. To that end, she vowed to keep the cottage locked up safe for them.

She walked into the kitchen and straight to the note that had been left for her on the table next to the key, which was strung on a rather long length of jute with the ends tied together. Martha smiled. Apparently, Aunt Hilda had written her note on the back of a piece of brown wrapping paper she had rescued from something she had purchased at the general store.

She left the key lying on the table and carried the note over to the window for a bit more light so she could see it more clearly and read aloud: "'Dearest Martha, With all of our children gone before us to Glory, we've decided to transfer ownership of our home and property to you. Since Thomas was away, we relied on his son-in-law, Micah, to help us. We've already signed the necessary document, and he assures us that it merely awaits your signature before he files it with the proper authorities. Please don't find fault with us for not telling you about our plans in person. We were afraid you'd try to make us change our minds. We pray you'll accept our gift as a token of our love and gratitude for all you have done for us and for so many others in Trinity, and we trust that you'll know how best to use our gift. With love and affection, Aunt Hilda.'"

Overwhelmed, Martha leaned against the window and pressed the note to her heart. Tears flowed and flowed, as much for the idea that Aunt Hilda had no intention of ever returning to the home she had called her own for over fifty years as for her aunt's generosity.

She glanced around the kitchen and shook her head. This cottage was a gift that reached straight to her heart and wrapped around the dream that she had had for the past ten years—the dream of having a home of her own—that she had given up as impossible to achieve.

Only Aunt Hilda knew how much Martha had cherished this dream and longed for the day when she would not have to depend on anyone else to provide a place for her to live. And now this gift, this very generous and unexpected gift, fulfilled that dream.

Most unexpectedly, this gift gave Martha the opportunity to live in her own home instead of remaining at the confectionery. Realistically, however, there were a host of reasons why she was in no position to claim a home of her own right now, whether here or anywhere else. She began pacing around the cottage, walking from the kitchen to the parlor to each of the two bedrooms and back again, note in hand, as she sorted through a host of conflicting ideas that troubled her.

Martha received the rewards she earned sporadically, and they were scarcely enough to maintain a separate household. Despite Aunt Hilda's good intentions, even if they did move into the cottage, Victoria could not be left alone here for days at a time. It would not be proper, especially now that she was betrothed, and it probably was not safe, given the number of unattached men who had come to Trinity to work on the new canal.

She paused in front of the bedroom Aunt Hilda had shared with her husband and sighed. Within a year or so, Victoria would be married, which would leave Martha living here alone, unless she married Thomas in the meantime, which meant she really had no need for this cottage since he had already prepared a home for them in the countryside.

It suddenly occurred to her that they might use this cottage when they returned to Trinity on weekends, but she could scarcely make that decision without discussing the possibility with him.

As long-buried emotions washed over her, Martha realized that the gift she had received required deep consideration, and it would take far longer than a few moments of prayer before she would know what to do with the cottage.

Still shaken by saying farewell to Aunt Hilda and over-whelmed by her gift, Martha was too distraught to be think-ing clearly about her future, but she had enough wits about her to realize that the safest place to keep this note was right here in the cottage.

She refolded the note and walked straight to the kitchen pantry, where she found an empty tin. Once she stored the note inside the tin, she put it back on the shelf and shut the pantry door. She found the key lying on the table, then took it with her as she locked the door from the outside. She slipped the circle of jute holding the key over her head like a necklace and started back to the confectionery.

For now, she decided, the gift of this cottage would remain a very deep secret from everyone, even Victoria, and it would remain a secret until she was able to sign the document Micah was holding for her and discuss the matter with him, as well.

The sun was warm and the breeze was soft as she walked along the narrow path through the woods toward home. Her heart was just a little bit lighter, and her steps were much surer as she made her way back, prepared to celebrate her aunt's generosity by devouring a rather generous piece of strudel.

Or maybe even two!

20

Martha was steps away from the back door of the confectionery when Will charged out and nearly ran straight into her.

Reacting purely out of instinct, she caught him by his shoulders and stopped his forward movement by locking her elbows and planting her feet. With her heart pounding, she held him in place. "Hold it right where you are, young man."

"I've been waitin' and waitin' for you for more than an hour. You gotta come out to the cabin. Right now!" he demanded as he wriggled free and tugged on her hands to make her turn around.

Annoyed that he would demand so rudely that she go with him, she tugged her hands free. "I'm not going anywhere right now—especially not so you can reclaim that spyglass—except to go inside for a bit of breakfast."

When he glared at her, she noted that his gaze was darker than she had ever seen before. "I ain't here for a dumb spyglass. Mr. Samuel's got himself hurt. He needs you."

Hurt? She had seen Samuel just the day before, when he had eased all of her concerns about Fancy's interest in protecting Cassie, telling her that Fancy had once had a daughter who had been accosted by a couple of rowdy youths and subsequently died. Samuel had been fine when they spoke then, yet now, somehow, he'd been hurt.

"Wait right here. I need to get my bag of simples," she said. It wasn't until they were on their way to the cabin that she gathered more information from him. "Can you give me some idea of how badly Samuel's been hurt?"

"Don't know for sure, but I think it's pretty bad. Mr. Fancy fixed him up a bit, but his arm still don't hang right," he offered as they followed the path behind the cemetery and into the woods. "You can fix his arm, right?"

"You should have gone straight to Dr. McMillan." She worried that Samuel's stubborn refusal to see a doctor under any circumstances in the past—even as he was going blind—might end up causing more trouble. She hurried her pace.

Will kept up with her, wearing a scowl. "He won't go to no doctor. Maybe you might wanna try forcing him to do something he don't wanna do, but I ain't gonna do that, and I don't think Mr. Fancy would wanna try, either."

"You're right," Martha admitted, grateful for the canopy of trees that blocked the sun. "Maybe you should just tell me what happened to Samuel, if you know."

"All I know is we found him layin' in the woods and dragged him back home. 'Course, if I had my spyglass, I cudda climbed a tree to scout the woods, and we cudda found him faster. He said he musta lost his way to the lake and run into a tree," he replied as they approached the isolated cabin.

Guilt about the spyglass lodged in her throat, and her hand tightened around the handle on her bag of simples. Will was just a boy, and Samuel was a good three times the size of Fancy, which made their rescue even more heroic.

There was no use arguing the point that she had warned Samuel that attempting to follow a path from the cabin to the lake to go fishing alone was entirely unsafe. Instead, she followed Will into the cabin with the intention of convincing Samuel to send for the doctor—especially if the salty old recluse was hurt as badly as Will thought he was.

She entered the sleeping room that had been added after Fancy joined them, but Will stayed just within the doorway. She found Fancy sitting on his cot. He offered her a look of relief and nodded toward Samuel, who was sitting rather calmly on his cot with his back against the opposite wall, one arm cradling the other.

The injured man's face was quite puffy, distorting the scarred tattoo on his cheek. Above his bloodied beard, both of his lips had cracked open. His nose was badly swollen, and the darkening flesh around his eyes had reduced them to mere slits. Matted with dried blood, his gray hair lay plastered against his scalp.

Some of the blood on his head and body appeared to have been washed away, but the front of his shirt and coveralls were so stiff with dried blood that she doubted either could be salvaged. Worried that Will had been right about the extent of his adopted father's injuries, she approached Samuel with a frown she was glad he could not see.

Before she took more than two steps, he grunted. "Widow Cade. I trust you weren't terribly inconvenienced when William summoned you all the way out here."

"Will you let me take a closer look at your face?"

He scowled and winced when he did. "Might as well, considerin' you probably won't leave till you do."

After setting her bag on the floor, she put one hand on the

wall to brace herself and leaned forward to study his head and face. She raised her brow when she saw that Fancy had apparently closed a gaping wound in Samuel's scalp with a number of crude stitches. "You cleaned this head wound first before you stitched it closed, didn't you, Fancy?" she asked, impressed that he had gotten Samuel to let him stitch it at all.

"Wasted good whiskey when he did," Samuel growled.

"Perhaps you might have taken a bit of whiskey, too, just to soften your disposition," she quipped as she studied the injuries to his face. They were far less angry-looking than the serpentine scar on his cheek, and she held back a sigh of relief that they were not severe enough to be life-threatening. "Your face is going to be awfully sore for a while. You can also expect to suffer from headaches for a few days, but I have some remedies that I can leave with Fancy to help ease the pain." She turned her attention to his torso, where he was still cradling his left arm with his right one.

"Can you move that injured arm of yours at all?" she asked, determined to send for Dr. McMillan to set it if it was broken.

"I can move it fine. Just need to let it rest a few days is all," he grumbled.

Fancy walked over to join her and gave her a skeptical look. "Show her."

Samuel pursed his lips, which unleashed a trickle of blood he licked away. "I can move it," he insisted. "I just can't bend it."

"Which means you've either broken your elbow or sprained it, which also tells me that Dr. McMillan needs to take a look at it," Martha suggested.

Samuel responded with a deep growl. "No doctor. If the elbow needs tendin', then you do what needs to be done."

She drew a long breath and held it for a moment before letting it go. She had only helped to set a broken arm once before when Dr. McMillan had been indisposed with a severe case of chicken pox. He had been there to give her the guidance she needed then, and she needed it now, especially since it involved Samuel's elbow and not the forearm, where that break had been.

"I'll do it on one condition," she cautioned. "I need to speak to Dr. McMillan first, and before you argue the matter, let me remind you that I'm not trained to set broken bones properly, while he is. Of course, that's assuming you'd like to regain full use of your arm. If not, I can just go ahead, put some sort of splint on your arm, and hope for the best. It's your arm. You decide what you want me to do."

When Samuel furrowed his brow, Fancy offered her a grin, something he would never dare to do if Samuel had still had his vision. She waited for several heartbeats until Samuel finally waved her off. "He knows better than to think I'd ever be his patient, and if you talk him into coming back here anyway, he won't get in."

"I'll be back as soon as I can," she stated and carried her bag out of the room, with Fancy and Will following on her heels. She took a small bottle of honey wine out of her bag and grinned. "I wouldn't tell Samuel, but a strong cup of tea laced with Aunt Hilda's honey wine helps ease the pain after bringing a new babe into this world. I suspect it'll work just as well for his pain, too," she whispered before handing it over to Fancy.

He grinned back at her, and Will shoved his hand against his lips to hold back his laughter.

"While I'm gone, try to get him to take some. When I get back, I can show you how to make a poultice for his face before I tackle taking care of that arm of his," she suggested, then hurried off to see Dr. McMillan. She could only pray he was at home and not off tending to a patient too indisposed to come to his office.

God answered her first prayer just as she had hoped, and Rosalind showed her into Dr. McMillan's office. As usual, the doctor's desk was covered with piles of books and medical journals, the leather box where he stored all the notes she had made for him about traditional remedies, and a stack of correspondence that threatened to topple over the moment anyone touched it. Surprisingly, Thomas was there, too.

She urged both men to keep to their seats and paused for a moment to catch her breath. "I'm sorry to interrupt you both, but I need some medical advice rather quickly."

Blushing, the doctor waved his hand over the top of his desk. "As you can see, Victoria hasn't been here recently to help make some order out of this mess. I finally read your notes this morning on using a poultice with burdock leaves, like you did for Mrs. Reed a few weeks back. Oddly impressive," he noted. "Mr. Dillon and I were just discussing business and a few matters of mutual interest, which can wait."

Thomas got to his feet. "In truth, I believe we're quite finished. I should leave the two of you to your work, but before I go, Martha, I want to let you know that I found Bella and brought her back."

She frowned. "I'm afraid I don't have time to talk about Bella right now, but you needn't rush off on my account. Samuel's gotten hurt, and I just need to talk to Dr. McMillan to know what to do for him," she replied and quickly described the injury to his arm.

She left moments later with the advice she needed, several splints, some thin cloth to wrap the splints into place, and a piece of heavy canvas cloth. She also made a quick stop at the confectionery to get a larger bottle of honey wine from the larder and ran up to her room to get one more thing. While she was there, she also took the key hanging around her neck and stored it in the trunk at the foot of her cot. She tossed a few more seeds into Bird's food bowl, then she headed back downstairs to explain where she would be for the next hour or so.

On her way to the back door, Jane handed her a hunk of buttered bread, which she had doused with a bit of honey, and Martha gobbled it down as she made her way back to the cabin. With her hunger abated and her courage strengthened by the time she reached the cabin again, she followed Fancy into the sleeping room, where she found Samuel resting exactly where she had left him. Will was sitting on the cot alongside of him, but he got to his feet the moment she entered the room.

She addressed Will first. "I need you to go outside and find a good strong walking stick for Samuel because he's going to be walking a bit off-balance until his arm heals, which may take several months. You'll need a branch that's thick enough not to break and long enough that he won't have to stoop to use it."

"Take the ax and choose well," Fancy cautioned. "And make sure you don't leave the ends of the walking stick sharp enough to cut his hand when he's using it," Fancy added before Will scooted out of the room without posing any argument to stay.

Samuel grunted. "I take it you're ready to do what you have to do now that the boy is out of the way, but it won't do the boy any good to be coddled."

"Actually, I think I agree with you, but Dr. McMillan assured me that I won't have to do more than put a splint in place to keep your elbow bent and held close to your chest so you don't flex your elbow."

She made quick work of wrapping the splints into place before she folded the heavier canvas cloth into a triangle and had Samuel's injured arm resting in a sling in no time.

"He told me that you'll have to wear the sling all the time, even when you sleep. And keep your arm lying on your chest," she cautioned, completely satisfied that she had followed the doctor's instructions to the letter.

He offered her a rather weak grunt in return but didn't argue when she urged him to lie down and rest a spell.

Satisfied for now, she took Fancy into the other room. After taking some dried parsley leaves out of her bag, she set them in a bowl of water to refresh them and showed him how to make a poultice for Samuel's face. "Lay this on Samuel's face when he's lying down, and you can refresh the poultice over the next several days as often as you like," she told him before going back into Samuel's room to gently press a kiss to the top of his forehead. "I'll stop back to see you in a day or two, but if you need me for anything in the meantime, just send for me."

He took her arm and pulled her close. "Thank you."

"You're welcome, dear friend," she replied, but before she left the cabin, she took Will's spyglass out of her bag and placed it on the hammock, where the boy slept. She knew without asking that Samuel would be out and about alone again, probably before he was fully recovered, and Fancy might need the spyglass, too, if only to keep track of his friend from a distance.

When she finally got back to the confectionery and walked in the back door, she could smell the lamb stew boiling on the cookstove and heard a bevy of voices coming from the kitchen. Martha grinned; she had made it in time to share dinner with everyone!

She hurried down the hall, but when she entered the kitchen and saw the young man standing there with everyone gathered around him, her mother's heart swelled with such love and joy that she grew weak in the knees and leaned against the door-frame for support.

Why or how Oliver came to be here in Trinity did not matter to her at all. All that mattered was that her son was here. He was actually here!

21

Standing only a few feet away from her son, Martha was in a state of pure euphoria from head to toe and hand to hand.

Every member of the household was gathered around her son. They were so enrapt by a tale he was telling that no one even realized she was standing there, and she took a moment to etch this image of Oliver among the many sketches of her children she had stored over the years in the scrapbook of her heart.

The finely tailored frock coat and trousers he wore clearly befitted his status as the grandson of a wealthy and prominent figure in Boston society, and it was nearly the same color as his dark brown hair. His tall, sturdy frame paid tribute to his heritage as the son of a man who loved life as a yeoman farmer, and he so closely resembled his father that she trembled.

In temperament, Oliver had always been a no-nonsense sort of boy who grew up preferring books and school over farming, rarely ever thinking with his heart. In hindsight, it gave him a decided advantage as a lawyer, where his clinical nature could shine.

Martha's one and only contribution to his physical appearance was the deep dimples in his cheeks that appeared on the rare occasions when he smiled. Quite surprisingly, she had had a continuous view of his dimples from the first moment she had laid eyes on him today. He looked healthy, but more important, he looked happier than she had seen him in a very, very long time, and she could not believe how much he had changed since last summer when she had stopped in Boston while searching for her then-runaway daughter.

Anxious to hold him in her arms again, if only to prove that she was not in the middle of a dream, she cleared her throat. "Although you appear to be reveling in being the center of attention, Oliver, might you spare a moment to give your mother a proper welcome?"

Oliver grinned the moment he spied her and immediately broke free from his audience. "You're back!" he exclaimed and embraced her as though he, too, needed reassurance they were truly together again.

She was duly unsettled by the amount of happiness that washed over her and his uncommon exuberance. "You're such a dear to come all this way." Martha stepped out of his embrace and stood on tiptoe to kiss his forehead. "When Victoria wrote to you with her news, we never even entertained the thought that you'd come in person to give her your reply. I just wish I'd been here the very moment you arrived. You look exceptionally well," she gushed, too excited to have him home again to worry about how that might impact the date Victoria and Dr. McMillan would ask to be married.

"And you look exceptionally tired. How's your friend Samuel

doing?" he asked, without explaining why he had come all the way to Trinity instead of simply writing.

"He'll recover, but I doubt he'll listen to reason. I expect he'll be out and about again before he should."

"Not everyone follows your orders, do they?" he teased, wrapping an arm around her shoulders. "If you ladies wouldn't mind holding dinner just a little longer, I'd like to take my mother out for a little while."

Martha looked around and realized that Victoria was not even there. "Where's your sister?"

"She suggested we meet at Dr. McMillan's to discuss a matter of great importance to all of us, which is what brought me here. She's waiting for us there," he replied and led her down the hall to the back door.

Concerned that he might have come all this way to oppose his sister's betrothal, she paused the moment they stepped outside and he closed the door. "Did Victoria's letter upset you to the point that you felt compelled to travel here?"

He took her arm and guided her down to the end of the alley before he answered her. "Apparently I left Boston before her letter even arrived. I had no idea she'd become betrothed until she told me so a few hours ago," he replied and stopped to let several riders pass by before escorting her across the roadway.

Martha's heart skipped a beat. Rather than worry about the nature of the news he wanted to share with them, she asked him outright. "What's wrong? Does your news have anything to do with your grandfather? Have you two had a falling out?"

He let out a long sigh. "What I've come to tell you has everything to do with Grandfather, which I'll explain once we're all together." He ushered her across the covered bridge and into the doctor's house without saying anything more.

Once they were inside, Martha learned Dr. McMillan had

left with Thomas not long after she had been there and had not returned. She led her son upstairs to the sitting room, where Victoria was waiting for them.

By this point Martha's mind was tormented by memories of Graham Cade that soured her mouth and lodged like a boulder in the pit of her stomach. If that man had caused any hurt to Oliver even remotely like the pain he had inflicted on the boy's father, she had every intention of riding straight to Boston to give him a good tongue-lashing.

She needed every inch of patience she possessed to rein in her questions. Hopeful that Oliver would get straight to the heart of the matter, she sat down next to her daughter on the settee and noted the look of concern and curiosity on her daughter's face that matched her own feelings.

Oliver picked up an upholstered chair, set it directly in front of them, and unbuttoned his frock coat before he sat down. His expression sobered. "I'm afraid I have some unfortunate news. A month ago, Grandfather suffered a mishap at home."

"What sort of mishap?" Victoria asked.

He moistened his lips. "He tripped and fell down the central staircase. Despite the efforts of some of the finest doctors in the city, he succumbed to his injuries several days later. As he set forth in his will, he was buried in the family plot in Boston."

When Victoria's eyes widened, Martha took her by the hand. Since the girl had had little contact with her grandfather, she suspected Victoria was reacting more to the idea of death itself rather than losing a grandfather she barely knew and had not seen for a good number of years. "I'm sorry, Oliver," Martha said. "I know you admired him a great deal."

He nodded. "He wasn't an easy man to know or to love, for any number of reasons, but he was very good to me, and . . .

and in the end, I believe he tried to be as fair as he could allow himself to be."

Martha cocked a brow. "How do you mean?"

Before he answered, he took a sheaf of papers from an inner pocket in his frock coat and laid them on his lap. "I didn't notify you of his death right away or come here sooner because I had to resolve a number of legal matters first. Rather than leave the executor to send you this news by post, I've brought his letter with me to confirm what I'm about to tell you."

Martha tightened her hold on Victoria's hand and tried to prepare herself to accept the likelihood that Graham Cade had favored Oliver in his will and left little or nothing of his considerable estate to Victoria.

"I hardly knew our grandfather, and I always knew he favored you. I don't expect to receive anything from him, so you needn't worry that I'll be upset," Victoria said and squeezed Martha's hand.

Oliver smiled. "Then prepare yourself to be as pleasantly surprised as I was," he replied and tapped the papers with the palm of his hand. "Other than generous donations to several of his favorite charities, Grandfather directed that his entire estate be split between the two of us according to custom, with two-thirds assigned to me and the other third to you, Victoria." He sorted through the papers to find the ones he wanted. "I've placed your inheritance into a separate equitable estate, which means that your inheritance will remain yours and yours alone. Even after you marry, your husband will have no legal claim to your inheritance," he assured her as he handed the papers to her.

Victoria held the papers with both hands and stared at them. "He did that for me? Truly?"

"He did, which means . . . well, it means we're each wealthy," he said, but his expression grew troubled when he looked at

Martha. "I'm so sorry, Mother. Grandfather left specific instructions to the executor to make certain you received nothing at all and—"

"That's utterly selfish and hateful," Victoria spat and tossed her papers to the side. "If it wasn't for Mother, you and I wouldn't be here. She deserved something from him."

Martha treasured her children's concern for her but waved it away. "Your grandfather always blamed me for your father turning his back on his birthright, so I never had any expectations of receiving anything from him. I'm just thrilled that he recognized *both* of you as his proper heirs," she countered. It was altogether amazing that both of her children would have lives of considerable comfort, as would her future grandchildren.

She drew in a long breath and smiled at both of her children. "Although your grandfather's death is sad indeed, I do believe it would be entirely appropriate to celebrate his generosity today."

Victoria beamed. "And to celebrate my betrothal. Since Oliver is here, maybe we can even set a date for my wedding," she suggested.

Oliver rose and stored the remaining papers back inside his frock coat. "If I may, I'd like to add something else we can celebrate," he offered as a blush spread across his cheeks and moved down the length of his neck.

"What other reason could you possibly have, other than the fact that you're now a wealthy and very eligible bachelor?" Victoria teased.

His flush deepened from pink to crimson. "Wait right here, and I'll show you. I'll be right back. I promise. Just don't . . . don't leave," he insisted before leaving the two of them sitting there altogether confused and decidedly curious.

Nearly an hour later, Martha and Victoria had exhausted every possibility they could imagine about what Oliver would be bringing back with him, and they could not decide which was more likely. Was Oliver going to bring back some sort of proof that he was going to move back to Trinity? Not likely at all. Was he going to show them an announcement that he was going to leave his grandfather's law firm to start his own? That made no sense. Or was he going to leave on a tour of Europe, something he had always wanted to do, but had never gotten the permission he needed from his grandfather? Maybe.

Martha was on the verge of sending Victoria to the confectionery to urge everyone to start dinner without them when footsteps coming down the hall kept her in her seat. When Oliver started into the room, she was about to chastise him for taking so long . . . until she saw that he was not alone.

He had a woman with him, along with two very little girls, each holding on to one of the woman's hands. Wearing a broad smile, he led them directly to stand in front of the settee. "Mother. Victoria. I'd like to present my wife, Comfort, and my new daughters, Lucy, who is almost four now, and Hannah, who just turned three."

22

Martha tried to wrap her thoughts around the preposterous idea that she had become both a mother-in-law and a grandmother in the little time it took for Oliver to utter a few words.

Comfort looked to Martha and offered her a nervous smile. "I'm honored to meet you, Mother Cade. Oliver has told me of the important work you do," she offered before turning to Victoria. "Oliver told me just a few moments ago that you'd just recently become betrothed. You must be incredibly excited."

Victoria clapped her hands, leaped to her feet, and stared back and forth between Comfort and her brother. "Married? You two are married? When did this happen?"

Oliver grinned. "Nearly two weeks ago, the day before we left Boston to come to Trinity."

Comfort blushed. "We decided to make this trip a wedding trip of sorts, and we both agreed that this would also be a good way for the girls to get to know their new grandmother and aunt."

As Victoria bantered back and forth with her brother and his wife about their courtship, which apparently had been rather short, Martha was still reeling from Oliver's news and his shocking decision to marry a widow with two young children.

Instead of interrupting them, she kept her focus on the woman who had claimed her son's heart. Comfort was a petite, slender woman with eyes the color of a strong cup of tea. Her dark gray gown was made of rather ordinary fabric and the design was a bit severe, but a band of needlework on the collar and the cuffs of each sleeve was exquisite. The top of her bonnet barely reached her son's shoulder, giving Martha just a glimpse of pale brown hair held firmly away from a delicate, oval-shaped face.

From a distance, Martha might have described Comfort as close in age to her son, who was twenty-four, but she was close enough to note the crow's feet at the corners of her eyes and the laugh lines near her lips. This woman was a good number of years older than her son, which made his decision to marry her even more curious.

But Martha was also close enough to see that Comfort's expression was kind, her manner was gentle, and her eyes lit with absolute devotion every time she looked at Oliver. And it was that look of deep and abiding love in her eyes that encouraged this mother's heart to accept the idea that Oliver had chosen a woman who truly loved him.

Martha felt a tug on her skirts and looked down to see that Lucy and little Hannah had slipped free from their mother's grasp. Dressed in gowns the same color as their mother's and just as beautifully decorated with needlework, the girls wore straw bonnets that bore a bit of dust and dirt, just like the hems of their skirts. Although their little faces had been scrubbed clean, Martha suspected their mother had kept them busy playing somewhere outside while they had been waiting for Oliver to fetch them, if only to get rid of the energy they had stored up during their travels.

"Grandma? Can you bake some cookies for us?"

"Me want cookies, too."

With one glance at those sweet little faces and the innocence shining in their dark brown eyes, Martha's heart melted and wrapped right around those two precious children. "I used to bake cookies for your new father when he was a little boy. I haven't baked anything at all for a long time, but I have an idea about how we might get some cookies for you," she replied. She then urged Lucy to sit down beside her and chuckled when Hannah scrambled right up into Martha's lap.

Amazingly, love for these two little girls was as immediate and all-embracing as the love she had felt the first time she held one of her newborn babes in her arms. "Would you like me to tell you where we might get some cookies for you?" she asked as she hugged Lucy close to her.

When they both nodded hard enough to make the blond curls poking from the bottom of their bonnets bounce, she chuckled. "I live just a short walk away with your Aunt Victoria at the confectionery, where my friends bake lots and lots of cookies. We're going to have dinner there very soon, I hope, but I think you'll be able to eat some of the cookies you like best when it's time for dessert, don't you?"

Hannah leaned her head back until it rested on Martha's chest, just below her chin, and grinned up at her, but Lucy squealed with delight to seal the first promise Martha made to her granddaughters.

She nudged Hannah off of her lap just long enough to stand up and take each of the girls by the hand. Once she cleared her throat, hard, conversation stopped immediately, and she smiled when Victoria and the others blushed, apparently realizing they had all been ignoring her, as well as the girls. "If any of you would care to join us, we're going to the confectionery for dinner. Otherwise, we'll see you all later—perhaps by then you'll have decided to include us in your gaiety," she teased.

Waving off their attempts to apologize for ignoring her, Martha led the girls away, and the others followed along behind them. She entered the confectionery with the girls by way of the front door, but she sent the others around to the back. Relieved to find the shop empty, she took Lucy and Hannah directly to the room on the left, where Fern and Ivy had displayed the cookies they had made earlier that day, and decided to make her first act as a grandmother a memorable one.

Lucy was just tall enough to be able to see cookies displayed on the tabletop, but Martha had to hoist Hannah up on her hip to give the smaller girl the same advantage. "There's a custom here in Trinity that both of you should know about before you choose your cookies. You might not be old enough to understand the tradition completely, but for now, you should know that the girls and the women who live here in Trinity get together on very special occasions to celebrate how important it is to love one another and to help one another whenever we have a problem. And when we're all together during a snowstorm, too!"

The memory of the women who had gathered together last winter, right here in this confectionery, to start this tradition while they hatched a plan to help young Nancy Clifford escape her abusive husband, warmed her heart yet again before she continued. "When we do get together, we celebrate by eating sweets instead of our dinner. Does that sound like something you'd like to do with me today? To have cookies for your dinner?"

Lucy grinned. "Yes!"

"Yes!" Hannah echoed.

"Then let's pick out your cookies and take them with us to the kitchen," Martha suggested and helped them each choose two cookies. Lucy wanted two of the sugar cookies, while Hannah preferred the molasses. Martha helped herself to several of each before she took them back to the others. "After we go to the kitchen, I want you to meet a little friend of mine," she said, certain the girls would be fascinated with Bird.

Everyone was here now, standing around babbling, but this time it was Comfort who was truly the center of attention. At least, she was the focus until Martha entered the room with those two darling girls.

Before they all surged forward, she held up her hand and stopped them cold. "My granddaughters and I are dining upstairs in my room, but there's no need to send up dinner. The three of us are going to follow a very important tradition today, which means we've got our dinners right here in our hands. I'll bring the girls down afterwards and give you all a chance to meet them."

Fern and Ivy covered their mouths with their hands but failed to smother their chuckles. Jane and Cassie wore expressions of total surprise, while Victoria and Oliver merely grinned and shook their heads. Martha, however, waited to see the most important reaction of all—from Comfort.

Her new daughter-in-law looked down at the cookies they were carrying and let out a very long breath that made Martha's heart beat just a little faster while she waited for the woman to comment.

"Traditions are very important," Comfort finally offered. "After eating their cookies, I think the girls will be very thirsty, so I'll bring up some milk for them. May I bring you something to drink as well, Mother Cade?"

Martha smiled. "A glass of milk for me too would be nice,"

she replied and took the girls upstairs, satisfied for now that God had indeed led her son to choose a wise and good woman for his wife.

❦

When Martha woke up, the girls were still asleep, nestled on either side of her, and the sunshine filtering into the room hinted that it was rather late in the afternoon. She closed her eyes again, just for a moment, to savor the feel of their little bodies curved against her own and the smell of their cookie breath while they slept on.

As far as she was concerned, there was nothing on this earth that could compare to having a child to cuddle up with for an afternoon nap, but having two grandchildren beside her felt like sheer heaven. She looked over and saw that Bird was still in his cage, taking a nap, too, and she chuckled. The girls had gotten more cookie crumbs on the floor than they'd managed to slip into the cage, and Bird had wisely decided it was safer to stay in the cage when there were two giggling little girls in the room who wanted nothing more than to take turns cuddling the little bird, a request Martha had refused for fear they might accidentally crush him.

Reluctant to disturb the girls, she eased very gently from her cot to answer a soft rap at her door.

Comfort peeked in, looked at the girls, and smiled. "I was hoping they'd take a rest. After a rather arduous journey, this has been an eventful day for all of us. May I come in? I'm certain you're curious, and I'd like to tell you a bit about myself and answer questions you must have."

"Perhaps we should talk somewhere else so we don't wake the girls," Martha suggested, even though there was little privacy to be found anywhere else in the confectionery.

Comfort chuckled and slipped into the room. "Those two girls sleep through heavy storms and thunder. I doubt a little conversation will disturb them," she countered, although she did keep her voice a little softer than usual.

When she sat down on top of the trunk at the foot of Martha's cot, Martha took a place at the end of the cot to be next to her. Before she could decide which question to ask about Comfort and the circumstances that had led to her marriage to Oliver, the young woman poured out her tale.

"I'm nine years older than Oliver, which I'm sure you noticed," she began, glancing down for a moment. "When I was twenty-four, I married a man named Jack Whitman who was a store clerk in the city. We were married for six years, but he'd struggled with periods of time when he was very depressed for many years before that. When Hannah was only a few days old, he . . . he committed suicide."

Martha clapped her hand to her heart. "Oh dear!"

Comfort smoothed one of the folds in her skirt. "I don't know how I could have prevented my husband from killing himself, but I blamed myself for a very long time before I was finally able to ask God to forgive me for anything that I did or failed to do to help him."

Martha's heart ached for the woman, and she placed her hand on her shoulder. "How very difficult for you."

"It was very hard," Comfort admitted. "As you might imagine, the girls and I were in rather desperate circumstances. I was thirty years old, a widow with two very young children, with few ideas of how I might support us all," she admitted.

"What about your parents? Couldn't you return home to live with them or another relative, perhaps?"

Comfort folded her hands together on her lap. "I was just about Hannah's age when I was placed in an orphanage, so I don't have any memories of my parents, and I just assume I don't have any relatives, at least any who would take me in. I was put out to service when I was twelve, trained mostly to do laundry and mending and such, and I served in half a dozen households before I came of age. Fortunately, I was able to stay on in the last household until I finally got married and made my home with my husband and, eventually, our children."

Moved by Comfort's tale of a difficult childhood and her very painful experiences as a young wife and mother, Martha also wondered how Oliver had come into her life. "After your husband died, how did you survive? What did you do to support yourself and your daughters?"

Comfort tilted up her chin. "It isn't possible to maintain a household and support two children on the wages I could earn doing menial work. The little talent I do have is with the needle, which is something I learned from watching the daughters of some of my employers. The wages paid for needlework would have been better, but there wasn't a seamstress in the entire city of Boston who would hire me without references for that kind of work, even though I carried samples of my work with me everywhere. Even if one had, providing board for me and my daughters would have been out of the question."

Reminded of her own dependence on others after John died and her own inability to maintain a home of her own, even now when she had Aunt Hilda's cottage to call her own, Martha's heart trembled. "Without family, a widow's lot is never, never easy," she said, grateful that God had surrounded her with family and friends.

"Not without divine intervention," Comfort offered with a smile. "We were only days from being forced to find a place at the poorhouse when I met Mrs. Callahan. When she took a bad fall outside the room where we lived, I helped her to get back home again in a section of the city I knew very little about. As it turned out, she and her husband worked for Oliver's grandfather. They had lived in a one-room cabin in the rear of his estate for many years, and they still do, bless their hearts."

Comfort paused to smile. "As I came to learn later, there's only one woman who's ever had the courage to stand up to Graham Cade, and that's Evelyn Callahan. She convinced him that her eyesight was failing and that she was no longer able to properly mend clothing or household linens and such. She told him she would have to retire as his primary housekeeper unless he hired me to take on those duties and set aside part of the garret for me and my girls to live there."

Martha chuckled and looked down at the girls to make sure they were still sleeping. "He could be a very difficult man when he chose to be," she admitted, without confessing that he had intimidated her, too, and preferred to think she did not exist.

Comfort also looked down at her sleeping girls. "Obviously, that's how I met Oliver."

"As part of the household staff."

"Exactly," Comfort replied, and her eyes took on a dreamy look. "I found him disturbingly handsome and quite the kindest and gentlest man I had ever known, but he was so far above my station and so busy with his work that it never occurred to me that he would . . . that he would ever be genuinely interested in someone like me. He was Graham Cade's grandson and heir, too, which made him one of the most eligible bachelors in the city. Fortunately, none of the young ladies who pursued him, or their status-seeking mothers who encouraged them, had any idea that two little girls whose mother mended Oliver's clothes would win his heart before any of them did. Or before I did," she added.

Martha cocked a brow. "I can't imagine that Oliver's grandfather approved of the match, did he?"

"Mercy, no! Had he gotten so much as an inkling that Oliver had any feelings for me at all or that I came to return that affection, I would have been dismissed immediately. Not even Mrs. Callahan would have been able to save me."

"God rest his soul, that sounds like the Graham Cade that I knew," Martha admitted, "but when all is said and done, he provided Oliver with a good home, trained him to excel in his profession, and provided well for both of his grandchildren. For that, I'll forever be grateful."

"And I'm grateful, as well," Comfort said. "If he hadn't let me come to work in his household, I'd never have met Oliver." She locked her gaze with Martha's. "I love him with all of my heart. It's dreadfully important to me that you'll be able to welcome me and my daughters into your family and your heart, too, but it means even more to Oliver. He wants so much for you to accept our marriage, and if there's anything I can do or—"

"Dear, dear girl," Martha crooned and put her arm around the young woman. "It's obvious to me that Oliver has chosen well, and although it's been a bit of a shock, your marriage pleases me. I suspect Victoria is more than overjoyed to have you as a sister, too," she reassured her and pointed to the embroidery on her collar that featured a trailing vine of flowers. "Did you stitch this design?"

"It's one of my favorites. I never could afford to buy expensive fabric for our clothes, but a bit of dye and a simple decoration tends to draw attention away from the fact that the fabric is ordinary muslin."

"There's nothing simple about that decoration, and your skill with the needle far exceeds mine," Martha argued. "My mother, Oliver's grandmother, was quite talented in that regard, which is a story I should keep for another day," she suggested when Lucy sat up and rubbed her eyes.

"Thank you," Comfort whispered. She immediately rose to tend to Lucy but glanced back at Martha. "You've been cooped up in this room all afternoon. I'll stay here with the girls. Why don't you go have a visit with Oliver? Victoria left with him a good while ago to introduce him to Dr. McMillan. They should still be at his house." She grinned. "Before they left, Victoria was trying to make all sorts of plans, including where the four of us might stay during our visit, and by now, I suspect he'd be grateful if you could rescue him."

"I can try," Martha replied before heading downstairs. In all the excitement today, she had not even thought about where Oliver and his new family would stay while they were here. But while she literally had the key to resolving that problem, she had no doubt that one of the plans her daughter was trying to make involved her entire family—which now included three generations—a certain anxious doctor, a minister, and a date on the calendar that was definitely *not* in December.

23

"Martha! I was just coming to see you!"

Just moments after Martha stepped out from the covered bridge and onto sunny East Main Street on her way to rescue Oliver, Anne Sweet's words sent a shiver of dismay down the length of her spine. She paused and plastered a smile on her face before turning around, and she prayed that Anne's mission was inspired by gossip, which would be typical, rather than an illness at her house or Thomas's, which would call Martha to duty.

Huffing and puffing her way down the cindered street, Anne hurried her way to Martha and put a hand to her heart as she caught her breath. "Mercy! The heat today is rather awful."

Martha chuckled. "It's always hot in July."

"I was at the general store earlier when I noticed a stranger with two little ones in tow," Anne began. After describing how she had discovered that Oliver had married a widow some years his senior with two young girls, she finally paused to take a breath. "That's quite a lot of responsibility for a young man like Oliver to assume, which must trouble you some."

"I'm just thrilled that he's here and with such good news," Martha insisted, refusing to take the bait Anne offered. Her heart soared when she saw Thomas come out of Dr. McMillan's and rush toward them.

"Anne? I believe you're needed back home," he said, taking the last of several long strides to join them.

"And I thought I might have a few moments to myself," Anne grumbled. The moment she hurried off, Thomas took Martha's arm and whisked her over to his buggy, which he had left parked at Dr. McMillan's house.

"As much as I would enjoy spending time with you, Thomas, I'm afraid I can't. I'm on my way to meet with Oliver and Victoria. He just arrived today, and they're waiting for me at Dr. McMillan's," Martha said.

"They're not there, which means you have a few moments to spend with me. How's Samuel doing?"

"Fine, and don't change the subject. How do you know where they are?"

"Because Rosalind told me a few minutes ago when I returned to give Dr. McMillan some documents to look over. The doctor had just left with Victoria and Oliver. Although Rosalind was a little vague about where they all went, she said they had something they needed to do and expected to be gone for at least an hour or so. They'll meet up with you back at the confectionery, which means you have at least an hour to spend with me. Now, let me help you up to the seat. Please."

Thoroughly disappointed that her children had not included her in their plans, she let him.

"It seems a little odd that you'd take your buggy to Dr. McMillan's."

He joined her on the seat and clicked the reins. "Actually, I only stopped by Dr. McMillan's on my way to the confectionery. I was going to invite you to take a ride with me to check on my cabin at Candle Lake, but after I heard Oliver was back in Trinity for a visit, I knew you'd want to spend time with your family. Then when Rosalind told me they'd all gone off somewhere together, I decided to rescue you from my sister."

She gave him a cockeyed smile. "I see the heat hasn't taken a toll on your confidence."

"Not at all, especially since you're sitting here with me instead of standing around being pestered by my sister's babble," he teased and drove them down past the workers creating the new canal toward the far end of Dillon's Stream, which remained untouched.

"I don't want to go too far, and I don't want to lose sight of town, just in case they get back earlier than they thought," she cautioned.

"That's precisely why I'm stopping right about here," he assured her and parked the buggy in such a way that they had a good view of both the town and the canal, but still a bit of privacy. "First, I suppose congratulations are in order," he suggested and took her hand. "You're pleased with Oliver's news, I assume?"

"Very much so. They haven't said anything about their plans yet, but I suspect they won't be here for more than a week or so. I'd like to spend as much time with them as I can; I hope you'll understand."

"I don't have any intention of intruding on your time with them, but there are matters we need to discuss, and I couldn't let this opportunity pass by." He handed her a thick package wrapped in brown paper. "I'm sorry I couldn't give you better news from your friend when I wrote to you, but at least I was able to secure all of the remedies on your list."

She laid the package on her lap and wrapped both her hands around it. "Thank you. Is there an accounting inside so I know how much I owe you?"

"There is, but rather than argue the point that I don't need your coin, I'd rather spend what time I do have with you doing something I can control."

She cocked a brow. "Such as?"

"Such as explaining why I stayed far longer in Clarion than I'd hoped," he offered.

Distracted by the feel of his shoulder pressed against her own, she pressed her lips together in a vain effort to stop them from tingling. "I don't expect you to explain everything you do, Thomas."

"But there are some matters that I want to explain," he insisted. "As you know, I went there to convince Micah's father to end this needless estrangement between them. Unfortunately, the man's no better than a fool led astray by his own pride. In the end, I'm afraid I couldn't even convince him to come to Trinity for a visit to talk to Micah and meet his only grandchild."

"He sounds an awful lot like Graham Cade," Martha admitted, then summed up Oliver's news about his grandfather's death, although she did not feel comfortable discussing the terms of the man's will. "I'm very pleased that you tried to help Micah. I suspect he's very grateful that you tried to resolve his trouble with his father, even though it didn't turn out well."

Moved by Thomas's concern for his family, Martha was convinced that she was incredibly blessed to have this man's love. "You have a good, good heart."

"I hope you're as understanding when I tell you about the tavern."

She squinted her eyes and furrowed her brow. "What about it?"

"Dr. McMillan asked me the other night if I was interested

in joining him as an investor in the tavern, which is why I was in his office this morning when you came seeking advice about Samuel."

Martha cocked her head. "What did you tell him?"

"I've agreed to invest in the tavern in principle, but I didn't want to sign the papers until I talked with you."

"With me? Why?"

"Because I know how hard it was for you and your brother when he had to sell the property and move away because he couldn't afford to rebuild after the fire. I didn't want you to think I wanted an interest in the property as some sort of ploy to persuade you to marry me any sooner than you want to. With all the growth I expect to see in Trinity in the next few years, the tavern is a particularly good investment for anyone, once a few problems are addressed. Would it bother you overmuch if I did?"

"No, I don't think so," she ventured and gave him a smile. "Telling me Bella had escaped again, on the other hand, would bother me to no end."

He chuckled. "Bella's safe and sound in her stall, at least she was when I checked on her a few hours ago," he said and took her hand. "Because of a few problems at the tavern, we're considering asking your brother to come back with his wife to Trinity to work for us and operate the tavern again, but for a portion of the profits, too."

Her heart leaped with joy. "James might be moving back?"

He squeezed her hand, as if trying to contain her excitement. "It may happen soon or it may not happen at all, so I'd ask you to keep all that I've told you in strictest confidence. By all rights, I probably shouldn't have even told you."

"I will, of course," she promised, although she had every intention of praying that James and Lydia would be living back in Trinity soon.

When Thomas pressed a gentle kiss to her lips, Martha found she didn't want to pull away. But after a lingering moment, Thomas whispered, "As much as I'd like to continue this, I'll probably have to get you back home soon. But there's still one thing I need to tell you before I do."

With regret shining in his eyes, he told her that he would be leaving for New York the following week to sell off his remaining investments there and would be gone for perhaps as long as a month. "Will you spend some time with me if by some chance Oliver and his family return East before I have to leave?"

"I'll try, but I doubt very much that will happen. To be perfectly honest, with all that's happened in the past two days, I'm hardly able to think beyond the next few hours," she replied, then told him that Aunt Hilda had left earlier that morning and made him promise to keep that news to himself for now.

"She'll be sorely missed, but I suspect you'll miss her more than most, won't you," he noted before his expression turned very serious. He cleared his throat, as if preparing to discuss something very important to both of them.

And indeed he was.

"Just in case this is the last opportunity we have to be alone together before I leave for New York, I have something I need to say that you might not like to hear," he said and cleared his throat again. "Courting you hasn't always been easy, and frankly, it's getting harder."

She nearly choked. "I beg your pardon?"

"I said that it hasn't been particularly easy for me to court you."

"Really?" she snapped, annoyed that she had heard him correctly the first time. "Courting young Samantha last year must have been so much easier for you. Up until the moment she refused to join the others to help put out the fire at the tavern and dashed your plans to announce your betrothal that very night, she never challenged you at all," Martha charged, without adding that the beautiful young woman was half his age and more interested in the life of ease that he offered her than in Thomas himself.

"No, she didn't," he admitted. "She didn't have a single thought about anything beyond the latest fashion or care a whit about anyone other than herself, either, which meant that marrying her would have proven to be a grave mistake at best. Fortunately, she saved me from myself by ending our betrothal before it really began, leaving me free to marry a far wiser, far better woman than I deserve."

He edged a bit closer to her and joined his hand to hers. "You challenge me, Martha. You always did. You have a clear and honest view of the world and your place in it as a godly woman, and you're more worried about other people most of the time than you are for yourself, but you always have been. You're unlike any woman I've ever known, and I love you with all that I am or hope to be."

Overwhelmed, she blinked back tears. Every word he had just whispered, every beautiful, loving word, would be branded on her heart forever.

Before she could find her voice, he tightened his hold on her hand. "Forgive me if I've upset you by asking you repeatedly to marry me and go to New York with me, but it's only because I'm afraid if you don't, by the time I get back you'll change your mind about marrying me at all, like you did once before."

The pain in his eyes and in his features was so deep, she knew it had to have come from deep within his heart. Her rejection so many years ago still haunted him.

The pain of their broken courtship so long ago came back to haunt her, too, and she realized that beneath the aura of self-confidence and charm that usually surrounded the man who was sitting beside her, he was just as uncertain of himself as any other man might be. But he was also being open and honest with her, which made him all the more dear to her and determined to be honest with him, too.

"I made a mistake all those years ago, but not when I ended our courtship. We never should have courted in the first place, but I was young and you were so handsome and a man so far beyond my dreams that I couldn't imagine turning you away. Once I realized that we had very different views on how we would live our futures together, I knew we had to live that future apart. I'm sorry, I know I wasn't fair to you back then," she said, praying she would find the right words to convince him that all of that pain belonged in the past.

"But this time," she continued, "it's different for both of us. You've given me the time I needed to carefully consider marriage. And while all my concerns may have felt unfair, I didn't accept your proposal until we'd resolved them. Can you put the past aside and trust me now that I'll keep my word and marry you as soon as I find my replacement?"

She waited for him to respond, one thudding heartbeat after another. She clung to the fact that he was still holding her hand.

Finally, he looked directly in her eyes. "I've had time to think about my proposal and your concerns, too. And you're right in one regard. You still aren't being fair to me by expecting me to wait, possibly for years, while you find a midwife to replace you before I can claim you as my wife and helpmate. I promised you the other day that if you'd marry me now, while you were still following your calling, that I'd be patient and understanding when you were summoned away. I renew that promise now. I'll even give you more time to consider it." He paused and grew very serious.

"I want you to marry me when I return from New York, whether or not you've found a woman to replace you. Forgive me, but I'm afraid I can only give you until then to make up your mind and no longer. Marry me then, or . . . or I'll ask you to set me free. This is my final proposal to you, and I'd like you to either accept it or send me away right now."

Surprised by the passion that simmered in his gray eyes, she was shocked by his demand, which was nothing short of an ultimatum. She swallowed hard and looked away. In all fairness, she could not expect him to wait for her indefinitely. Would any man? *Should* any man?

The answer that slipped from the very depths of her soul made her heart quiver and left her with a dilemma unlike any she had ever confronted before: Marry Thomas and trust in the promise he made to be patient every time she was summoned away? Or set him free, afraid he would not be able to keep that promise, and lose him?

Her heart pounded, and she drew a long breath. "I accept your new proposal, Thomas." She swallowed hard. "I'll either marry you the very day you return, or I'll set you free, as you've asked, to find and marry a woman who deserves you so much more than I do."

His expression softened, and he accepted her promise by pressing both of her hands between his. They sat together in silence, side by side. No more words or promises were necessary.

24

Martha needed time by herself to fully absorb all the ramifications of Thomas's new proposal before her children returned.

Anxious to avoid customers in the confectionery, she decided against using the front door and walked to the alley, but the moment she turned the corner of the building, she spied Bella tethered next to the back door licking off the remains of several baking pans and felt an all-too-familiar dread pool in the pit of her stomach.

How or why that troublesome horse was here mattered a whole lot less than the simple fact that Thomas was not here to get her back into a stall at his house. He had already left to check on his cabin at Candle Lake.

Which meant Martha had no choice but to do it herself.

She blinked back tears of frustration. "At least she looks tethered well," she grumbled and proceeded very, very slowly down the alley so she would not spook the horse. She also kept her distance from the horse as she tugged all the baking pans away. She cautiously set them inside the back door, never fully turning her back on the mare, and noticed the crude note tied to the horse's mane.

Whispering gentle words, she reached out to work the note free. She got a head-butt on her arm in the process and stepped well beyond Bella's reach to read the scribbled message:

> *I found your horse behind the new bank.*
> *Ask Mr. Dillon to put the reward on my account at the store.*
>
> *Luke Morgan*

She crumpled the note and glared at the horse. "For goodness' sake, Bella, why can't you run away to someplace where you can find a decent home and folks won't keep bringing you back here for a reward that isn't supposed to be a reward anymore? As soon as my son gets back, I'm going to ask him to walk around town until he finds someone willing to take you for free so I can be well rid of you."

When Bella snorted and pawed the ground with her front hoof, Martha lost her temper. "Fine. Have it your way. That's exactly what I'm going to do. I'm going to give you away and . . . and I'm going to put up posters with your new owner's name!"

"I'll take her, Widow Cade!"

Still fuming and thoroughly embarrassed that anyone witnessed her diatribe, Martha turned about to find Will standing in the middle of the alley wearing a wide grin. "What on earth would you do with a horse, considering you think all horses are dumb and useless?"

He shrugged, then approached and handed her his school report. "She likes me, so I guess she's not that dumb." He walked around her to stand alongside Bella and stroke the mare's neck. "I wanted to keep her the first time I found her, but Mr. Samuel said I couldn't 'cause she belonged to someone else. He'll let me keep her now if she belongs to me. I know he will."

Martha glanced at his school report, smiled at his achievements in the classroom the past school year, and returned it to him before she put her hands on her hips. "I doubt you're able to ride a horse or know anything about taking care of one."

Will arched his back and stiffened his shoulders. "Can't be too hard to learn. You did."

She suppressed a grin. "And just where do you think you're going to keep her?"

"Right in that pasture where I found her a couple of weeks back. Me and Mr. Fancy can build a fence for now and a lean-to near the cabin for when it gets cold. We got lotsa time for that now 'cause school's not in session," he insisted, and his eyes began to sparkle.

Truly tempted to give the boy what he wanted, she had to be certain he could handle the responsibility of owning the animal. "Before I give you Bella outright, you need to prove you're up to the task of caring for her and that she won't keep running off, so I'm going to hire you to take care of her for the rest of the summer. I'll tell Mr. Sweet at the general store that you'll be stopping by from time to time to get feed for the horse. And you'll have to give her some sweets now and then so she doesn't keep running back here."

He narrowed his gaze. "How much you payin' me?"

When she cocked a brow, he shrugged. "If you're hirin' me to take care of your horse, you must be willin' to pay me, but if she was my horse, you wouldn't hafta pay nothin'."

"I'll discuss your wages with Samuel, after you get his permission, of course," she insisted, rather doubtful that Samuel would consider this idea for more than half a minute before rejecting it. "In the meantime—"

"I'll take her with me," the boy countered. "Don't worry about Mr. Samuel and Mr. Fancy. Nobody can resist her once they get to know her. 'Cept for you," he added with a grin.

"Take her," Martha replied, "but if Samuel upends this plan of ours, just walk her back to the stables at Mr. Dillon's, and I'll find someone else who wants her."

"Mr. Samuel won't do that," Will insisted. He untied the horse, turned her about, and walked her past Martha. Bella was just as docile as you please.

Still stymied by not knowing the name of the anonymous giver of this "reward" in the first place, she went back inside. With all that was happening in her life right now, this was one problem she could do without, and now it looked like she could—at least until Samuel nixed it.

Trouble, however, was waiting for her back in the kitchen. Cassie was still sitting at the table, as pale as a sugarloaf, and she had a bloody towel wrapped around one of her hands. A paring knife and the pile of carrots she must have been peeling lay on the floor, splattered with blood.

Blinking back tears, Cassie offered her a tremulous smile. "Poor Miss Fern. She almost swooned when she saw all this blood."

"What about you?" Martha asked, but before she could reach the girl, Jane flew down the steps and hurried straight to her daughter.

"I've got what I need now," Jane stated. Noting Martha standing there, she nodded toward the water pump. "I could use some fresh water and a clean cloth, as well as some bandages to wrap Cassie's hand. Miss Fern is just changing out of her blood-stained gown, but I'd rather not wait for her to help me."

Struck by the oddity of following orders instead of giving

them, Martha secured everything Jane had asked for, placed them onto the table, and removed the ruined carrots to give her more room to work.

Jane had already removed the bloody towel and quickly used a fresh towel dampened with water to clean her daughter's hand. When she did, Martha saw that the girl had sliced the flesh from the tips of her four fingers, which were thankfully no longer pulsing out huge amounts of blood. While the injury itself was not serious enough to be life-threatening, it did pose the possibility of easily becoming infected.

Jane poured a good amount of honey onto the tip of each finger and wrapped each with bandages to keep the healing honey in place. "I hope you don't mind, but since you weren't here, I helped myself to some of the lavender you had in your room to make her some tea to help ease the pain."

"Not at all. I'll heat some water," Martha responded, quite impressed not only by how calmly and efficiently Jane was handling the emergency, but also, again, by her apparent knowledge of healing remedies, particularly the honey. Curious to know how Jane had acquired such knowledge and skill, she asked her point-blank.

"Credit should go to my mother, I suppose," Jane said. The crisp tone of her voice left no doubt that she had no interest in saying anything more, leaving a silence in the air as uneasy as it had been when Martha asked her to consider being her replacement. Martha did not know if Jane's reluctance to discuss the matter further was due to some sort of strained relationship with her mother or not, but she was wise enough to let the matter drop for now.

Fortunately, the tea was ready, and Martha turned her attention to Cassie. Martha placed the cup onto the table in front of her and asked, "Would you like some honey in your tea?"

"Just cream, please."

Although she had never heard of anyone putting cream into lavender tea, Martha smiled and added the cream. "Why don't you let your mama take you upstairs so you can drink your tea and rest awhile? Don't worry about all this, Jane," she added. "I'll clean up here and finish up the carrots, but I'd be grateful if you could check on Miss Fern while you're upstairs."

"I'm right here," Fern announced, stepping aside from her place at the bottom of the steps to let Jane escort her daughter upstairs.

"It's all my fault," she said as she approached Martha. "I should never have given that girl such a sharp knife. She's just so anxious to help that sometimes I forget to keep an extra eye on her. Mr. Fancy seems to be doing a lot better job at that than I do. He watches out for that girl like she was his own blood and more precious than all those gaudy jewels he's got poked in his ears."

Martha quickly shared with Fern what Samuel had told her about Fancy's late daughter.

"Even so," Fern said, "I just can't figure out how he manages to be here every time she leaves on an errand—though we're all not grateful."

When the vision of a certain spyglass came to mind, Martha chuckled. "Old seamen tend to be a bit quirky, at least the ones I've met so far. And you can't watch her every minute any more than you can keep her from trying to be helpful or learning to do as much as she can. It's not your fault she cut her fingers. It was an accident." Martha cleaned up the table and donned a clean apron before she sat down. "I've got nothing else to do while I'm waiting for my children to return, so I might as well help you finish up these carrots."

"If you peel the rest, I'll start grating these," Fern suggested. "Did you happen to see that that awful horse was tied up by the back door again?"

"I did indeed," she replied and quickly explained the arrangement she had made with Will.

"Do you think Samuel will let the boy keep the horse?"

Martha chuckled. "I doubt it, but once I explain how much longer that boy will be content to live on land if that horse is around instead of wanting to run off to sea again, I'm hoping I can convince him it's a good idea, at least for the summer."

Their conversation was interrupted when a group of people poured into the kitchen from the front of the confectionery. Oliver, Victoria, and Dr. McMillan were the first to enter the room, but Comfort and the girls were not with them. When Reverend Welsh filed in last, Martha couldn't keep a small gasp of surprise from escaping. She hadn't known he'd returned. And she couldn't help but wonder if somehow her daughter and her future husband, aided by Oliver, had convinced the minister to marry them while Oliver was here visiting—and had brought him here to convince Martha to agree to the idea.

To be fair, Martha had suggested a similar idea, although at the time, she thought it would be at least Christmas before Oliver would come to visit.

"If ever I needed Your guidance and wisdom, it's now, Lord," she whispered, silently praying that He would help her to convince everyone else, even Reverend Welsh, that it was far too soon for Victoria and Dr. McMillan to exchange the vows that would make them husband and wife.

Far too soon.

For Victoria?

Or for herself?

25

Fern rose and offered the minister a huge smile. "Welcome back, Reverend Welsh. We've all missed you, haven't we, Martha?"

"Very much," she managed, then noticed the wrapped confections he was holding in each of his hands. Perhaps she had misjudged the purpose for his visit to the confectionery. "I hope Mrs. Welsh is feeling better now."

"She is, indeed. Sarah and I missed everyone here in Trinity while we were gone." He chuckled. "But I have to confess that we missed these sweet desserts, as well."

Victoria approached her mother wearing a nervous smile. "We'd just gotten back from taking Comfort and the girls with us to show them the farm where we grew up when we saw Reverend Welsh, so we . . . well, we invited him to join us all . . ."

"At Dr. McMillan's home," Oliver added quickly. "Comfort's already taken the girls there, along with a good assortment of treats from the confectionery, and she's asking Mrs. Andrews to make some lemonade for us. Please come."

"Go on, Martha. I can finish up here," Fern insisted. "We'll make our supper a late one."

Apparently, Martha had been so engaged talking with Thomas that she had not even seen that her children had come back. Sabotaged by everyone else present, Martha had no choice but to agree to join them for some refreshment. She paused just long enough to wipe her hands before retrieving her bonnet and tying it into place. "I'm glad we have the opportunity to be together since I've got something very important to discuss with you all, including Reverend Welsh," she ventured, putting them all on notice that she was not about to relinquish her role as the matriarch of this family. She wasn't certain whether or not they understood her subtle message that she knew what they were about to propose, but if they did, they would have a good chance to think about that while walking back to Dr. McMillan's house.

And so would she.

Reverend Welsh's presence helped to mitigate the fact that the sitting room at Dr. McMillan's house was not a neutral domain. While the girls were downstairs with Rosalind, Oliver and Comfort sat together on the settee. Victoria and Dr. McMillan sat side by side in a pair of wooden chairs brought into the room and placed next to the newlyweds. Martha and Reverend Welsh, appropriately, sat facing the two young couples in very comfortable upholstered chairs.

Once the refreshments and fanciful conversation were well spent, Martha was ready to initiate a conversation that would address more pressing needs than Victoria's marriage.

"I wonder if any of you have given thought to where Oliver and his family are going to be staying while they're here. Obviously, there isn't room enough at the confectionery for everyone."

Dr. McMillan smiled. "Since I have all sorts of empty rooms here, I've offered them a place here with me."

"I have another idea that's much more suitable for a family of four, but you all need to keep what I'm about to tell you in strictest confidence since not all of the details are quite worked out yet," Martha stated.

Reverend Welsh raised a brow. "Are you certain that you want me here?"

"Absolutely. I might need you as my ally. Is there anyone else who has any reservations?"

Everyone, including Oliver, shook their heads, but her son's expression was dubious at best.

"What's wrong?" she asked him.

He shrugged. "Nothing more than a healthy dose of curiosity. It's difficult to imagine that anywhere I choose to stay with my family during our visit would require such secrecy."

Martha smiled and quickly explained that Aunt Hilda and her husband had left Trinity for good, but as far as anyone else in town was concerned, they were simply on an extended trip, on the odd chance that one or both of them might one day return. She also added the thought that the cottage would provide more room and some privacy for a family of four.

Oliver furrowed his brow. "If she doesn't have any plans to return, why did she even keep the cottage?"

Martha drew a deep breath. "She didn't. She gave it to me."

Oliver cocked a brow, but Victoria gasped. "She gave you the cottage? You *own* it?"

"Not quite yet," Martha admitted. "I won't actually own the cottage until I sign a document Aunt Hilda left for me and it's recorded properly. There's no rush to do that, though."

"That was a generous and kind thing for her to do," Reverend Welsh added.

Comfort, however, looked thoroughly confused, and Martha eased her concerns by suggesting that Oliver could explain her relationship with Aunt Hilda later.

"In the meantime," Oliver suggested, "I can take a look at that document for you."

Before Martha could reply, Victoria interrupted. "Does that mean we'll be moving out of the confectionery soon?"

"No. Not that I wouldn't love for us to have a home of our own again, but for now, there are a number of reasons why we won't be moving into the cottage. For one, since I'm often called away for days or weeks at a time, it wouldn't be proper for you to live there on your own when I'm gone," she cautioned. She paused to organize her own thoughts before she admitted that she had not decided what to do about the cottage since her own plans for the future were a bit uncertain.

Oliver grinned. "I think it's a grand idea for us to stay in the cottage. It's just a short walk to town, and we wouldn't have to worry about overstaying our welcome with anyone. What do you think, Comfort?"

"I think I'd like to see the cottage first. The girls are very young, and I'd hate to spend all of our time there worrying about whether or not they'll break something valuable while they're playing or—"

"Once you see the cottage for yourself, you'll realize that's not something you'll have to worry about," Martha insisted. In order to get back in time for supper and allow Oliver to get his family all settled in before dark, she asked Oliver to bring his family to the confectionery with her straightaway to get the key to the cottage and invited Victoria and Dr. McMillan to go with them.

Everyone agreed to leave right away, except for Oliver. "Before we go, I have a question or two to ask you, Mother, and whether or not you decide to be stubborn about answering them honestly might keep us here until long after dark."

She huffed at him before she pursed her lips. Having her lawyer son speak to her about being stubborn did not sit well, but rather than provoke an argument, she nodded for him to continue.

He grinned at her. "Let's assume that you're already the legal owner of the cottage. Would I be wrong to assume that your primary concern about moving into the cottage is first and foremost financial?"

Martha was embarrassed to discuss her financial situation with her children or with Reverend Welsh, for that matter. Her cheeks started to burn, but she could not lie to Oliver, any more than she could simply refuse to answer his question.

"Since your father died, I haven't had much choice," she began. Speaking frankly but carefully, she explained that financial considerations would be first and foremost in any decision she made about where she might live or what she might do. "You've been gone a long time, Oliver, but the rewards I receive for the work that I do haven't changed. Frankly, some of the women and children I've treated now seek out Dr. McMillan instead of me." She glanced at the doctor and smiled. "It's the way it is, and with Trinity growing, I know there's a need for an extra pair of hands more often than not."

Oliver looked at his sister for a moment before he leaned forward, took a document out of his pocket, and handed it to Martha. "Consider your problem solved. Victoria and I want you to have this."

When Martha's heart started to pound in her chest, she pressed the document to her lap. "What are you talking about?"

"We're talking about loving you and wanting the best for you," Victoria offered. "We asked Reverend Welsh to be here with us, just in case you get all stubborn and need a bit of convincing to accept our gift."

"Why is it that both of my children find it quite appropriate to call me stubborn?" Martha snapped.

"Because you are, Martha," Reverend Welsh said. "Apparently, you've got two fine children who've turned out to be just like their mother, at least in that regard."

"I wish you'd all stop worrying about my faults and just tell me what you've done," Martha said and waved the document in the air without looking at it.

Oliver smiled. "We did what was right."

"And what was fair," Victoria added. "Grandfather Cade had every right to design his will any way he chose, but Oliver and I have rights, too. We want to take care of you properly, and since Grandfather Cade chose not to do that, we did. Oliver and I have talked this over a great deal, and we discussed it with Comfort and Benjamin, too. And we all agreed that this is what we wanted to do."

"That document you're scrunching up in your hand is rather important," Oliver cautioned.

Martha immediately smoothed the paper against her lap, but her heart was still racing. Feeling guilty for assuming that her children had planned this little meeting to get Martha to agree to let Victoria marry within a matter of days or weeks, she had a hard time absorbing their true intentions. "What . . . what does it say?"

Oliver quickly explained that she now had a rather substantial sum of money deposited in her name at the First Bank of Trinity, enough to guarantee that she would be well able to afford most anything she needed or wanted.

Her eyes widened. The fact that she did not have to depend on her rewards or the charity of others to provide a home for

219

her was just as foreign as the idea that for the first time in her life, she was a woman of means, free to spend every day of her life exactly as she pleased.

Victoria smiled at her. "What we're really giving you, Mother, is an opportunity to freely choose how to spend the rest of your life and know that your financial situation won't dictate what that choice has to be."

Martha shook her head, almost too overwhelmed by her children's gift to think very clearly. "B-but what about you? You can't just give away your inheritances. You have long lives ahead of you. You'll need—"

"We won't need any more than what we have left," Oliver argued. "Trust me, Mother. We still have quite enough. Grandfather Cade was a lot wealthier than any of us imagined."

Martha turned in her seat to face the minister and blinked back tears. "What should I do?"

Reverend Welsh took her hand. "As I see it, you can do one of two things. You can be stubborn and reject your children's gift. Or you can accept their generosity and enjoy the freedom that wealth brings to those who have it, as well as the responsibilities. Naturally, I suggest you do the latter."

Sniffling, Martha searched in her pocket, found her handkerchief, and wiped away her tears. Earning enough funds to survive was all she had worried about as a widow, and the prospect of having more funds than she might ever need was almost more than she could comprehend. "Did you have to call me stubborn, too?"

He chuckled. "It's a sin to lie, Martha, and over the years I've discovered that being stubborn can even be a blessing at times. But it's a greater sin not to recognize a blessing when you receive it, and that's what this is. Your children's gift is a blessing. Can you accept that?"

Martha let out a long, long breath. She bowed her head for a moment and with every beat of her heart, she sent gratitude to heaven for a God who never abandoned her, for children who were very special indeed, and for a future where she could make all her choices based on what God led her to do—for herself and for others.

When she lifted her head, she looked at Oliver and Victoria first. They were both encouraging her to accept their gift by nodding their heads. She found Comfort smiling her approval, and even Dr. McMillan was nodding in agreement. Fortunately, the choice she had to make now was not a dilemma at all, and she pressed the document to her heart. "Rather than disappoint you, I accept your gift. Thank you."

Oliver grinned, Victoria beamed, and Comfort wore a sheepish smile. "Can we go to see the cottage now?" she asked.

"Not before we all agree to keep Mother's gift confidential. I've only been back a day, but I've already noticed that the gossipmongers are just as fierce as they were the last time I came for a visit," Oliver cautioned.

When no one objected to his comment, Martha started to rise, but Victoria urged her to remain in her seat. "Before we go, there's one more thing we should talk about first." Victoria took Dr. McMillan's hand. "We don't want to wait until Christmas. We want to get married now, while Oliver's here," she blurted and locked her gaze with her mother's. "It's only a matter of moving up our marriage a few months. Oliver's promised to try to make arrangements to stay for another few weeks, and now that they have the cottage to stay in, that shouldn't be a problem and . . . and Reverend Welsh said it would be all right if he only read the banns once or twice instead of three times and . . . and . . . please? Won't you let us get married now, Mother?"

The yearning to marry the man she loved resonated in Victoria's voice. It was just as deep as the longing in Martha's heart to marry Thomas, and she sighed. Resigned to the fact that there was really no good reason to deny Victoria's request, other than selfish ones, Martha also felt vindicated that she had not been entirely wrong about one of the purposes for this meeting. After suggesting that she would discuss the matter with the betrothed couple on their way to the cottage and then sending Oliver and his family to the confectionery to fetch the key, she got to her feet.

"Excellent proposal," Reverend Welsh announced, then gave Martha a hug and whispered in her ear, "I believe you mentioned to me once that when you and John Cade wanted to marry, Trinity wasn't even town enough to support a full-time minister. As I recall, you also mentioned that you only had to wait a matter of a few weeks for the minister who rode this circuit to arrive and marry you, rather than the many months you're asking this young couple to wait. I might be tempted to share that tale with them if you decide against giving them your blessing."

Horrified, she pulled back and stared at him, only now remembering the very same thing. "You wouldn't!"

"That's entirely up to you, but I think you might want to tell them yourself. Children rather like the idea that their parents are just as human as they are," he whispered and left her standing there, surrounded by her ever-growing family and the reality that in a matter of weeks, her responsibility to provide for both of her children would end and an entirely new phase of her life would begin.

The gift they had given her today, however, meant she actually had some very, very hard choices to make about her own future—choices that would impact her life as well as Thomas's.

How she wished that she could ask Aunt Hilda for her advice, but she was not here any longer. In fact, the only one she could turn to who could guide her and who could truly lead her to the life she was meant to enjoy in the years ahead was her Creator and her God.

Which meant she needed lots of time to pray in order to silence her own mind so she could listen to the answers God was sure to whisper to her heart.

26

Even the weather seemed to know that today was a special day when the third Sunday in July dawned bright and clear and comfortably warm.

Only three short days after Thomas left for New York, Victoria would become Mrs. Benjamin McMillan. The wedding would take place in just a few hours.

Today should be a day of celebration and joy for Martha, not a day spoiled by disappointment that her brother and his wife could not be here or bittersweet memories of the day she had married John Cade. While she did regret that Thomas was not here to share this momentous day with her, she had tucked away the dilemma of his final ultimatum deep within her heart, unwilling to let anything distract her from enjoying the last few days she had Victoria at home with her.

When she pinned the brooch from Dr. McMillan to the collar of her gown, she could scarcely believe that over the past eight days, she had managed to safely deliver two precious babes, regretfully eliminated one more woman from the dwindling list of potential candidates to replace her as midwife, tended to an entire family suffering from ringworm, and visited with Oliver and his family, especially her two darling granddaughters. And she had still managed to help Victoria pack for her wedding trip and help make arrangements for the celebration they had planned for later that morning with the entire congregation.

The moment she slipped out of her room, the tantalizing aromas filtering up from the confectionery testified to the fact that the entire household had been just as busy preparing for this day as she had been. She hurried to Victoria's room, where she found her daughter looking out the window.

"It's a perfect day! It's warm and sunny and there's not a cloud in the sky!" Victoria exclaimed as she turned around. "We can have our celebration outside after the ceremony just like we hoped."

Martha caught her breath. She had always thought Victoria was an attractive young woman. Wearing the lavender gown she reserved for Sunday services and special occasions, her daughter was a pure vision of loveliness. The excitement of the day had painted her cheeks just rosy enough, and her eyes shimmered with joy that must have flowed straight up from her heart.

"You look beautiful," Martha said. "The needlework Comfort added to the collar of your gown makes a lovely backdrop for your brooch."

Victoria swirled about the room, swishing her skirts and grinning. "I'm so happy. I just wish I had wings so I might fly all the way to the meetinghouse. I can't wait to marry Benjamin."

Martha chuckled. "Even if you could fly there straightaway, you'd still have to sit through the services before Reverend Welsh performs the ceremony."

"While everyone else is waiting to sample some of the treats that Miss Fern and Miss Ivy have spent the past week making for today," Victoria teased. She crossed the room and wrapped Martha in a long embrace. "Thank you for not making us wait any longer."

"You should thank Reverend Welsh, too. If he hadn't given you permission to marry on such short notice, you would have been forced to wait, regardless of whether or not I approved."

"We already did," Victoria replied and her eyes twinkled even brighter. "Don't you think it's exciting that we're going to follow Oliver and his family this afternoon to go to Boston for our wedding trip?"

Martha hugged her daughter back, inhaling the scent of her to store away in her scrapbook of memories. "I'd be a whole lot happier if I could be certain that you and your new husband won't be so taken with Boston while you're visiting some of his relatives there, too, that you'll change your mind about returning to Trinity. I don't think I could bear it if both of my children lived so far away from me."

Victoria tried to step back, but the betrothal brooch she had pinned to her gown caught on Martha's, and she froze. "It looks like we're pinned together at the moment, which may be a sign that you needn't worry. I've had my fill of city living, although I'd love to go back to New York someday to visit Mr. and Mrs. Morgan and to see how Nancy is faring. But don't worry. As far as I'm concerned, our home will always be right here in Trinity, and Benjamin feels the same way," she insisted and frowned for a moment before she found her smile again. "Maybe we could all go to New York early next spring, right before our articles appear in that magazine. We could see Nancy and the Morgans and then go to Boston to visit Oliver!" she exclaimed and lowered her voice to a whisper. "Maybe by then you'll be married to Mr. Dillon, unless you decide to just enjoy the gift we gave you instead. Better still, you could do both," she teased.

"We'll . . . we'll see," Martha replied. She could not stop the warmth creeping up her neck that threatened to paint a blush to her cheeks. "There. That should do it." She stepped back after freeing their brooches and examined the needlework on Victoria's collar. "No damage done. Now, is there anything else you need to do up here, or can we start downstairs? There's only an hour or so left before we have to leave for the meetinghouse."

Victoria hooked her arm with Martha's. "That's just about enough time for you to get your fill of sweets," she teased and ushered them out of the room and into a future that was waiting for them both.

Immediately following the Sunday service, Reverend Welsh invited Victoria and Dr. McMillan to join him at the front of the packed meetinghouse.

Even though Oliver and his family were sitting with her in her customary bench and the meetinghouse was completely filled, Martha felt like she was all alone inside of a large, translucent bubble, unaware of everyone else there. As Victoria and Dr. McMillan pledged their lives and troth to one another and became husband and wife, she thanked God for the privilege of being here to witness this moment and prayed that God would forever be the center of this young couple's lives.

Following the very brief ceremony, Martha followed the newly married couple out of the meetinghouse, where they were joined by the rest of the congregation in the side yard. A soft breeze chased away the heat of midday, and friends had set up a long row of planked tables that were decorated with vases of wild flowers and covered with plates of sweet treats from the confectionery, along with bowls of punch.

While the newlyweds were off receiving congratulations and

Oliver was introducing his new family all around, Martha received her own well-wishes from longtime friends, including Anne Sweet, who did not miss the opportunity to question Martha discretely about her own future plans—questions Martha left unanswered.

After an hour or so, with the excitement of the day still holding exhaustion at bay, she welcomed an opportunity to stand alone and simply watch everyone else.

Bless their hearts, Fern and Ivy were watching over the treats on the tables, refilling the serving plates as they emptied, and chatting with Rosalind Andrews, who had insisted on helping today. Jane and Cassie were assisting, too, busy at work keeping the punch bowls filled.

When Martha spied something sparkling at the edge of the woods at the rear of the property, she saw the outline of three familiar figures standing within a copse of trees and realized that the sun must have caught on one of Fancy's many earrings.

In truth, she was not surprised that Fancy was nearby, keeping a watchful eye on Cassie, but she was surprised to find Samuel so close to so many people. She waved to catch their attention when they turned to leave and held up one of her fingers to urge them to stay there. After quickly filling several plates with goodies, she carried them over to the odd threesome.

As she handed the plates to Will and Fancy, she saw the sugar crumbs stuck at the corners of the boy's lips and grinned. Will had obviously ventured out of the woods to snatch a few treats, but he was not about to turn down more. "I've been looking and looking for all of you," she scolded gently as she put a plate of desserts into Samuel's hand. "I'm pleased to see that the bruises on your face are fading, and I'm glad you're still wearing that sling," she offered, but she did not comment about the walking stick leaning against a nearby tree.

Samuel shrugged. "Can't say I don't welcome the sweets," he said, ignoring her comments about his health before he shifted the plate to the hand sticking out from the sling so he could pick up a cookie. "You know I don't take to bein' around so many people, especially all in one place, but I waited for young William to let me know that you saw I was here before we left," he said before he popped the cookie into his mouth.

"I wanted to thank you again for letting Will take care of Bella for me, too. It's a relief not to have to worry about that horse," she admitted, still surprised that Samuel had needed no convincing at all.

He snorted. "Responsibility is good for William, but I'm guessin' it must be a bit humblin' for you to admit you finally met somethin' you couldn't control."

She frowned and decided not to offer a retort and turned to address Fancy. "I trust you're making good use of Will's spyglass."

"Yes, ma'am, as a matter of fact, I am," he said between bites of strudel. "No harm's gonna come to young Cassie. Not as long as I'm around."

"Even so, I appreciate that you're looking out for her, and so is everyone else at the confectionery," she offered before turning her attention to Will. "As for you, young man, I was wondering how you and Bella were getting along. Mr. Sweet down at the general store tells me you've been in to get the feed you need for her."

He shrugged his shoulders and shoved two molasses cookies into his mouth. "She ain't bad, for a horse. Me and Fancy started on a lean-to already. She'll be needin' it come winter," he replied, although he had so much in his mouth that his words were garbled.

"She will at that, assumin' I decide you can keep her," Samuel argued. "You still got half a summer left to prove yourself. I don't have eyes that work anymore, but Fancy does, and I got a good pair of ears. You might do well to remember that."

"Yes, sir," Will grumbled.

Martha kept a chuckle from escaping her lips. She didn't need to worry about how well Will was taking care of the horse. She trusted Samuel to handle that. And she trusted Fancy in that regard, too.

"There you are, Martha! Yoo-hoo! Yoo-hoo! Martha!"

When Martha turned around, she saw Fern waddling in their direction and waving her handkerchief in the air. "I'd better go."

Obviously anxious to leave, Samuel held out his half-filled plate, but she urged him to keep it. "Take the plates with you. I'll stop by the cabin in a few days to get them," she insisted and hurried off to meet Fern to see what she wanted.

By the time they met, Fern was practically gasping for breath. "If you don't hurry, you're going to miss them. They're all ready to leave, but they can't go before they say good-bye to you. Come with me. I'll take you straight to them."

Martha's heart skipped a beat, then settled into a series of dull thuds. She had looked forward to many things on this day, but saying good-bye to her children and grandchildren was not one of them. Even though she knew right where to go, she followed Fern back to the front of the meetinghouse where Oliver and Dr. McMillan had positioned their carriages.

The crowd that had gathered around them parted to let her through, and she approached Oliver and his family first. After hugs all around and promises to visit again soon, she waited for her son to get his new family settled before she walked over to the carriage where Victoria and Dr. McMillan were standing, waiting for her.

Beaming with pride, Dr. McMillan held Victoria's arm, but

230

he left her side to embrace Martha. "Don't forget to remind folks that if they really need a doctor that they should send for Doc Williams in Sunrise, although I'm rather certain you can handle most any emergency. And if you can find it in your heart not to be stubborn about it, you might want to reconsider using the office I'd set aside for you months ago while I'm gone. And don't worry. I won't keep your girl away forever. We'll be back in a month or so," he promised.

"I'm going to hold you to your word," Martha teased and hugged him back.

When he stepped aside, Victoria moved right into her mother's arms and held on tight. "Benjamin will take good care of me, and Oliver will be right there in case he doesn't. And I'll write. I promise," she said before she lowered her voice to a whisper. "And I'll be thinking about the secret we share, too."

Martha was surprised at how quickly her tears welled and overflowed, and her throat constricted as she embraced her daughter, who had no idea of how Thomas's proposal had changed. "I know, dear girl. I know," she managed.

"Safe travels. All of you," Martha cried when both carriages finally pulled away. While the guests showered Dr. McMillan and Victoria with wild flowers, Martha gave up trying to stem another flow of tears and simply dabbed them away.

She watched with blurred vision as the carriages headed out of town. Today was a life-altering day for her daughter, who had set aside her place as a child and a daughter to assume the adult role of a wife, but it was also a day that marked a significant change in Martha's life. Now that both of her children were grown and married, her primary role as a mother was basically finished.

When Fern and Ivy took a place on either side of her, she let out a long breath. She did not argue when they urged her to go back to the confectionery with them, leaving Rosalind behind to take charge of recruiting others to help clear away the remnants of the celebration in the yard.

As the two sisters bantered back and forth about how lovely the day had been, Martha barely heard them because she was too caught up in the thought that now that the rest of her family was gone, she would finally have time to make one of the most important decisions of her life.

"Finally, home is within view," Fern announced.

With no traffic on West Main Street, they crossed right away, quickly rounded the far end of the confectionery, and turned down the alley. As they passed the side window, Ivy took Martha's arm. "We haven't seen you for more than a few moments after the ceremony, and I'd surely love for the three of us to be able to sit a spell and chat."

"You mean gossip, which will have to wait if you're absolutely determined to lower yourself to the same level as Anne Sweet," Fern noted with a huff and glared at her sister. "Honestly, Ivy, can't you see that Martha is thoroughly exhausted? She needs a good nap, not a gossip session."

"I'd love to have your company and have a cup of tea with both of you," Martha offered, "but as far as gossiping . . ." Embarrassed, she paused to stifle a yawn. Whether she was tired from lack of sleep or overwork or simply a case of experiencing too many emotions today, the thought of a nap was tempting indeed, but she favored some time with her friends to savor the excitement of the day a bit more.

"Fern's right," Ivy suggested when they reached the back door. "I'll fix a cup of tea for you and bring it up to your room. We'll have plenty of time to chat together later. It'll be just like old times," she said as she opened the door and stepped back to let Martha and Fern enter before her.

"Old times," Martha repeated. She did not want to argue with Ivy, yet she was quite certain the days ahead would be anything but. With Dr. McMillan gone, she could look forward to long days of work that would often extend into all hours of the night, and on less busy days she would be consumed by her search for her replacement and the question of how she would make use of the gifts she had received from Aunt Hilda and her children. When she would finally crawl into her bed at night, however, she had little expectation she would get any solid sleep.

Not until she resolved her dilemma and decided exactly what she would tell Thomas when he returned. And in the end, it all boiled down to which two simple words she would say. "I do" or "I won't."

Those words were not really so simple to say at all, were they?

27

The cottage had needed a good scrubbing after a family with two young children had called it home. It had taken Martha nearly a week to put a shine on the cottage again, but she had finally finished today.

She took one last look around the sitting room before she secured the front door. As she retraced her steps and returned to the kitchen, she tucked the new memories she had created here with her own family, most especially her precious grand-daughters, right next to her lifelong memories of Aunt Hilda.

Martha paused for a moment to arch her back and eased away an annoying kink. She wished she could chase away the pain and worry in her heart as easily.

With Thomas's return drawing ever nearer, she was no closer to knowing what she was going to tell him than she had been before he left. In addition to working here at the cottage and helping occasionally with household tasks at the confectionery, she had been called out to duty for one ailment or another nearly every day for one of her patients or Dr. McMillan's. She'd simply not had enough time to resolve all the uncertainties in her life.

More determined than ever to end her days as a midwife, however, she had used the one totally free day she'd had yesterday to borrow a mare from Thomas's stable. After riding out of town to see the final two women on her list of likely replacements, she returned to Trinity in failure—not that she could argue with either of the two women. Daisy Pyne's elderly parents had moved in and required too much care for her to leave them, and Esther Mitchell simply said she had absolutely no interest in becoming a midwife, in part because of her husband's disapproval.

Disheartened, Martha resolved it was time to decide whether or not she should marry Thomas. Right now and right here.

She glanced over at the rocking chairs in front of the hearth and shook her head. No, not here. The cottage was definitely not the place she should make her final decision about whether she would marry him or not—not with images of what it might be like to live with him here as his wife.

But she knew exactly where she had to go.

She walked out of the cottage and locked the back door, then took her time as she walked along the dirt path that led through the woods. She was grateful for the shade that protected her from the hot, late-July sun.

She noticed some of the mountain laurel lining the path on either side of her was still in full flower, the best time to make remedies from the evergreen. Stooping down, she put on gloves and stripped some leaves from their crooked stems in order to dry them. Others she would pound into a powder she could use to reduce fevers. She took even more to bake in lard to make a different remedy and made a carryall with her apron to cradle her fragile collection.

She resumed her journey, but decided to stop and stoop down one more time to take a few pale pink blossoms from another mountain laurel.

"I like to pick flowers. Can I help you pick some?"

Startled, Martha nearly let go of her apron but caught herself just in time. When she looked up, she found Cassie standing just a few feet away. "Goodness, child! I didn't even hear you coming down the path."

Cassie giggled. "That's because I walk quiet, like a little deer. At least that's what Mr. Fancy says. He's around here somewhere, but you don't need to worry. He'll walk along out there and watch over us on our way home," she offered, looking deep into the woods.

Martha heard just the hint of a man's chuckle coming from the woods and shook her head. She was curious about what Cassie was doing here. "Did you come all this way to find me?"

"Mama asked me to fetch you back. Miss Fern wants everyone home for supper on time tonight."

"It's a good thing she sent you. I haven't given a thought to the time," Martha admitted as a flush of guilt warmed her cheeks and reminded her she had been late for the past two days.

"That's okay. Mama says you've been working real, real hard."

"Too hard, I fear," Martha said, then turned and started them both walking back home again. She never did see Fancy, but she heard him in the woods as they made their way along the path and caught just a flash of the sun when it hit one of his earrings, just as they turned down the alley leading to the back door of the confectionery.

Although a host of tantalizing aromas greeted their arrival, Martha found the kitchen abandoned. Other than a dozen skyberry tarts cooling on the table, there wasn't a single pot on the cookstove or a place set to eat, and she looked to Cassie for an explanation. "Would you happen to know where everyone might be?"

"They're waiting for us in the yard, right behind the place where they're building the new church."

Martha cocked a brow. "Of all places, why are they waiting for us there, especially since Fern is so worried about having supper on time?"

"Because we're not having a regular supper. We're having a picnic supper tonight! Won't you please, please hurry and wash up? I want to get to the picnic," Cassie replied, a grin teasing her lips and delight lighting her eyes.

Martha nearly groaned but managed to return half a smile. She'd had every intention of having a quick supper and hanging up some of the mountain laurel leaves in her room to dry before calling it a day, although baking the rest of the leaves in the oven would wait until tomorrow.

Feeling a bit grumpy, she deposited her bounty on top of the table. "Maybe you can put these flowers into some water so they don't wilt. Just don't touch anything else, especially the leaves," she cautioned and headed for the staircase. She wondered if she should take a good dose of belladonna to forestall the new aches and pains in her back that she knew would be coming after sitting on hard ground instead of a chair to eat her supper, but she decided to wait until right before she went to bed.

Yet less than half an hour later, she was sitting on something worse—the front seat of a farm wagon. With her travel bag, birthing stool, and bag of simples bouncing around in the back, she was traveling some thirty miles north with Kenneth Rhoads to deliver his wife of their fourth child.

Unaware that Liza Rhoads was even pregnant in the first place, she could not argue the point that calling for a midwife a few days before the woman expected to deliver was a good idea, especially when there was such a long distance to travel. She could, however, take argument with her back, which did not wait for more than a few miles before it protested every bump in the unpaved road with spasms that nearly took her breath away.

Gritting her teeth, she was grateful that she was able to salvage one element of the picnic supper she had left behind. After making certain that Mr. Rhoads had no interest in sharing her treat, she nibbled at one of the three skyberry tarts she had packed for herself. And she was just brassbound enough to finish the other two, despite the fact that she knew very well that sweets were no substitute for the belladonna she had forgotten to take for her aching back before she left.

Indeed, if she had her way, a spoon of honey and a piece of a sugarloaf would be the only remedies anyone would ever need to cure their ailments, but they weren't.

Pity that.

Three days after Martha arrived, baby Rhoads had yet to decide it was time to enter this world. She did not expect that would happen for another couple of days, although she did hope the rain that had pelted the area since she arrived would stop.

She had expected to be living temporarily with a typical homesteading family in an isolated cabin on an ordinary plot of farmland in the wilderness, but she had not been to the Rhoads homestead for more than three years. What she did find when she arrived was astounding.

Kenneth Rhoads's cabin was now one of five that made up a family compound where he and his three brothers, as well as their respective families, lived in separate households in cabins arranged closely together in a pattern that resembled the crescent of a waning moon. They worked the land together, worked a common kitchen garden together, shared the fruits of their collective labor, and served God together as one very large extended family.

With each short break in the rain, adults and children alike were able to escape from one cabin to play or work in another, and the three sisters-in-law made sure the very pregnant Liza had an hour or two each afternoon to rest by taking in her children. Martha also had the opportunity to visit with each of the four families while waiting for Liza's labor to begin. She also took turns sharing her meals with each family.

But at the end of the day, instead of sleeping on a cot in a crowded household, she retired to a fifth cabin, located at the western end of the crescent next to Kenneth and Liza. Come fall, the cabin he originally built when he first arrived would become home for Mr. Rhoads's younger sister, who was expected to arrive with her husband and only child. One bedroom had been set up as a birthing room, and Martha had been given the other room, an oasis that offered her another surprise: privacy.

Lying in bed for the past two nights, Martha had listened to the rain tap a constant, but peaceful, rhythm on the roof above her. Drop after drop, the rain shifted time and time again from a sprinkle to a soaking downpour, creating nature's hymns to accompany her prayers.

Tonight when Martha knelt down by her bed, she was determined to decide how she would spend the rest of her days. She prayed silently but fervently, worshiping God, praising Him, and asking Him to guide her to make the right decision. When she finished, she crawled into bed, curled on her side, and folded her hands beneath her cheek before weighing her options.

"Should I marry Thomas when he returns or not? I suppose

the answer depends on two very different things. What do I really want and what can I have?" she whispered.

What *did* she want?

First, a home of her own. Thanks to her children's generous gift, she could have that home, with or without Thomas, although she did not take the time to consider how different her home would be if she lived there with Thomas or alone.

She also wanted the companionship and support of a loving spouse that she thought she had lost forever when John died. She could only have that if she married Thomas. He was a most unexpected gift, one that would satisfy longings buried so deep in her heart that they had only recently resurfaced.

She sighed and snuggled deeper under the covers. There were other things she desperately wanted, too. Wearied by her work as a midwife, she wanted a different life, a respite from nonstop work that would allow her to choose how she would spend her days.

She wanted the freedom to travel to Boston to visit Oliver and his family or to spend time here in Trinity with Victoria and the grandchildren she hoped would come in time. Now that she had the funds to do all that, the only thing holding her back was the fact that she had yet to find a woman willing to replace her as midwife, and she feared she would not find her anytime soon.

She lay very still and let all of these thoughts simmer together in her mind as her longing for Thomas stirred her emotions.

Yet no matter how very deeply and surely she wanted to marry him, doubt gave her pause. He had promised her that if she married him when he returned, he would be patient and supportive until her duties as a midwife were over.

For the first time since he had renewed that promise and presented her with a new proposal, she knew that the questions she had about his ability to keep that promise were the crux of her dilemma and the reason that she had not been able to make a decision before now.

She knew he meant to keep that promise, but would he? Truly, *could* he? Not very likely, if she considered that he had originally promised to be patient and wait to marry her until she had found someone, only to prove himself otherwise within days. How many times had he asked her since then to marry him, often twice in the same day, so they could go to New York together as husband and wife? Three or four? Or more?

Troubled, she wrapped her arms around her waist to consider what might happen if she did marry him when he returned. What if it turned out that he could not be as patient as he had promised to be? What if he grew so frustrated when their lives together were constantly interrupted when she was summoned away that he eventually lost his patience and insisted that she give up her work as a midwife, even before she had a replacement? What would he do if she refused? Would he try to use his authority over her as her husband to force her to stop? Would she let him?

Her eyes welled with tears. She loved him with all her heart and trusted that when he had made this promise to her, he had every intention of keeping it. As often as she had been frustrated by the fact that he knew her well, to the point that he could almost read her thoughts, she realized that after twenty-five years, she knew him well, too.

Well enough to know, in her heart of hearts, that even though he meant to keep his promise to be patient as she continued her work as a midwife, he would resent all the time they would spend apart. Eventually, his resentment would build, and her disappointment in him would grow to the point that the love they had for each other would slowly but surely be destroyed, along with their marriage.

She refused to let that happen.

Swallowing hard, she tightened her resolve and wrapped it tightly around her heart, where her love for him would always be true, protected by her dreams of what could have been.

She now knew what her answer to Thomas must be—and would be—unless by some miracle one of the women she had approached was waiting for her to return to tell her she had changed her mind and would take over Martha's duties. Or, by a more incredible miracle, a woman who was already a midwife in her own right arrived in Trinity.

Her tears began to trickle down her cheeks. That such a miracle would occur seemed impossible, even for God. She had only one hope left: to eliminate her dilemma by convincing him to wait to marry her until she was no longer bound by her duties as a midwife.

If she failed, the only answer she could give him then would break her heart and his.

And this time, there would be no second chance . . . for either of them.

28

Baby Alexander arrived the next morning, but to Martha's profound dismay, she did not return home to Trinity for many, many days.

Summoned by families in the hinterlands who took advantage of the fact that a midwife was in the area, she had remained for nearly four weeks. She had even been desperate enough to expand her search for her replacement to include this area and had spoken to more than half a dozen women, despite the fact that it would take a good two years to train any one of them. As she had feared, none were interested, primarily because it would have meant relocating the entire family to be closer to Trinity, and the offer of having a rent-free cottage to live in did not sway them at all.

She was bone-weary and travelsick by the time she finally made it back to town. And she carried no small measure of guilt for abandoning everyone in Trinity for so long. Now that the month of August had almost entirely been spent, she held no hope that Thomas was still away, which meant she would probably be giving him her decision in a matter of hours. Victoria, though, was probably back from her wedding trip, which meant there was a joyous reunion waiting for her, too.

She deeply feared the outcome of the former, but she looked forward to the latter.

It was well after dark when she returned and long after everyone else in Trinity had taken to their beds. Except for a lantern she needed to guide her way, she left all the rewards she had received in the alley near the front of the building, rather than the back door, to keep noise to a minimum. The kindly tinker who had brought her the final ten miles home had stacked a fair number of boxes and crates there, but she was confident they would be perfectly safe there until morning.

With her heart racing in anticipation, she entered the back door and slipped into the confectionery. Although no baking had been done for hours and hours, the aroma of sugar and spice and everything sweet and gooey lay heavy in the air.

She grinned. Yes, *now* she could believe she was actually home!

She tiptoed down the hall carrying the same things she had taken with her. With her still-lit lantern and travel bag in one hand and her birthing stool and nearly empty bag of simples in the other, she would have looked like a pack horse if anyone had been awake to see her. She felt like one, too, and only one thought kept her from literally falling asleep on her own two feet: Tonight she would finally sleep in her own bed.

The blistering heat of the day, unfortunately, had barely abated. Her well-soiled travel gown was limp, and her chemise was pasted to her skin. Covered from head to toe with fine travel dust, she moistened her lips and tasted pure grit.

Anxious to quench her thirst and wash her face before crawling into her own bed, she set down everything but the lantern at the bottom of the staircase and turned around to walk to the pump and fill a pitcher of water to carry up to her room.

"Jane!" she gasped. Shocked to find anyone in the kitchen at this hour, especially in the dark, she rocked back on her heels and stared at the woman, who looked like she had been dozing at the table before Martha startled her awake.

Wearing only a thin robe and nightdress, Jane leaped to her feet, nearly knocking over the glass of water in front of her. "Martha! I'm so sorry. I-I didn't mean to frighten you by being here, but no one else is ever up at this hour. I never even heard you coming down the hall, let alone the alley. I must have dozed off for a bit," she explained in a voice just above a whisper.

"There's no reason to take any blame for not hearing me. I was deliberately trying to be very quiet." Martha followed Jane's lead and kept her voice low to keep from waking the rest of the household.

"You would've seen me if I'd bothered to light a candle, but that might have been even worse, considering the fact that I fell asleep."

After Martha put the pitcher of water onto the table, she set her lantern on the floor so the light would not shine directly into their eyes and plopped down into a chair. "Is there a particular reason why you're sitting down here in the middle of the night?"

"Other than the fact that I've had more trouble sleeping lately than I usually do, it's the heat, and tonight is especially warm," Jane admitted. "I finished the water I'd taken up to my room and came downstairs to get more, but it was so much cooler here I thought I'd sit awhile." She rose, took a glass from the cupboard, and set it down in front of Martha.

Martha swiped away a limp lock of hair that fell in front of her eyes before taking her seat again. "I'm hoping you'll be able to tell me that my daughter is back home again."

"You'll be happy to know that she is. Or at least she was. She stopped by the day before yesterday to tell us that she and Dr. McMillan were leaving for a few days to visit her Uncle James and Aunt Lydia in Sunrise, but that she was hoping you'd be back home again by the time they returned. In fact, there's a letter from her that came some weeks ago waiting for you upstairs in your room. And you have several letters from Mr. Dillon waiting for you to read, too. From all I've heard around town, he's been delayed in New York, and I don't think he's expected back for a good while yet. I put all your letters in your room to keep them safe."

Overjoyed to learn that her daughter had returned from her honeymoon, she was equally disappointed that their re-union would be postponed for a few days, though it pleased her Victoria had gone to visit family in Sunrise. Martha also couldn't deny she was relieved to know of Thomas's delay. "How on earth did you get Wesley Sweet to turn over my mail to you?"

Laughing, Jane shook her head. "I didn't. Mr. Fancy did. He used the note you'd written out once before, giving him permission to collect your mail, as well as your daughter's. Since you keep such irregular hours and might return when the general store is closed, he said he wanted your correspon-dence to be here waiting for you so you wouldn't have to wait to collect it."

Martha furrowed her brow for a moment before she smiled. "I'd forgotten all about writing that note for Fancy. I hope Bird didn't cause any trouble for you while I was gone."

Jane rose to refill the pitcher and chuckled on her way back to the table; she filled both of their glasses and sat down again. "No trouble at all. I kept food and water in good supply, changed the cage once a week, and put the cover on the cage at night, just like you do. Miss Ivy and Miss Fern will be very glad tomorrow to find that you're home again. They both think it's long past time for Bird to go back where he belongs."

Cringing, Martha took a couple of deep breaths and sighed. "They're probably right. I'll take him out with me in a day or two to see if he's strong enough to fly off," she promised and mopped her brow. "Mercy, it's hot."

Jane nodded. "It can be steamy in Philadelphia in August, but I never expected to find the same heat here. Fern and Ivy insist that it's not typically this hot in late August, but I suspect they've stretched the truth a bit."

Martha drank her water and refilled her glass again. Prompted to take advantage of this time alone with Jane to learn more about her past, she posed a question. "Would you ever consider moving back to Philadelphia?"

Jane grew paler, if that was even possible. "No. I've seen quite enough of that city."

Martha swallowed hard but followed her intuition. "Forgive me for even asking, Jane, but I think that we've become friends over the past few months, and I'm concerned about you. Did something happen to you in Philadelphia that still troubles you and perhaps keeps you from sleeping well?"

Jane closed her eyes for a moment, and her breathing quickened. She moistened her lips before opening her eyes, then folded her hands atop the table. "I've come to know you and respect you as a fair-minded woman. I'd like to think that we've become friends, too, but I haven't been completely honest with you, or Miss Fern and Miss Ivy, either," she admitted.

She paused for a moment to draw a deep breath. "As far as the sisters are concerned, all they knew when they offered me a place here with them was that my last position had been caring for Mr. Pennington. What no one here knows is that before that, I had been a midwife in the Philadelphia area for over twelve years."

Too shocked by Jane's admission to interrupt, Martha tried to concentrate on what the woman said next.

"I worked very hard to maintain an unblemished reputation as a skilled and compassionate midwife, which became crucial as more and more doctors took over caring for women and children, forcing many of the other midwives out of the city. I lost that reputation and so much more several years ago."

Martha reached across the table to take one of the woman's hands. When she found it cold to the touch, she covered it with her other hand. "Go on."

"The last time I was called to a delivery, I had no reason to expect there would be any problems at all. I had helped Priscilla Ward to birth her first two children without any trouble at all. I did everything I could think of to do. Everything, even prayer. But I couldn't get that babe to draw a breath," she explained, and tears began to trickle down her cheeks.

"I've buried two of my own babes," Martha said, "and in my work as a midwife, I've lost a babe, too. Several, in fact. It's the saddest ending to what should be a miraculous event."

Jane sniffled. "And the mother? Have you ever lost the babe's mother, too?"

Martha caught her breath. Losing both a mother and her babe was the worst possible outcome while attending to a birthing. Grandmother Poore had had that happen only once, but Martha had been spared that nightmarish experience, and she shook her head. "As much as we'd like to think otherwise, not everything is within the midwife's control. Nature can be very unpredictable, but knowing that doesn't make it any easier to bear when we lose both the mama and her babe, does it?" she asked, using the very words her grandmother had used to prepare Martha for the possibility that it might one day happen to her. "You must have been devastated."

Jane looked down but squeezed Martha's hand hard. "I truly was, and as much as I loved my work and considered it a calling, I—I knew I never wanted to be faced with such a tragedy again and decided I could never be a midwife again. Never. When I saw the ad for a caretaker for Mr. Pennington and got the position, I considered it an answer to prayer. After he died, I stayed on but had little luck finding work there because the area was so remote and I had no funds to leave. If it hadn't been for Miss Fern and Miss Ivy, I don't know what I would have done."

"I've always been taught that God sends people to help us when we need them the most," Martha suggested. A hard tug to her conscience, however, forced her to take her own words to heart and embrace the idea that God had sent Jane here as an answer to Martha's prayers, too. Unfortunately, the midwife he had sent was broken in spirit, and He had left it to Martha to find a way to help her to heal.

"I'm so sorry. If I had known that you'd had such a tragic experience with Priscilla and her babe, I never would have approached you about replacing me the way I did. You're obviously still grieving for the mama and baby you lost, as well as the calling you set aside."

Jane held tight to Martha's hand and used the back of her free hand to wipe the tears from her cheeks. "Ever since you asked me to take your place, I've been lying awake, praying and praying, night after night, asking God to give me the courage to tell you the truth and accept the idea that God had led me here to take up my calling again by replacing you, but . . . but I can't. I just can't. If anything like that happened again, it would destroy me. And it would be even worse this time, because I would be letting you down, as well as the women and children here, too. I hardly think that's part of God's plan for either one of us, do you?"

Martha thought about what Jane said for a moment before she answered. "In all truth, Jane, I find it to be more than just a coincidence that God sent you to a town that needed a new midwife, and I'm tempted to think my grandmother was right. I'd like to tell you a faith story that was a favorite of hers, if I may."

Jane nodded.

"According to my grandmother, God's plan for each of us is so grand that He's the only one who knows how those plans are often intertwined. When I was a little girl and didn't want to go to sleep at night after I'd said my prayers, she would tell me that she believed that God always listened to all of our prayers, but because there were so many, He only sifted through them at night while we were all asleep. Some He answered right away, but He waited awhile to answer others. If He found two prayers that were related to one another, He'd play matchmaker and put them together, with one answering the other. But He couldn't answer a single prayer until we were all abed and fast asleep."

Jane chuckled. "I assume you went to sleep pretty quickly after hearing that tale."

"Only when I was praying and praying for something I wanted," Martha admitted. "And as far as the two of us are concerned, I'd think God put our prayers together. You're the answer to mine, and I'm the answer to yours. I also think that if we can pray together each night, you'll find the courage to take up the calling He has blessed you with, and He'll give me the strength and will to continue as midwife until you do. What do you think?"

Jane blinked back fresh tears. "I think you have a greater faith than I do, but . . . but I'd like to try. Perhaps I could accompany you when you're helping a woman or child who is sick and I don't have to tend to my duties at the confectionery. I'd also like to be there with other women to help you with a birthing, although I'd rather wait before I even attempted to deliver a babe again myself. Can we . . . would you . . . that is, do you think we could pray together now?"

That's exactly what they did. Hand-in-hand, their arms stretched across the table, and heart-to-heart, they prayed aloud together for a good long while, asking God to bestow His grace upon them and to guide them in the future He had designed for them.

29

Just before midnight, everyone in the household was asleep except for Martha.

Anxious to read her letters, she set the lantern on top of the trunk at the foot of her cot, sat down on the floor, and leaned her back against the trunk for support. She separated Victoria's letter from the pile and decided to read that one first.

Just as she was about to start reading, Bird chose that particular moment to let himself out of his cage. When he settled himself on her shoulder, she did not have the heart to lock him up in his cage again and let him stay.

She broke the seal on Victoria's letter and unfolded the single sheet of paper. Just as she'd hoped, the lantern cast light perfectly over her shoulder, and she was able to see Victoria's handwriting without any trouble at all.

The letter was from late July, and she whispered the words as she read them. "'Dearest Mother, I am truly the happiest I have ever been. Truly, truly happy! While in Boston, we've been staying with Oliver and visiting with some of Benjamin's relatives. I'm keeping a journal of our visit so I won't forget a single thing to share with you, except one secret that Oliver insists that I keep. Since it's his secret, I can tell you no more, except to say that I think you're going to be very, very pleased!'"

Martha chuckled out loud. Oliver would most definitely not love the idea that his sister had divulged the fact that he had a secret at all. Martha continued reading the rest of the letter aloud. "'As a surprise, Benjamin has decided to take me to visit the Morgans, so we are leaving for New York City in a few days. I hope to have a pleasant time with Nancy, too, and have more news for you about our magazine articles when we return to Trinity. I pray you're taking care of yourself. Your very, very, very happy daughter, Victoria Cade McMillan. P. S. Although I do like the way the name Mrs. Benjamin McMillan looks on paper just as well, I thought it was a bit formal to use with my own dear mother. I must learn the proper signature for a married woman!'"

Martha chuckled even harder this time when she reread her daughter's double signature, refolded the letter, and pressed it to her heart. How well she remembered the joy of those first few weeks and months of married life. Her heart trembled with the idea that she might not experience that joy with Thomas, however.

She turned just enough to set Victoria's letter on top of the trunk before laying out all three of Thomas's letters on the floor by her side. She broke the seals and opened them, just enough to check the dates so she would read them in the correct order. Before she began to read, she said a quick prayer to ask her heavenly Father to be by her side as she read Thomas's words, hoping that one of his letters contained a miracle: that Thomas had reconsidered and rescinded his ultimatum.

Her soul was trembling when she read the first letter, dated only a week after he had left:

My dearest beloved,

I have arrived safely, but within days, I've already realized that my plans to be away from you for only a month may have been wishful thinking. I'm still disappointed that I wasn't there with you to witness and celebrate Victoria's marriage, but I'm certain she'll want to share the details of that special day with me when I return.

As you ponder your decision concerning our marriage, I pray with all my heart that you will be guided by your heart. Forgive me if I also pray that you will give me the answer I yearn to hear.

With deep devotion,
Thomas

Apparently, he did not have second thoughts early in his journey. She quickly turned to his second letter, dated two weeks later, skipped over the identical salutation, and read this one aloud.

"'Being apart from you is harder than I ever imagined it could be. I'm sustained only by thoughts of the wonderful life we'll have together when we're united as one, and I pray you're ready to become my wife when I return. My negotiations here to liquidate my investments are challenging, and you will no doubt find it amusing that some here find me to be most difficult and stubborn at times. I've assured them that the woman I love is often twice as stubborn as I am, but it is a quality I tend to find endearing more often than not. As you can imagine, they did not view my qualities in the same light. I long for the day we are together again. With devotion, Thomas.'"

She paused and swiped at the tears that blurred her vision. He was a stubborn man at times. In that regard, she had every expectation that when he returned, he would not back down from his ultimatum if she asked him to wait to marry her for a while longer.

Praying she was wrong, she decided to simply read his third and final letter. She took hope that he might have changed his mind about his demands from the fact that this letter was far longer than the other two and was dated just a few days after the one she had just read:

> *Dearest Martha,*
>
> *The business of selling off my investments here gets more and more complicated by the day. I will be traveling back and forth between here and Albany to finalize the sales. Thus, this will be my final letter to you before I return, which may be as late as September, although I will make effort to be back with you before then. . . .*

She caught her breath and held it for a very long moment. This letter was her last opportunity to know how he felt about his ultimatum, and she would not know if at a later point—perhaps weeks later—he might have changed his mind. Prepared for the worst, she continued reading:

> *I want you to consider coming to New York with me after we marry as part of our wedding trip, and I've already made arrangements for our stay here. I've also made a few discreet inquiries and now have a list of several women here who each have a good reputation as a midwife.*
>
> *I haven't taken the liberty of contacting them, but if you come with me to New York, I'm convinced you'll find at least one of them who suits you as a new midwife for Trinity. Thus, the days you're summoned away once we're married will be as few as possible once we return home. . . .*

His words only proved how impatient he was for her to cast off her duties as midwife and how easily he dismissed the possibility that she might refuse to do exactly as he had just suggested. Her heart dropped, but somehow she found the courage to read his final words aloud.

"'By now, you must realize that I have no doubt that you've made a decision in my favor, just as you must never doubt you are precious to me and you are loved. I vow to respect your opinion on all matters in the years ahead, although I would ask you to reconsider your obvious and deep attachment to Bird, as I assume you have yet to set him free. I cannot fathom the possibility that you have less an attachment to me. But if you choose not to marry me the day I return, do not worry that you'll have to utter the words that will set me free. I shall do so myself, if only to keep my heart from hearing the echo of your words for the rest of my days as we part for the final time. With affection and longing, Thomas.'"

She dropped the letter and buried her face in her hands, cried, and then cried some more, comforted only by the presence of the little yellow warbler on her shoulder, as faithful and loyal as ever. "You're a stubborn, stubborn man, Thomas, and yes, I'm probably doubly so. Jane won't possibly be ready to assume my duties by September and may need much, much longer, which means that there's no hope you'll ever agree to wait and give me more time before we marry, is there?"

Long hours later, as dawn broke, she was still sitting on the floor. Her tears had stained his letters and blurred his words, but they were already burned into the heart of her memory. With her hope to convince him to wait for her until Jane was ready and willing to take over for her completely tottering on the precipice, she slid headlong into the depths of a deep, soul-numbing despair, where faith and miracles did not exist.

30

With Dr. McMillan away again, Martha anticipated she would spend the next several days answering one summons after another. Folks would be expecting her to tend to all the minor ailments they had or to listen to them complain about the ones they had endured without her or the doctor there to help ease their suffering.

In the past, that is exactly how she would have spent every single day, and that is precisely how she spent the first three days after her return.

But not today. Jane had proven herself so competent lately at handling most any complaint, Martha was quite content to leave her midwifery duties in Jane's hands for the day.

"If folks waited for me for four weeks, and Dr. McMillan doesn't have any problem leaving again, they can see Jane. She's proven herself completely competent at handling most any complaint, or they can wait to see me this afternoon," she whispered to Bird.

She slipped Bird into his covered basket, filled a canvas bag with goodies until it was nearly overflowing, and managed to slip out of the confectionery before anyone else came downstairs, ready to start the day's work. She did, however, remember to leave a note on the kitchen table stating she had gone out and would not be back until the afternoon, just so they would not worry about her.

Outside, the sleeping town lay still under a blanket of eerie silence. No wagons or horses traveled down West Main Street. Mill workers and canal workers had yet to report to work. Shopkeepers had yet to offer their wares for sale, and their customers were only dreaming about the purchases they intended to make later.

Confident that no one had seen her, Martha reached the protection of the woods and followed the familiar dirt path that would take her to the clearing above the falls. She took her time now, inhaling the heavy scent of the lush landscape and enjoying the coolness that a late summer sun would bake away before noon.

Bird started to chirp the moment she started up the incline, as if he knew they were almost at the clearing, and memories of her picnic here with Thomas were bittersweet. She did not even wait until she reached the border of trees at the edge before she set the canvas bag down and lifted the lid on the basket. Bird flew out before her heart took another beat, ignored her outstretched finger, and soared over her head, reaching heights she had never seen him reach before.

"You've really missed flying, haven't you!" she cried, clapping her hands when he flew higher still, until he was only a speck in the sky. Her heart filled with fear that he was doing too much after being cooped up in a cage for a month. Then a chilling fear—that he was flying away forever before he was really ready to survive on his own and without giving her the opportunity for one final good-bye—made her heart tremble.

Eventually, just when she was ready to admit that he was leaving for good, the tiny speck in the sky grew larger and larger, and before she knew it, he landed right down on her shoulder. Relieved, she nudged him gently with her cheek. "You did very well today, my friend, and I suspect you've worked up a bit of an appetite." She took a seat on the trunk of a tree that must have been downed by lightning while she was away.

She polished off a number of molasses cookies, and Bird ate all of the crumbs she laid out for him, too. Still hungry, she offered Bird a piece of two sugar cookies before munching them down as well. "The last time I had a special moment with cookies just like these was the day I introduced my new granddaughters to the idea that once in a while, it was perfectly fine to have nothing but sweets for a meal. I wish they were here, but I'm glad you're still here with me today."

When she was finished with her treats, she brushed the sugar from her hands. Before she realized it, Bird had flown off again. And then again and again, soaring lower and lower each time. She grew exhausted just watching him circle and soar about. Afraid that he had pushed himself too hard on his first day out, she scooped him up the first time he landed next to her and put him back into his basket, even though he offered a bit of a protest.

"If you can fly for me like that another time or two, then I won't have to worry that you're strong enough to fly off for good and take care of yourself properly." She refused to consider that Thomas had been right to complain that her attachment to Bird was the only reason she had yet to set him free.

Ready for her next mission, she carried the basket and the canvas bag with her as she retraced her steps halfway back home again before veering off to follow a narrower path to visit Samuel.

Unfortunately, because the trees on either side of this path were big and packed closer together, the sun had not evaporated the water left by a recent rain. To avoid puddles of water and thick mud, she had to step from one tiny island of dry dirt to another all the way to Samuel's cabin.

She set the basket off to the side and warned Bird to behave and be quiet. She was about to knock on the door when it swung partway open.

Will poked his head out and offered her a grin, along with a full view of the spyglass he was holding. But his gaze was clearly focused on the canvas bags she was carrying. "Me and Mister Fancy were out taking care of Bella when I saw you comin'," he whispered.

She cocked her head and frowned. "Then perhaps you might have met me along the way and offered to carry my bag," she said, following Will's lead and keeping her voice low.

"Had to get back here right quick and warn Mister Samuel you was comin'. That stuff you got in the bag. That for us?"

"It is, but I'd rather not open it up out here. Is there a reason why we're both whispering?"

"Mister Samuel's sleepin', and since he ain't been sleepin' too well lately—"

"Hard for a man to sleep day or night with all the commotion around this place," Samuel bellowed. "Come on in, Widow Cade. William, you need to get yourself right back out to that meadow and help Fancy repair that fence instead of wasting time fooling around with that spyglass of yours. See that you give it over to Fancy for now. When you two get back, I'll consider the idea of sharin' whatever it is Widow Cade's brought along with her. Now scoot!"

"Yes, sir." With his cheeks flaming, Will stepped out of the cabin and took one last longing look at the treats sticking up from the top of Martha's bag before he charged off into the woods.

Chuckling, Martha let herself inside and closed the door behind her. "A fence? That sounds permanent," she suggested as she made her way over to Samuel, who was sitting in one of the two chairs in front of the warming stove.

"Are you gonna keep chatterin', or can you hold off until you pick out one of those cinnamon rolls from the treats you brought with you?"

"Apparently I need to take care of your sweet tooth before I try to have a conversation," she teased and set her bag on the floor. She was not surprised that he knew what was in her bag. He might be blind, but like his hearing, his sense of smell was well beyond normal. Seated next to him, she sorted through the bag to get to the pan of cinnamon rolls on the bottom and studied him out of the corner of her eye.

He might be just a bit thinner than before, but his clothes were clean and his beard was neatly trimmed. He was not wearing his arm in a sling anymore, either, another good sign. With no tell-tale bruises on his face, she felt reassured that he had not been out and about by himself, bumping into trees or bushes again.

Pleased that he was faring well, she went right to work. When she finally found the pan she wanted, she gently separated a double roll and placed her hand beneath his before laying the sweet into his palm.

"Nice and sticky," he remarked and gobbled the entire roll down in a few quick bites. Swiping at the crumbs on his beard without actually seeing that they were there, he patted his stomach. "Wouldn't hurt to have another. Once Fancy and that young'un get a crack at these, won't have much of a chance of more."

She nudged the bag close enough to his leg that he could feel it. "I've brought plenty, but you might want to keep some of these aside for yourself."

He grinned. "You tryin' to sweeten me up for any good reason?"

"No, I'm just trying to thank you for letting Will help me with Bella," she said as she tore another pair of cinnamon rolls from the pan.

He shrugged. "Didn't do more than what I wanted to do."

"Here. Two more and that should do you for now," she said and placed the sweets into his palm again. While he munched away, she licked the sugar from her fingers and waited until he was nearly finished before she tried to get an answer to her earlier question. "That fence you mentioned earlier. If that's for Bella, it sounds as if you're actually going to let the boy keep the horse. Is that right? Or am I jumping to that conclusion simply because it would make life so much simpler for me if you did?"

He polished off the rest of the cinnamon roll and wiped his hands on his trousers. "About that horse of yours . . . maybe . . . maybe it's time to admit that it was a mistake to get involved with that horse in the first place. I mean to say—"

"Don't bother yourself about changing your mind," she said and groaned in spite of herself. "I was surprised you even let him keep Bella on a temporary basis. I'm just being resentful, I suppose, because now I have to take responsibility for something I never asked for in the first place. I'll stop at Thomas's on the way home and let them know to get a stall in their stable ready for her. After that, I'm not quite sure what I'll do, but once—"

"But for once, you might think about listenin' instead of chatterin'," he snapped. "You gonna let me talk or not? 'Cause if you're not, you might as well hand me another something sweet to eat before you head out the door."

Startled by the brusque tone to his voice, she folded her hands on her lap. "I'm listening."

He cleared his throat. "Like I was sayin', takin' that horse turned out to be a mistake, but I'm not talkin' 'bout lettin' William take it from you. There's no easy way for me to admit this to you, but the mistake I made was givin' the horse to you the way I did. Without askin' you first if you wanted it. After all you done for me, I just wanted to do somethin' special for you. Just didn't turn out so good, and I'm real, real sorry about that and hope you won't be so mad you won't wanna come back and visit me from time to time."

Stunned and in total disbelief, she turned and stared at him. "You? You're the one who left Bella at the confectionery door with an anonymous note claiming she was payment for a reward you owed to me? *You* did that?"

"Don't be daft. I couldn't do that on my own. Not with these useless eyes of mine. Fancy helped me. He even used the spyglass tryin' to keep a watch on you and the horse, just like he does for Cassie, but you can't blame him for anythin'. It was all my idea. He just helped make it happen. Said she was a right pretty horse, not like that ugly one you had before. I don't suppose it occurred to either of us that the horse might not take to women so good, but bein' seafarin' men, I guess we didn't know as much about horses as we should have 'fore we got one for you."

The image of these two retired seamen, one of whom was blind, negotiating to buy a horse created one giggle and then another and another that burst out of her lips in one giant guffaw. "I'm . . . sorry. I—I . . . I don't mean to laugh at you, but thinking about the two of you trying to choose a horse for me is a bit like having me pick out a sailing ship for you. Whatever possessed you to do such a thing?"

"You never took nothin' from me, all the time you spent tryin' to come up with one remedy or another when my eyes was failin' me. I had a debt I wanted to repay," he argued gruffly.

She took his hand. "You've repaid me ten times over with your friendship, Samuel. That's all I've ever wanted and far more than I ever expected, and if you think I'd want to end our friendship because you made one little mistake, then you're wrong."

He cocked his head. "Little mistake?"

She laughed until she had tears in her eyes. "You made a whopper of a mistake with Bella, didn't you?"

His chest rumbled when he laughed. "'Bout the biggest one I'll ever admit to makin'." When their laughter was spent, he tugged on her hand. "Don't have much right to ask a favor of you, but I'm askin' anyway considerin' we're friends."

She let go of his hand and reached down into the bag again. "I'll give you one more cinnamon roll. Just one."

"It's not about my sweet tooth. It's about William."

She let go of the pan of cinnamon rolls and sat up straight again. "What about him?"

"He don't know yet, but I'm gonna let him keep the horse. So far, he don't have a clue that it was me and Fancy that got Bella to you in the first place, and I'd be beholden to you if we could keep it that way."

Recognizing how important it was for him to save face with the boy he had adopted, she nodded and then voiced her approval. "I think I can do that. On one condition."

"I shudda known you wouldn't make this easy. Go ahead. Name your price."

"It's not so hard. You just have to promise me that the next time you even form the thought that you'd like to give me something in return for whatever I do for you, you'll let it go and remember that all I want is your friendship."

He snorted. "You sure 'bout that? I've given you nothin' but trouble so far. Can't see that changin' much from now on, neither."

"That's not true. You're my friend. If I ever need help, I know I can always depend on you, can't I?"

"'Course you can."

She grinned, took one more cinnamon roll out of the bag, and handed it to him. The morning she had claimed for herself could not have turned out any better. Bird had had a chance to fly again, Bella's future was now set, and Martha did not have to worry that Samuel would ever make the same kind of mistake where she was concerned again.

She headed back to town and prayed the work she had waiting for her in town would also turn out to be less than she expected it to be. Maybe if it did, she could use all of her energy to climb out from despair and find hope again that she and Thomas would still have a future together.

31

The rest of the afternoon did not turn out to be as good as Martha had hoped. It turned out even better. Not a single person had come to summon her away the entire afternoon.

Not one!

After an early supper, Martha headed upstairs to finally unpack her travel bag and settle properly back in her room again. She found Bird asleep on her pillow and decided to leave him there for now.

It was easy to believe that there had not been a teeming woman ready to deliver today, but Martha found it impossible to believe there was not a single soul in Trinity who had not been feeling poorly enough to need her help.

Well, there had been one. Apparently Cassie had complained most of the morning about a toothache, but Jane had given her a clove or two to chew on. By the time Martha returned from Samuel's, just in time for dinner, the girl's tooth was feeling just fine and Cassie was back to her usual happy self.

She took her soiled clothes out of her travel bag and shook her head as she tried to think of a reason why the afternoon had been so quiet. It was possible that some folks did not seek her out because of the hot, humid weather. They'd had fewer customers than usual at the confectionery, too.

Considering the night air was still steamy, that made some sense to her, and she piled her soiled clothes in the corner, where they would stay until tomorrow. If Jane was not doing laundry, Martha intended to do it herself, since she had only one clean gown left to wear. Besides, getting wet while she was scrubbing her clothes clean was not a bad way to cool off.

She stopped for a moment to mop her brow before she removed her notes from the travel bag and slipped the bag under her cot, right next to her birthing stool. She was still searching her mind for an explanation for the quiet afternoon, though. There were lots of things changing in Trinity these days, but she was confident that gossipmongers had not given up their self-appointed roles as the town's network of news and keepers of people's comings and goings.

Unless the hot, humid weather had made the spread of gossipmongers' news as sluggish as the folks who did venture out to shop around town today.

She then opened up the trunk at the foot of her bed. She retrieved her grandmother's diary, which was actually a box filled with the records Grandmother Poore had kept of every birth in and around Trinity since the town's beginning. After adding her own notes from her recent trip, she left the remaining notes right where they were and returned the box to the trunk.

With lots more work ahead of her, in part because she had let things pile up, she pulled out her record book, where she kept a listing of her rewards. She spent a little more than an hour recording what she had done recently, when she had done it, and what reward she expected to be given for her work, leaving the furthest column blank until she received it. By the time she was done, her hand was tired from all that writing, and she made a mental note to never, ever let so many notes pile up again.

She was ready to store the record book away again when she realized she had forgotten to make one important entry about a reward she had recently received. When she found the one she wanted, she smiled:

16 June Thursday   Bella, white mare   Left anonymously

With a flourish, she crossed of *left anonymously* and wrote, *Given by Samuel Meeks in error and given back to him.* "And happily so," she murmured and closed the book. She was all set to close the trunk when there was a knock at her door.

"Martha?"

"I'm coming, Jane," she replied, then closed the trunk lid and opened the door. "I suppose I'm being called away this late now, when I've been waiting all day?"

Jane's eyes were twinkling. "You're needed, but only downstairs. Cassie begged me to ask you to join us downstairs in the sitting room. I know you're probably too busy or tired enough to want to go to bed, but—"

"I just finished up doing what I truly had to do. I can always do the rest tomorrow. Just give me a few minutes to freshen up a bit first."

Jane grinned and handed her an old cotton nightdress that was so big she could have wrapped it around her twice. "Since we're all wearing something a little unusual, you might want to remove your gown and some of your petticoats and change into this. I'll tell her you'll be down soon," she said and was halfway down the back staircase before Martha had a chance to ask her what exactly they were doing in the sitting room.

Completely intrigued, Martha got as far as the kitchen in less than ten minutes. She was as surprised to find the air so much cooler downstairs, almost as much as she was intrigued by the oddly pitched voices coming from the sitting room.

The voices got louder and stranger the closer she got to the sitting room.

She opened the door very slowly, took one look inside, and clapped her hand to her mouth to keep a cackle from bursting free. Jane and Cassie and Fern and Ivy were all inside, as she expected, but what they were doing together stretched well beyond the realm of her imagination.

Totally absorbed in what they were doing, they took no note that she was even there. She did not need anyone to explain that they were in the midst of a rather unusual play, and they were indeed wearing costumes, of a sort.

All of the furniture normally in the sitting room had been pushed to the walls. Four wooden chairs were lined up side by side in the center of the room. Cassie was standing on the first chair, with the other three stretched ahead of her. She was wearing one of Ivy's better gowns, her mother's only Sunday bonnet, and a ruby necklace that Martha recognized as one of the pieces of Fern's valuable jewelry she had left.

Fern stood next to Cassie. She was dressed in a feathered cap and a man's robe, the source of which further defied Martha's imagination, and she was holding out one of her rolling pins like a sword. For her part, Ivy held on to a ribbon that was tied to Cassie's wrist. Her costume consisted of a pair of burlap bags held together with string, to resemble a long jacket. Jane stood an arm's length away like a soldier on guard, if you imagined the broom she was holding against her shoulder was a rifle of some kind.

"Surrender your jewels, or I'll have one of my crew take them before you walk the plank," Fern commanded in a ridiculously low voice.

Cassie knelt down on the chair seat and steepled her hands. "Please, Captain, they're all I have left. I'd willingly share them with you if you'd spare my life. I am a godly, Christian woman. Have mercy on me."

Fern scowled. "I show no mercy, and I share booty with no man or woman!"

Ivy pointed toward her sister. "You'll share with me, or you'll walk the plank with her!"

Fern puffed out her bottom lip and looked over at Cassie. "I thought you said I was the captain. Can't I keep all the booty from this woman that we captured?"

"No, you can't. I already told you, remember? The captain has to share all the booty with every member of the crew. And Miss Ivy, you can't talk to the captain like that," Cassie insisted. The girl looked like she was about to cry with frustration until she saw Martha standing at the door.

She yelped with joy, jumped down from the makeshift plank, and ran straight to her. "Miss Martha! You really did come to play pirates with us. Now we'll have a proper captain. You don't have to change costumes with Miss Fern unless you want to. If you don't, she can be the pretend captain and you can be the real one she captured and put in irons. But now you escaped and want your ship back," she said.

Martha knew just who to blame for the girl's obvious fascination with pirates, but she had no idea how Cassie had convinced these three grown women to join in her play. Since she did not have the heart to disappoint Cassie, Martha did not even try. Instead, she decided to make that four grown women instead of three and joined in the play.

Two hilarious hours later, after each of them had switched

character roles again, Martha was about to walk the plank, planning to pretend to jump to her death, when there was a loud knock at the back door. "I've been rescued," Martha exclaimed and stepped down very carefully from the chair and held up her hand. "I'll go. The caller is most likely looking for me."

Grateful that she was wearing a gown now instead of a night-dress, she answered the door expecting to be summoned away. Instead, she found her entire family standing there—including her two precious granddaughters, who were standing on the top of the steps and looking up at her with expressions of great expectation on their little faces.

Her heart leaped and banged against the wall of her chest.

"Hi, Grandma," Lucy said. "Papa said you could give us some more cookies, and if we're really, really good, you'd let us see Bird again. We promise to be good, don't we, Hannah?"

"Really, really good," Hannah promised.

Torn between disbelief that they were here and sheer joy that they were, Martha was absolutely speechless, possibly for the first time in her entire life. While she struggled to find her voice, she glanced up at Oliver and Comfort, who were standing behind the girls, and saw that Victoria and Dr. McMillan were there, too. She could not decide which one had the widest grin.

When the girls started tugging on Martha's skirts, obviously anxious to get their grandmother's full attention, Oliver started to chuckle. "Before we explain why we're all here, it might be a good idea to let the girls have a cookie or two like I promised since there won't be any peace until you do."

"Cookies," Martha repeated, glanced down at the girls, and took each of them by a hand. "Of course we have cookies at the confectionery, and I'm going to let you pick out exactly which cookies you'd like to have today," she promised and bent down to press a kiss to the top of their blond curls before she let them inside. "Along the way, maybe your father can explain what you're all doing back in Trinity."

Lucy skipped her way down the hallway. "We're gonna get a new house and live here."

Hannah walked along more sedately and tugged on Martha's hand. "And we're gonna get a puppy and a kitten and a . . . and a—"

"A pony. Papa said we could get a pony, but we have to share it," Lucy added.

Martha stopped dead in her tracks, which forced her granddaughters to do the same. She turned and searched Oliver's face for some sign that the girls were mistaken.

He returned her quizzical expression with a grin. "The girls have vivid imaginations, but in this case, they're absolutely right."

Martha's heart trembled. "They are? You're moving back to Trinity with your family? Truly?"

"That's my intention. I thought about telling you our idea when we were here last, but we hadn't decided then exactly what we were going to do, which is why I kept it a secret from you. Now I'm just trying to decide whether or not we should buy an existing house, build one of our own here in town, or settle farther out on some kind of homestead. In the meantime, we'll be staying with Victoria instead of the cottage so we're all a bit closer to town."

"In other words, the girls will be closer to the confectionery—so they can visit with their grandmother more often. You might want to warn Miss Fern and Miss Ivy that they'll need to bake more cookies than usual," Comfort teased.

Martha chuckled and turned to Oliver. "I can't even begin to tell you how happy I am with your decision to come home to Trinity and raise your family here."

Before they could continue their conversation, everyone in the household poured out of the sitting room and pandemonium erupted. Before conversation reached a level that would frighten the girls, Martha let Cassie take the girls into the shop to pick out their cookies. Once they were gone, Victoria came up behind Martha and whispered in her ear, "Thanks for not telling Oliver you knew he had a secret."

Martha turned and gave her daughter a hug. "I trust my secret is still safe with you, as well?"

"It is, but I'm ever so curious to know what you've decided to do. Are you going to marry Mr. Dillon or not?" she asked, keeping her voice low.

"We'll make that decision together when he gets back, which may not happen until sometime in September," Martha whispered as she studied her daughter's features. "You look wonderful and so very happy. Maybe tomorrow we can find some time to be together and you can tell me all about your honeymoon travels."

"We will, assuming you're not called away and Lucy and Hannah agree to share you with me," Victoria teased before Oliver reached his mother's side and claimed her attention. They all spent the rest of the evening together, and for the first time, Martha created memories with them that were all the sweeter because the days they would have together now stretched ahead with endless promises of many more.

The only possible way those memories could be any better would be if Thomas could be part of those memories, too.

She prayed together with Jane briefly because they were both uncommonly tired. Martha had promised to take her granddaughters swimming tomorrow afternoon and needed all the energy she could muster. She was headed back to her room to change into her nightgown when she heard a pounding at the back door. Grumbling under her breath, she passed Ivy in the upstairs hallway, insisted on answering the door herself, and hurried downstairs.

When she finally got to the back door and opened it, she found Eleanor's husband, Micah, standing there, and her heart started to race with worry.

Before she could ask him if it was Eleanor or little Jacob who had taken ill, he handed her a note. "Mr. Dillon just got back from his trip. He asked me to give you this and wait for you to write back your response. I'll wait out here, if that's all right."

She felt her blood drain from her face and nodded before she closed the door. Her hands were shaking as she unfolded the note and walked rather unsteadily down the hall to the kitchen. She waited until she had the better light there to read his words:

> *Darling Martha,*
>
> *I have finally made my way back to you. Because of the lateness of the hour, it would not be proper for me to call on you now, especially since I pray we'll be asking Reverend Welsh to marry us within hours of our reunion.*
>
> *I'll pick you up with my buggy tomorrow morning at ten o'clock, unless you're as anxious as I am to begin our future together and prefer that I come earlier. Out of respect for your desire to keep our plans secret, please write your response and have Micah bring it back to me.*
>
> *Thomas*

Martha's eyes welled with tears. Jane had yet to attempt a birthing on her own as midwife and still needed much more time, which meant there would be no miracle to save Martha's future with Thomas. Now that he was home, she had to keep her promise to give him her answer. He deserved her answer. And as her stubborn streak rose from the ashes of her despair, she realized she was not going to give up hope there was still a chance for them to be together as husband and wife.

She wrote her answer below his name:

Meet me at ten o'clock above the falls, where we had our picnic together.

M

Sniffling, she folded up the note and carried it back with her down the long hall. Her emotions were in such turmoil, she felt as if she were doomed to walk the length of a plank instead of just pretending, like she had been when playing with Cassie.

She returned to her room with a heavy heart. Her love for Thomas, however, was too precious to let go without making one last effort to convince him to change his mind, again, and agree to wait for her just a little while longer.

And that was exactly what she intended to do tomorrow morning.

32

Martha started up the incline to reach the edge of the clearing above the falls just before nine o'clock. The extra hour she expected to have by arriving early in order to rehearse what she was going to say died the instant she reached the top.

Thomas was already here.

He was standing with his back to her, just beyond the fallen tree in the middle of the clearing. Even though she could not see his face, she would have recognized him from twice the distance.

She gave an involuntary gasp of surprise, and when he did not turn around to greet her, she assumed he had not heard her coming and had no idea she was there. She swallowed the lump in her throat easily enough, but she grew impatient waiting for her heart to stop pounding and her pulse to drop back to normal.

Her gaze never ventured from his image. Sunlight glistened on his ebony hair, which she noted had been neatly trimmed.

Long and lean and straight in stature, he was wearing the same dark blue frock coat that he wore to Sunday services and every other important occasion, at least in her recent memory.

She was tempted to step back down again, ever so slowly, to reclaim the hour she had wanted to organize her thoughts and practice what she wanted to say to him, but she never had the chance to take a single step.

He turned around, caught sight of her, and nodded, as if making certain that she knew he had seen her there.

When he did not start toward her and remained in place, she made her way to him, step by cautious step, until she was standing within arm's reach and separated from him only by the trunk of the tree . . . and the stubborn will that each of them possessed.

"You're early."

His voice was deep and strong, just as she remembered it, except that now it was tinged with disappointment.

She moistened her lips. "Apparently you arrived even earlier."

Her answer nudged the first hint of a smile from him. "I thought I might be able to find a spot up here to watch you leave the confectionery on your way here. Obviously, I didn't."

"That's why I favor this particular place. It's very private," she remarked, curious as to why he still held his place and kept the trunk of the tree between them. Or why he allowed a thick silence to grow until she found it unbearable. "I hope it wasn't as hot back East as it's been here. And I hope your journey was as successful as you'd hoped it would be."

"I didn't come here this morning to talk about the weather or my journey, Martha."

"Neither did I."

"I came to hear the answer you promised to give me today, assuming you've made up your mind, one way or the other."

"Yes, I have." She worried her lips together for a moment. "I was hoping we might talk about this together, but it feels a little awkward with this tree trunk lying between us. If for some reason you don't want to step over it, I'll walk around it so we can sit together and talk—"

"Please don't."

She pulled her head back and furrowed her brow. "Don't what?"

"Don't take a step from where you are. Please," he said, and his gaze grew troubled. "If you're any closer to me than you are right now, if there isn't something between us as sturdy as this tree trunk, I'll lose control the moment I get a whiff of the scent of your hair and kiss you. And I'm trying very, very hard not to kiss you. In fact, I've promised myself that I'm *not* going to kiss you."

"May I ask why?" she asked, disappointed that she would not be able to use at least part of her plan to get him to listen to her, just long enough to convince him to give her more time.

When his gaze softened, her heart trembled. "Because I know you, Martha, better than I know anyone else in this world. I knew the exact moment you reached the clearing. I waited for you to come to me, excited to tell me that you would marry me today. But you didn't do that, did you?"

"No, I didn't, but I—"

"You held back. But in all truth, I knew your answer the instant I turned around and saw you were dressed for a day of work, not for a day you expected to be married. Even then, I still held out hope, but the moment I was close enough to see the expression in your eyes, I knew you weren't going to marry me today. Instead of setting me free, you've got an argument all planned out that included more than a few of your sweet kisses—used to convince me to wait until you have a midwife

278

to replace you before we marry. Then to ask me to believe you won't change your mind by then."

"But I only—"

"Am I wrong?" he whispered, and his eyes were filled with a longing that left her trembling. "Please. Tell me I'm wrong."

Half of her heart wanted her to leap over that tree trunk, hurl herself into his arms, and stay there until his kisses convinced her to marry him this very day. The other half begged her to stay right where she was, because if she didn't, her heart would end up broken in the end, never to be whole again.

"It's all right. You don't have to tell me. It's written all over your face. You've set me free without saying a single word. Maybe . . . maybe it's best you do," he whispered, his voice hoarse with regret, and started to walk away.

"That's it? You're leaving? You're not going to give me a chance to tell you why I'm willing to beg you, if I must, to wait for me? I have a woman who has agreed to replace me, but she won't be ready to deliver a babe on her own for at least another few months and quite possibly more than that. But she will. I'm confident she will. Why can't you wait just a little while longer for us to marry, like you promised before you changed your mind? Why is it that you get to change or conveniently forget a promise you've made to me whenever you feel the need, or to push me into accepting your last proposal, which was really an ultimatum, even though it's unfair? But I only get one chance to keep a promise I've made to you? And I can't take it back or . . . or replace it with another or give you an ultimatum you don't like, either?"

He paused in mid-stride and walked back to her, but he remained on the other side of the tree trunk. "That's not what I'm doing."

"That's exactly what you're doing," she argued gently. It took all of her willpower not to step right over the tree and to march right up to him. "I love you, Thomas. I always will. But I know you very well, too. I need more time before she's able to take over for me completely, and she'll probably need my help until then. I believe you have every intention of keeping your promise to be patient with me when I'm summoned away, even if it takes a good while before I can give up my calling completely. But I also know that the longer it takes for me to stop, the thinner your patience will get."

"Even if—"

"Even if I'm gone for a month at a time, like I was for almost the entire month of August? Or now? Dr. McMillan is back, which means I won't have to care for his patients any longer, but there may still be days when I'm not home for more than a few hours at a time. Can you honestly say you won't grow to resent the fact that you're almost always alone and eventually break the promise you made to be patient about that? No man could, Thomas. That doesn't make you any less than a man of his word. It just makes you what you are—a man who wants his wife by his side, day in and day out."

She paused just long enough to grab hold of the thought that had just flashed in front of her mind's eye. "Did it ever occur to you that I might grow impatient and resentful, too? That as your wife, I'd want you to be by my side each and every day? I never really thought about it before right now, but I have to admit that I would. And I'm not willing to take the risk that if we marry now, we'll end up hurting one another when all we should do is love one another. Am I wrong, Thomas? Please, tell me something . . . anything . . . to convince me that I'm wrong," she pleaded and reached her hand out to him, along with her heart.

His eyes churned and deepened in color. His jaw twitched, as if he were fighting against the words she needed for him to say, and his shoulders slumped so slightly no one else would have noticed. "No. You're not wrong, Martha, but the longer I have to wait for you, the more I'll fear that this woman you claim to have found will change her mind or that you'll eventually do what you did once before. You'll turn me away. I can't let that happen. Not ever again. We have had our second chance to be together. Forgive me, but I can't ever let there be another." Then he broke his earlier promise to himself and kissed the back of her hand before he turned and walked away.

And when he did, he did not only take her heart with him. He took her hopes. He took her dreams. And he left her with only one place to live—all alone, destined forever to live in the shadows of a life shaded by what might have been.

33

The first few weeks of September flew by quickly, but not easily.

In all truth, she had been blessed with days filled with the joy of spending time with her children and especially little Lucy and Hannah. With Dr. McMillan back and with Jane to help, she had far fewer calls to duty, which left her more time to spend with her precious grandchildren, a decided blessing. Jane had proven herself to be as skilled at diagnosing illnesses as she was with knowing which remedy to use and how to prepare it. Both Fern and Ivy agreed that Jane would be an excellent replacement for Martha, who had been encouraging Jane to do even more. Even so, Jane had yet to deliver a babe on her own. They continued to pray together every night that she would be blessed with His grace and given the courage to do so, but Martha still expected it would be months and months before that happened and even more before Jane was both willing and able to take over that essential core of Martha's duties.

On the other hand, she was so filled with grief that Thomas

282

had rejected her completely, she had to fight her malaise just to function. It took every ounce of her energy just to get out of her bed and dressed, in part because she had barely touched her meals—and not a single sweet treat in the confectionery had tempted her—and because her knee had recently been injured, and the pain added to her unrest.

Her soul, too, was numb, to the point that she still had no desire to pray to God for relief and had not even bothered to try after praying for Jane. She had even made an excuse not to go to Sunday services this week.

Already haunted by too many painful images of Thomas, she could not bear to add even one more. She avoided going anywhere near his house and averted her eyes when she had no other choice. Although she tried to keep her grief hidden and refused to discuss anything related to Thomas with Victoria, she knew she'd ended up being nothing short of completely grumpy with everyone except her grandchildren.

When she greeted the first light of the day today, however, she decided that things were going to change, because she could not continue to live this way. She forced herself to get out of bed and dressed for the day. After she brushed her hair, she plaited it to form a single braid she left hanging down her back instead of shaping a knot at the nape of her neck. "That's just one change," she murmured.

She went over to take Bird's cage, her swollen knee causing her to limp. He chirped to life at once, and she tossed a few seeds into his food bowl. "I know I haven't taken you up to the falls for over a week, but as soon as this knee is better, I will. And we'll take the girls with us, too," she promised and sat down on top of the trunk at the foot of her cot to think about how she might lift herself out of the doldrums.

A series of six yawns in a row convinced her that when she

went to bed tonight, she needed to get a decent night's sleep. Instead of lying awake and remembering her last meeting with Thomas over and over again in her mind and wondering what she could have done or said to keep him from leaving her, she had to think about something else.

She just had not thought of what that would be yet.

Today, at least, she did not have to worry that Fern and Ivy would continue to harass her about what was troubling her. Hoping for relief, she had let them wheedle the truth out of her— simply put, that she and Thomas had been planning to marry but had changed their minds. She hoped they would leave her in peace to mourn now, which would be welcome and needed. She just was not ready to be as honest with Victoria, in part because she knew her daughter would not let the matter rest.

As she looked ahead to her day, she knew there was nothing she could do about the weather. Extremely hot, humid air continued to drape the town like a wet wool blanket, helping swarms of mosquitoes, flies, and other annoying summer critters to flourish, and there was no relief in sight.

Already feeling the heat, she undid the top button on her bodice. "I can certainly try not to wallow in self-pity today. Everyone else who calls Trinity home is suffering, too—although the relentless heat is at the root of their misery rather than a broken heart."

And since they had been suffering from the heat for a while, they had changed their daily routines. Canal and mill workers took a long break at midday when the heat was most intense. Most people strolled along Main Street only in early morning or late afternoon, and wagon traffic grew sparse. Good tempers and patience seemed to be as rare as a cooling breeze, and more than a few folks could be found with their gazes glued to the sky, searching for any sign that a good storm was coming to save them from the heat. She had heard Reverend Welsh had even led everyone in prayer at services the other day to ask for God's mercy and divine intervention.

The other members of the confectionery household had also found ways to adjust. Fern and Ivy had actually stopped baking three days ago, much to Lucy and Hannah's dismay, although the confectionery remained open to offer what was left of the tins of hard pretzels and soda crackers. They also limited using the cookstove to every other day until after the sun had set, and Jane and Cassie performed only the most necessary of limited household tasks.

For her part, Martha had developed a routine that usually allowed her to avoid the greatest heat of the day when treating her patients, and she also reduced the number of occasions she was out and around town. She spent most mornings in the room Dr. McMillan had set aside for her use months ago in his office, although she continued to make visits to those in town who weren't able to come to her.

After taking time for a midday rest back home and a bite of dinner, she would return to the office and spend every moment she did not have a patient with her granddaughters. She had taken the time to write a note to Thomas and had sent it over to his house days ago asking him to meet with her, but he had never replied. In fact, she had heard just yesterday that he had moved out to his cabin on Candle Lake.

She drew a long breath and gently rubbed her swollen knee before wrapping it tight, hoping it would not swell any more than it already had. "I can't control how many people get sick and need me, but I can try to stop grumbling so much," she said and eased onto her feet. "I'm afraid that's about all the change I can handle for today," she admitted and headed off to see how successful she would be.

By the end of the morning, Martha had grumbled more, not less, than yesterday and twice as much as the day before. Grumbling under her breath yet again, she limped her way back to the confectionery, swatting at flies attracted to her soiled apron along the way. She plopped her bag of simples on the bottom step of the staircase that led up to her bedroom, untied her apron, and dropped it on top of her bag.

She had not seen anyone here so far, and without a single sound to indicate anyone else was even at home, she was more than curious to know why.

She plopped down into a chair in the kitchen to wait for them, anxious to finally prop up her knee. Despite the tea she had been drinking and the wrap she had applied to her knee, the pain still stole her breath away every time she put her foot to the ground, and her knee throbbed almost nonstop, even when she rested it.

Flushed and overheated from walking the short way home, she tugged at her bodice, which was stuck to her skin. She was sorely tempted to scratch at the welts left by mosquitoes, who had feasted on her flesh again last night, and barely managed to resist it.

Jane entered the kitchen just as Martha was easing her leg up to rest on the opposite chair. Looking even more overheated than Martha felt, Jane went straight to the sink, where she pumped out enough water to wash her hands and wet a cloth that she pressed against her flushed cheeks. "I'm sorry I'm a little late in getting dinner started. I was over at Mrs. Reed's tending to the garden and lost all sense of the hour. I'm surprised Miss Fern and Miss Ivy aren't here waiting for me with you. They expected to be back long before now."

Martha mopped her brow. "I thought I told you that what's left of the garden during this hot spell can wait until it breaks. Do you know where Fern or Ivy went? Did they take Cassie with them?"

"They left after breakfast, but they didn't really say where they were going. Cassie didn't go with them, though. I gave her permission to go fishing at a lake with Will and Mr. Samuel today, although I suspect she'll have more fun just dangling her feet in the cold water and splashing around a bit to cool off. Mr. Fancy will be there to watch over all three of them."

Jane glanced out the window. "I'm getting worried about those two sisters. They shouldn't be walking in this heat, and if you'll forgive me for saying so, I might say the same about you—especially since you promised to let me help you care for your patients more often, especially with that knee of yours."

"Don't bother. I'll say it myself and save you the trouble," Martha replied, unable to keep herself from a moment of self-pity. "You're right. I should have let you take over all of my work at Dr. McMillan's office. It's nearly been my undoing."

"Nearly?" Jane frowned, moistened another cloth, and handed it to Martha, who promptly pressed it to her forehead. "I know you said it wasn't intentional, but when poor old Widow Pitt whacked your knee with that stick two days ago, she actually *was* your undoing. Unfortunately you're too stubborn to follow the very advice you'd give to one of your patients and stay off your feet for a while."

Martha sighed. "It wasn't a stick. It was her cane, and she really wasn't aiming at me. She was trying to strike out at her son because he'd brought her out in all this heat to see me," she countered. "Poor old woman. She's not very congenial, even when she's feeling well." She paused. "In all truth, I think it's time you took over my duties with anyone who is ill. I'd much rather be cooling off with Cassie instead of going back to my office at Dr. McMillan's this afternoon."

"Except you'd never be able to walk that far with that knee," Jane teased. "I'll take care of anyone who needs help this afternoon as long as you promise to keep your weight off of that knee. Unless you're summoned to a birthing, of course."

"I don't expect I will be, but let's hope I'm not called out to a birthing for at least a couple of days, since I'll never be able to kneel down on the floor with this knee of mine to deliver a babe. If I am, I'll just have to let Dr. McMillan take my place . . . unless you think you might be ready to go for me."

Jane moistened her lips. "You'd really trust me to go in your stead when I haven't even attended a birthing with you yet?"

"Only if you can trust yourself to go," Martha replied. "Do you think you could?"

"I think I might be able, but I'm not sure," Jane admitted.

Martha nodded and gently patted her sore knee. "I think I will accept your offer to rest my knee this afternoon. But before you start dinner, I wonder if I could bother you for a fresh cold cloth."

Jane furrowed her brow. "I do believe this is the very first time you've ever asked me for help with something you always do for yourself," Jane teased and walked away. She had the cloth ready within minutes, but instead of handing it to Martha, she motioned for her to pull up her skirts.

"It'll be easier if I do it," she offered, and Martha posed no argument to the idea.

Jane took one look at the knee and the cloth Martha had wrapped around it and scowled. "That knee is twice the size it should be. You need to do more than drink a cup or two of sneezewort tea each day and wrap it." She removed the cloth and set it aside before going directly to the larder.

She returned with a bottle of apple cider vinegar. After saturating the cloth with the liquid just short of leaving it dripping, she wrapped the cloth around Martha's knee. She wrapped it again with a thicker towel and put a folded towel underneath her foot to elevate her leg. "There. That should do it. If you'll let me change that poultice every time it dries out and keep off your feet for a few days, you'll be good as new. But if you insist on hobbling your way to and from Dr. McMillan's office and all around town, you just might damage your knee permanently, which is precisely what I warned last night to Miss Fern and Miss Ivy."

Martha wrinkled her nose, put off by Jane's remedy and the fact that the three women had been talking about her. She could not remember the last time anyone had admonished her for her choice of remedies, and she did not take it well. Not at all.

34

The following day, Jane's faith in God and in herself was put to the very test that both she and Martha had discussed together.

At midday, when the two of them were sitting together in the kitchen and no one else was home, a series of slamming doors and pounding footfalls through the confectionery frightened them both. The door connecting the shop to the kitchen crashed open, and a hulk of a man burst into the kitchen. He was carrying a very pregnant, very pale woman, who was writhing in pain. "They told me I'd find the midwife here," he said as he glanced from Martha to Jane and back again. "Name's Clemmens. Richard Clemmens. My wife, Claire, needs the midwife. Our babe isn't due for another month yet, so we thought we could join her folks in Ohio before . . . before this happened. Luckily, we weren't far from town. Please! Which one of you is Midwife Cade?"

"I am, and this is my friend Jane Trew. Unfortunately, I won't be of much help to your wife with this knee of mine." Martha pointed to her leg, which was propped up on an opposite chair, before she turned to her companion and friend. "Jane, if you feel up to delivering this babe, you can use the sitting room, or would you rather show them the way to Dr. McMillan's?"

The man shook his head. "I just left there. His housekeeper said he was out on a call and won't be back till late tonight. It's our first babe, and . . . and I don't think we can wait that long."

Confident that God was in total control of the situation, Martha whispered a hurried prayer that Jane knew that, too.

Jane's gaze darkened for only half a heartbeat before her eyes shimmered with determination. "I can take care of your wife and deliver the babe," she said and got to her feet. "Let me show you to the sitting room."

He hesitated. "Are you a midwife, too?"

Jane tilted up her chin. "Yes, I am, and unless you want your wife to deliver that babe right here in the kitchen, I suggest you follow me. Now," she added firmly, in the same tone of voice Martha always used to force a father-to-be to follow her directions.

Whether it was Jane's command or the poor laboring woman's scream, the man did as he was told. And what mattered most was that Jane had accepted the challenge God had placed in front of her, and Martha prayed with all of her might that He would stay by her side and help her to deliver this babe safely into this world and into its mother's arms.

Martha had gotten to her feet by the time Jane came rushing back into the kitchen. "My bag of simples is sitting right on the floor in my room, and the birthing stool is stored under my cot. I'll get everything else ready for you here," Martha suggested. "I may not be able to do much, but if you are worried about doing this on your own, I can be there with you when you deliver the babe."

Jane shook her head and smiled. "I can do this, Martha. I know I can, because I won't be helping this babe into the world all by myself. God has blessed me with my calling, and He'll be with me. That's not to say I wouldn't mind having you there, too. I won't need you to tell me what to do, but I could use your help with our mother-to-be, if it wouldn't put too much strain on your knee."

"Let's go help this little one meet some very anxious parents," Martha replied. They gathered up what she had assembled for Jane to use with the birthing and carried everything to the sitting room, where she found Claire lying on the settee with her worried husband standing by her side.

Relinquishing her usual role as midwife to Jane, she was not surprised when Mr. Clemmens was sent out into the hallway. Working quickly but efficiently, Jane helped Claire off of the settee, and Martha assisted the laboring woman until Jane had covered the settee with a birthing cloth and laid the woman down again.

Martha held the woman's hand while Jane rolled up the woman's gown to examine her. Within minutes, Jane was frowning. "The babe is in a posterior position and appears to be stuck. From what she's already told me, she's been suffering from forcing pains for several hours. She's very weak at this point, and I'm afraid the babe is, too," she said to Martha before she turned her attention to Claire. "I need to help your babe, and it's going to hurt. A lot. But once I do, you'll have your babe in your arms in no time," she promised, although Martha was far less confident than Jane appeared to be.

Deathly pale, poor Claire managed a smile before gritting her teeth against the pain of another contraction. "Hurry. Do whatever you have to do, but please hurry! It hurts. It really hurts!"

"I know, sweet woman. I know," Jane crooned, but her demeanor changed in an instant. She squared her shoulders and nodded to Martha as she lubricated her right hand and arm. "I'll need you to help Claire hold as still as she can."

Martha stood at the end of the settee and took hold of Claire's shoulders. "I'm ready."

Jane nodded, and without saying another word, she went straight to work. With confidence and skill, she managed to help that baby in far less time than it would have taken Martha. Claire had passed out from the pain, poor dear, but she roused when her husband returned. Jane barely had time to get the worried man to take a seat on the birthing stool and his wife seated properly on his lap before little Michael Paul Clemmens entered this world.

True to her word, Jane placed the squalling babe into his mother's arms just a few minutes later. Once again moved by the absolute glory of birth, Martha saw her feelings mirrored on Jane's face and more. She saw confidence and courage and joy. Such wonderful, immeasurable joy!

When Jane's work was over and the new mother and babe were resting together under the watchful gaze of the proud new father, Martha was pleased when Jane led them to all pray together, a custom Martha had always followed after every birth.

"Heavenly Father, we thank you for the gift of precious Michael Paul, who is living proof of the perfect love You have for each and every one of us. Martha and I thank you for the privilege of attending his birth. We pray that You will shower his parents with grace, that they might raise this child to know You, love You, and serve You so that he will grow to manhood and live a long and full life as a model of Christian love and integrity that will bring You and our savior, Jesus Christ, the honor and praise that You are due. So pray we all. Amen."

When the echo of their combined *amen* had yet to fade, she and Jane left the new parents alone and returned to the kitchen together.

Martha could not help noticing that Jane's eyes were still aglow. "You did a wonderful job with Claire and little Michael. How do you feel, now that you've delivered a fine, healthy babe and placed him into his mother's arms again?"

Jane swirled around the room as if freed, once and for all, from the fear and doubt that had taken her calling away from her. "I'm . . . I'm excited. Amazed. Grateful. Blessed. Happy. And oh so ready to be a midwife again," Jane crooned and danced over to Martha to give her a hug. "I don't know how to thank you for helping me rediscover my faith in God as well as in myself. I thought I'd lost both forever. I know there may come a time when something will go horribly wrong, but if and when it happens, I'll be better prepared to hold on to my faith and to help the parents I serve to do the same. Thank you, Martha. Truly. I owe you so much."

Martha hugged her back. "Not at all. It was all part of God's plan. For each of us. He's the one who brought us together," she replied, but her voice caught on her words. Despite her lack of faith, God had indeed sent her a woman who was a fully competent midwife. He had just sent her too late for Martha and Thomas to have a life together.

It suddenly occurred to her that maybe that was part of God's plan . . . because He did not want her to marry Thomas at all.

A final tug on her conscience, strong enough to shake off the numbness in her soul, set her faith free again and reminded her she must always bow her will to His. And she could only do that in the days and nights ahead with prayer.

Too overwhelmed by the many possibilities for her future, and too hurt to imagine her life without Thomas, Martha had an ache in her heart and her head almost as bad as her knee, which had survived her work today with no more damage.

Her first prayer tonight and every night for the rest of her life? To ask God to help her to follow the path He had set out before her . . . without Thomas.

⁂

The busy household was even busier for a couple of days, but once Mr. Clemmens left with his wife and little son to continue their journey to Ohio, life in the confectionery returned to a normal, but slightly different, routine.

Fern and Ivy were surprised to learn that Jane was, in fact, a midwife, then promptly made the same arrangements with her as they had made with Martha—and they already had a few ideas about how to go about hiring more help to run the household.

They were less than enthusiastic to learn of Martha's plans to move into her cottage. When they walked into the sitting room, where Martha was resting on the settee after dinner, and closed the door behind them, she had a feeling she was not going to like what they had to say.

Although the settee was clearly designed for two, the sisters plopped down, one on either side of her. Now she knew she was not going to favor the conversation they apparently had planned.

Fern took the lead. "My sister and I need to talk to you."

"If it's about moving into my cottage—"

"It's not. It's about you and Thomas," Ivy argued. "We love you both, and we just don't understand why the two of you can't settle whatever disagreement you had and get married."

"We don't want to know what's come between you," Fern explained. "That's none of our concern, of course, but we just can't stand by, day after day, and see how unhappy you are without doing something to try to help you. I can't imagine he's faring any better, either."

Disappointed that she had not been better able to hide her deep disappointment, Martha hoped to ease the concern etched on their faces. "At the moment, having a little more room to breathe would be a good start," she teased.

Fern shook her head. "We're not letting you off of this settee until you agree to sit down with Thomas and try to work things out."

Martha drew a deep breath. "We already did try. Truly, we did—but we just couldn't agree on . . . on some things that are important to each of us. It wouldn't do any good for me to talk to him about it again."

Ivy squeezed herself off of the settee. "Then if you won't even try, my sister and I will. We'll ask around tomorrow and get someone to drive us out to that cabin where he's holed himself up and talk some sense into that man."

Martha's heart started to pound, and she got to her feet. "No, please. Please don't do that. I appreciate your concern, but it wouldn't make any difference if you did. He's made it very clear he isn't interested in anything more I might have to say. And please, if you're tempted to talk to him anyway, please don't do anything unless we talk about it first. Promise?"

They nodded, eventually, and in unison.

She gave them both a hug. "There is something you can do that would cheer me up a bit," she suggested, looping her arms with each of theirs. "Cassie mentioned you tried a new recipe for chocolate fudge this morning, and I'd like to sample some."

Ivy cringed. "It's a bit gooey."

"And we added a tad too much cocoa," Fern added.

Martha chuckled. "I happen to love gooey cocoa fudge."

With the mood between them lightened, they spent a good

while together before finally deciding that perhaps using another recipe for fudge might be in order. When both sisters insisted on trying out the recipe then and there, Martha made her escape, grateful her knee had finally healed. She headed out, hoping for a visit with her grandchildren, and on the way happened to meet Victoria, who was carrying two baskets.

"I was just coming to see you," her daughter said after they kissed each other hello.

Martha smiled. "I was hoping I might see you, too, but in all truth, I was rather hoping I might take Lucy and Hannah out for a spell."

"Sorry. Comfort put the girls down for an early nap, so you're stuck with me. I just happen to know where there's a whole patch of blackberries that are ready to be picked, and I thought you might want to join me, even though you'll probably only want the leaves or something other than the fruit for one of your remedies. Unless you actually do want the berries now that you're turning over most of your duties." She handed one of the baskets to her mother. "See? I even remembered to bring some gloves for you."

Martha chuckled. "If there are enough for both of us, I'll pick some berries for Fern and Ivy, but I'll take some leaves, too. I may not need to make a lot of remedies for sick folks, but I'll still need a few to keep at the cottage."

"It will be nice to have you all to myself," Victoria noted and led her to the edge of the woods behind the cemetery to a rather small but lush patch of blackberries. Working side by side, they each gathered up enough blackberries to make a pair of pies and shared lighthearted conversation. When they finished, Victoria helped Martha to select a good cup's worth of healthy green leaves.

Ready to head back home again, Martha was surprised when

Victoria held her back from picking up her basket. "You might think it's none of my concern, but . . . but I'm worried about you, and since you're my mother, then I think I have a right to be concerned."

Martha tightened her hold on her basket. "What are you concerned about? I'm perfectly fine. I've found a lovely woman to be Trinity's new midwife. I have a new home of my own that I'll be moving into in just a few days, and thanks to you and your brother, I have more than enough to live on. You and Oliver are both living back in Trinity, too, which means I have everything to make me happy."

Victoria cocked a brow. "Everything, Mother?"

"If you're referring to Mr. Dillon and our decision not to marry—"

"Whether or not you marry him isn't the point. And I'm not worried about him, either. I'm worried about you. If you're as happy as you've insisted today, then tell me why I don't see anything but deep sadness in your eyes. Even when you're playing and laughing with little Lucy and Hannah, that sadness is still there. Most people probably wouldn't notice, but I'm your daughter. I know you, probably better than anyone else."

Martha felt tears welling and blinked them away. For the second time that day she had to defend herself, but it was much harder to do with Victoria than it had been with Fern and Ivy. It was easier, however, to talk more openly with her daughter. "Fern and Ivy talked to me about the very same thing just a few hours ago. You're right. I'm terribly sad that Mr. Dillon and I aren't going to marry. I just . . . I just thought we'd be able to work things out, but since we couldn't, I'm trying very, very hard to accept that it's all part of God's plan. That He has another future for me, and for Mr. Dillon, too."

Victoria hugged her mother and held her tight. "God doesn't

design a plan for any of us that will make us sad or disappointed or leave us suffering. His plan for us is always joyous and filled with His grace. Isn't that what you always taught me?"

Martha treasured being held in her daughter's arms, but she found little comfort in having her own words used against her. "I did," she admitted. "Not that you always listened or believed me," she added, without mentioning that Victoria never would have run away with that theatre troupe if she had taken those words to heart.

"No, I didn't, but I know better now, and you should, too."

35

The waning days of October brought cooler air and autumn colors to the landscape, offering proof that another season had begun.

Martha had witnessed almost all of Jane's capabilities—from birthing to treating ill women and children—for long enough now to be fully satisfied that Jane was not just a midwife, she was a very, very good one. She was also younger, stronger, and possibly a bit kinder than Martha, too, which helped to reaffirm Martha's decision to pass her calling on to her and gave her confidence that the women and children here would be well served.

Jane had completely taken over Martha's place as Trinity's midwife only yesterday, and Martha was ready to begin another phase of her life, too.

Having Oliver and his little girls so near helped immensely. She spent a lot of time with Victoria, too. Although they had never spoken again about the root of Martha's sadness, Martha was not able to match her daughter's faith and embrace what she had said, even though she had tried.

As part of her journey from dismal disappointment to eventual acceptance that she and Thomas were destined to live separate lives, Martha had started by moving her things into the cottage. After a final supper with Fern and Ivy three days ago, she had moved into the cottage and finally claimed it as her home. She had spent every night since she had moved here praying and praying for God to help her to be grateful for all that He had given her and asking Him to forgive her for resenting what He had not.

She returned from an unsuccessful walk in the woods to look for late-blooming flowers to brighten the cottage, unlocked the front door, and stepped inside wondering how she might spend another free afternoon. With a glance around the sitting room, she had to admit that the cottage finally looked like it was her own home now, instead of Aunt Hilda's. She just did not feel that way and wondered if she ever would.

She did not have to walk into the kitchen to know Bird's cage was probably empty, and she wandered from one bedroom to the other to look for the little bird.

She started in her bedroom, and she was surprised that she did not find Bird sleeping on her pillow like he had been doing lately. Freshly laundered, her mother's hand-stitched quilt lay atop the bed. She had taken the old curtains down, replaced them with new ones that were a little less lacey, and had put a hooked rug on the floorboards. As pretty as it looked, she would have been happier if the room had been plainer, as long as she shared the room with Thomas.

In the other bedroom, Bird was still nowhere in sight. Her grandmother's diary and her record book were lying on a small table she had purchased to sit between the pair of cots her grandchildren had used while they had been here.

She swallowed hard. Turning that diary over to Jane would be one of the hardest things she would ever have to do, but it would not be fair or right to keep it. The diary belonged to Trinity, and Grandmother Poore and Martha had only been its guardians—an obligation that she really should have passed on to Jane yesterday. She decided to do that tomorrow.

She turned and walked back to the sitting room. She could still detect the scent of the beeswax she had used to make the floorboards nearly as shiny as the trim on Aunt Hilda's furniture. Bird was not here, either, which meant he must have made himself at home in the kitchen.

She still had not set him free, in part, she admitted, because once she did, she would be living here totally and utterly alone. How sad to think that she was living here now, only to discover that living alone with her independence intact was not going to be as satisfying as she once thought it might be.

She left that thought behind when she walked into the kitchen. She had hung a number of plants and herbs from the rafters to dry, including the blackberry leaves she had picked with her daughter, and they would stay there until Jane made room for them at Dr. McMillan's.

Finally she spied Bird. He was perched rather happily on a bunch of pine branches she had hung up just the other day. She pulled a chair over, stood on the seat to lift him off, and then changed her mind. "I don't think you'll be here with me at the cottage for very long, so you may as well get used to sleeping in branches again," she said. She put the chair back, removed the embroidered cloth from atop the ancient kitchen table to safeguard the elegant stitching, and glanced over at the hearth.

She had stacked more firewood by the hearth, just in case of a chilly spell, and there was enough to fuel the cookstove for a few weeks, too. The rocking chairs in front of the hearth gleamed with fresh polish.

She opened the pantry door and stood face-to-face with happy memories of Aunt Hilda. The jug of her honey wine sat in a place of honor in front of enough sweets from the confectionery and staples to keep her cottage well supplied for a few weeks. She tucked the key to the cottage into the tin where she had stored the document Micah had given her, which made the cottage legally hers—as well as the letter Aunt Hilda had left for her—and closed the pantry door.

With nothing left to do that interested her, she had just decided to take a midday nap when there was a knock at the kitchen door. Praying neither Fern nor Ivy had come to pester her again about talking to Thomas to see if they could resolve their differences, she opened the door and practically gasped. "Samuel?"

"Thought I'd see if I could find my way to you out here."

"By yourself?" she exclaimed.

"Fancy walked me as far as the path up near Main Street. Managed the rest by myself. You gonna keep askin' questions or let a man inside to rest a spell?"

"Come in, of course. There's a table straight ahead. Here. Let me help you," she gushed and managed to get him seated without incident. "You're my first official visitor. Did you know that?" she asked as she took a seat across from him.

He shrugged. "Don't see much reason for folks to walk all the way out here, other than curiosity."

She was glad he could not see the disappointment she knew was written on her face. "Is that why you came? Because you were curious about where I lived now?" she asked.

"Some. Had a hankerin' for some of that honey wine you gave me a while back. Considerin' you've been too busy to visit lately, I figured I'd come to ask if you had any more."

"I'm sorry. My days have been a little hectic," she offered with no small measure of guilt. "I've got a jug in the pantry you can take home."

He shrugged. "Wouldn't turn down a sip now, if you offered it. Otherwise, a glass of water would suit."

"I'm not a very good hostess, am I?" she said by way of apology. She left the table and put a small glass of honey wine into his hand when she returned.

He took a sip and set the glass on the table. "Not sure I understand why you're livin' out here all by yourself instead of marryin' that young fella Dillon whose been chasin' your skirts for almost a year and managed to win your heart."

His words nearly knocked her clear off her seat. "You know about Thomas? How on earth could you possibly know anything about him? Or . . . or us?"

"I just do. Well? You got an answer for me instead of a question?"

She huffed, too annoyed to mince words. "A very simple answer. He doesn't want to marry me, and before you ask how I know that, it's really very simple. He told me so."

He chuckled. "And you believed him?"

"Of course I believed him. And even if I didn't, there isn't anything I can do about it, because he's already told me he wasn't interested in listening to anything I had to say on the matter. Besides, he's moved out of Trinity to his cabin on Candle Lake."

"Oh. So that's it. You're gonna let a good man walk right outta your life. Just like that. I guess what I heard about you lovin' him weren't right. 'Cause if you did, I know you'd be stubborn enough to put up a fight and get him back instead of mopin' out here feelin' sorry for yourself."

"I'm not moping around. I like living out here," she argued, and her pulse quickened. "But I will admit I'm sad. But only because I'm trying to accept that we're not meant to be together and that God's plan for us is something else . . . something we each have to discover," she said, repeating the same argument she had used with Victoria.

"Guess you know what you're doin' then," he said and got up to leave. "I'll get Fancy to show me the way to the confectionery and set Miss Fern and Miss Ivy straight."

She bolted out of her seat and held on to his arm to keep him right where he was standing. "You know Fern and Ivy? You *talked* to them?" she asked, surprised the recluse had talked to anyone in town other than her.

He snorted. "I ain't been blind forever," he argued. "Just 'cause I don't like livin' close to folks don't mean I don't know most of them in Trinity, except for the ones crowdin' in lately. I weren't too keen on lettin' those two women inside when they came callin' a few days ago askin' me to convince you to talk to Dillon, but I smelled that bag of sweets they had with 'em and decided it was worth listenin' to what they had to say."

Martha was getting annoyed. "Fern and Ivy mean well, but they had no right to involve you in something so . . . so private and personal," she argued, her heart pounding now.

"Don't get your skirts all twisted up. Like I said, I'll set 'em straight. Shudda known they had everythin' backwards. Women usually do, 'cept for you, of course. Never knew you to wobble about anythin', 'specially somethin' you wanted or needed to do. Shudda remembered that. Now, you got that jug of honey wine you promised me?"

"Yes, I do," she said and made sure the cork was tight before she handed it to him. "You're a good friend, Samuel. I'm sorry if I didn't act that way with you just now."

He shrugged. "You got a whole army of friends ready and waitin' to help you any time. Family, too. All you gotta do is ask." He took a few steps and turned around to face her again. "I'm not much of a church-goin' man. Never have been. Don't claim to know much Scripture, either, but I know enough 'bout God to believe in Him. And I sure don't think He filled two people's hearts with love for each other if He didn't mean for 'em to hold on to it."

Martha was too wound up to take a nap after Samuel delivered his faith lecture and left her standing at the back door.

She had a good mind to march back to town, sit Fern and Ivy down, and set them straight herself. Instead, she left that for Samuel to do and paced around the cottage, walking from one room to the next and back again. Over and over again. Until her frustration with those two meddling sisters was under control.

Her visit with Samuel, however, still haunted her, and she knew that until she made some sort of peace with all that he had said, she would pace a hole in the floorboards in every room of that cottage. And while she was at it, she may as well try to make peace with what Victoria had said to her, too. Since that might take a while, she walked around the outside of the cottage for fear that if she walked any farther away and meandered through the woods, she would only end up getting lost.

"I'm living out here in the cottage because I want to be here. I do," she insisted. When her conscience argued back, she ignored it and spied several curved pinecones lying on the ground, which would make a remedy for congestion. Out of habit, she bent down and selected just one, since the others were damaged, and carried it along with her as she resumed her way.

Unfortunately, her conscience was wholly dissatisfied with her answer. "All right, fine," she admitted. "I don't really want to be alone or to live here alone, but that's the way it is, and I'll just have to learn to accept it," she grumbled.

In frustration, she balled her hands into fists, but the edges of the pinecone pricked her flesh, and she tossed it away, "Drat it, Thomas," she cried, leveling deeper disappointment at the real source of her misery as she rounded the side of the cottage. "You made a mess of everything with your demands, Thomas. You stubborn, stubborn man!"

With her chest heaving and tears blinding her eyes, she stopped in her tracks. It was pointless and futile to point blame at everyone else when she deserved blame for the way things ended between them, just as much as he did. Was she the only one who had thought their love and their future together was a gift from God, or had he felt that way, too? Or had they both been wrong, misled by broken dreams when God had other plans for them?

She brushed away her tears and walked away from the cottage and into the woods. In her heart, she knew there was only one way to end the confusion and the torment that was tearing at her soul.

She kept walking until she finally found a grassy clearing where the tree canopy that surrounded her could not keep the sun from shining down upon her. She dropped to her knees and began to pray that God's grace and His peace would be able to find her, too.

She humbled herself before Him and truly opened her heart to Him for the first time in many, many weeks. "Heavenly Father, forgive me for turning away from You and for losing my faith in You. I need You now more than ever before because I don't know what to think or what to do anymore. I'm so confused and . . . and my heart hurts. It really *hurts*, and I don't know how to make the hurt go away without You. I know that Victoria and Samuel are right. The ache in my heart doesn't come from

You, because You are a gracious and loving God. You don't break hearts or fill them with pain. You fill them with hope and with peace and with Your abiding love to comfort them until the pain we find so unbearable goes away."

She paused and gave her prayer a chance to rise up to the heavens and rest at His throne before she continued. "If the love that Thomas and I have for each other is truly a gift from You—that You want us to share as husband and wife—please fill my heart with hope and give me the wisdom to know what I can do to have him set aside his fears and embrace Your gift, too. But if that's not what You want for us, if You have other blessings waiting for us to embrace, please fill my heart with peace so I can wait until You reveal them to me, and help Thomas to do the same. Thy blessed will be done."

She remained on her knees, praising Him, worshiping Him, and thanking Him for loving her and showering her with His grace while her soul rested in the comfort of His love.

Hours later, as the sun began to dip low, she felt her heart tremble as every bit of heartache slipped away and made room not for peace, but for hope—precious, empowering, loving, and blessed hope.

Overjoyed, she offered a litany of praise and gratitude, and she held tight to her faith and her hope, with God's grace showing her the way to win Thomas back.

She hurried back through the woods to the path that led to town. She went to Dr. McMillan's house first to talk to both of her children, then off to the confectionary before rushing off again to a few other homes. She had a stitch in her side by the time she reached her last stop, which was Samuel's cabin, and she had to wait a moment to catch her breath before she knocked on the door.

When Fancy opened the door, she charged past him, ignored

Will, who was sitting on his hammock practicing knots again, and went straight to Samuel. "I talked to my family first, and they've agreed to help me. You told me I had an army of friends who'd be willing to help me, too, if I asked them. I've already been to see the others. Now I'm asking you and Fancy, too. Will you help me convince Thomas to give me another chance?"

He grunted. "I told Fancy you'd be here before dark. Tell us what you want us to do."

Will jumped off of his hammock. "You got somethin' I can do to help?"

She grinned. "Only if you bring your spyglass."

36

By seven o'clock the next morning, Martha's volunteer army was in place, waiting impatiently for her to call them into action and follow the orders she had given to each of them.

As planned, some of her friends were stationed out of view of Thomas's cabin on the shores of Candle Lake. Will was farthest off so he would have the best vantage point. He was high up in a tree with his spyglass, ready to give one of two prearranged signals. Below him, Fancy was at the base of the tree keeping an eye on Will and standing ready to bring him back with the others when his job was done.

Samuel, however, was waiting with Martha and the rest of her friends from the confectionery household, including Cassie. They were hidden now behind a thick copse of evergreen bushes, and they filled their time waiting by eating a breakfast they had brought with them and keeping their voices low while they discussed what each of them thought might happen here today.

Her family had taken up positions a bit farther away from the property itself, while friends would be arriving a little bit later.

Martha was wearing the fine gown she had worn the day Victoria had gotten married, a visual cue important to her plan. She munched on an apple fritter as she glanced around at her friends and smiled. She was not leaving until Thomas listened to every word she had to say. How long she would stay beyond that depended entirely on how stubborn he would be.

She polished off her fritter, licked the crumbs from her fingertips, and chose another before she walked over to inspect the array of goods piled together on the ground. A couple of rolling pins, a frying pan, a fire poker, and two brooms with dust pans could be dangerous weapons, especially when they were wielded by determined women. She had other uses in mind for them, but she counted on Thomas remembering just how dangerous any one of those household items could be. Ivy had mistakenly taken him for an intruder last winter and had smacked him in the face with a poker, and he still bore a tiny scar that cut through one of his eyebrows to remind him.

Chuckling, she looked a little farther in the woods, where they had left the wagon they had traveled here on. It was laden with baskets of food they had packed for the after-battle feast they would enjoy. Jane was positioned there so none of the animals who called the forest their home discovered the feast.

Martha now fetched one particular covered basket, and Bird started squawking and knocking against the sides. "It's almost time," she crooned and carried him deeper into the woods. She found a tiny clearing where the sun was able to break through and she still had sight of the wagon.

She took a deep breath and lifted him out of the basket. Bird hopped on her finger before flying off, higher and higher. When he landed on a high branch, he looked around as if realizing for the first time that he was in a different place with a different landscape he could explore.

Today, Martha's heart was in a different place, too, and she walked over to the tree where he had perched and looked up at him. "You've been well enough to fly away for a while now, but you haven't done that because I think somehow you knew I needed you, and I wasn't ready to see you go," she whispered. "But I'm ready now, Bird. I'm not afraid that you won't survive on your own anymore, either. I have every hope that you will, because I know God will be watching over you, just as He'll be watching over me and Thomas. Good-bye, my friend."

Then she turned and walked away.

And she never looked back.

She did, however, catch a brief glimpse of him through a break in the canopy. He was flying overhead, directly toward a flock of birds. Blinking back a tear, she hoped they had come to welcome him home.

Soon after Martha returned to wait with the others for a signal from Will, Victoria arrived with her husband, as well as Oliver and his family. They had just joined the others when a series of chatters that closely resembled the sound of a pair of squirrels fighting over a nut sent Martha's heart racing. "That's Will's signal that he sees Mr. Dillon walking around inside the cabin. We all need to be quiet now, but we don't need to move into position just yet," she whispered, hoping the other folks who were coming were on their way here.

Scarcely five minutes later, her heart skipped a beat when she saw the front door open. When Thomas walked out carrying a travel bag, her heart skipped two more. He was leaving, which thoroughly upended her plans. Desperate to salvage them, even though both Victoria and Oliver were already in position well beyond the property to keep those plans alive, she needed to get everyone in place so she could reach him before he drove off in his buggy.

"Hurry up, everyone. The moment he steps a foot inside that stable, where he won't be able to see any movement at all out here, we have to get into position. You know where to go and what to do. And hurry. We need to be ready when he comes out."

Her heart pounded harder and harder with every step she took as she walked toward the stable. Her legs were shaking so hard, she had to make a deliberate effort to keep from tripping over her own two feet.

But she soon reached the place she had chosen so that she would be the first thing he saw when he walked out of the stable. A sense of calm she had not expected washed over her.

When she heard his footsteps and the clip-clop of a horse's hooves, she swallowed hard, lifted one last prayer to the heavens, and tilted up her chin . . . just enough to let him know she had found her way back to being stubborn again. She only hoped he could find his way to seeing that quality of hers as endearing again, too.

Thomas came into view and nearly stole her breath away, but he was not driving his buggy. Dressed in his finest frock coat, he was holding the reins to his horse, which walked behind him. He braced to a halt the instant he saw her standing there. With his eyes wide, he cocked his head and stared at her. "What are you doing here?"

"I thought we should talk, and since you never responded to my note and moved out of town, you didn't leave me any other choice but to seek you out here, and . . . and I really don't intend to leave until you agree to talk to me," she said as gently but as firmly as she could. "And if you do, my children and their spouses are waiting along the roadway to intercept you."

When he broke his gaze and looked beyond her, he had a

twinkle in his eye she had not seen for a long while. He dropped the reins and took a step forward. "And if I refuse, I assume you've brought an assembly of your friends, including a blind man and a couple of children, who are armed with nothing more than a few brooms or rolling pins to convince me otherwise."

She smiled. "Don't be ridiculous. I have other plans for them today. And for us," she said and boldly took a step closer to him.

He frowned. "I'm afraid I don't have time for a long chat with you, which I suspect you had planned down to every word you wanted to say as well as every word you wanted to hear *me* say. In case you haven't noticed, I'm dressed for a very important meeting. I was just leaving, and you've completely disrupted very important plans that I've delayed making for far too long." He pointed to the travel bag tied to the horse's saddle.

"Then I'd ask you to change your plans. What we need to talk about is more important than anything else you expect to do today," she whispered, surprised when he took another step toward her. Drat. Did he have to look so strong and so handsome? And did her lips really have to tingle and beg for his kiss? Really, now? When she had to keep her mind focused on more important things?

That twinkle in his eye got brighter when he closed the distance between them until there was almost no room to put a hand between them. "If I told you where I was planning to go today and what I was hoping to do, you might think differently."

With his breath fanning her cheeks and his gaze so intense, she could scarcely breathe. "There isn't anything you could say that would convince me to think any differently at all," she replied, too mesmerized by being this close to him again to step back, even if she tried.

He really was going to make this hard for her, wasn't he?

He made it even harder when he took her hand and held it.

"What if I told you that I was planning to ride back to Trinity and pound on your cottage door until you let me in and listened to every word I had to say?"

Every word, every thought, every plea she had carefully organized in her mind to use when she talked with Thomas today flew right out of her head, leaving only disbelief behind. "Y-you were?"

He nodded, and his expression softened. "I've been a stubborn, overconfident, unreasonable fool. I lost faith in you and I lost faith in myself, but far worse, I almost completely lost my faith in God. Even if I had to beg for your forgiveness until my voice was hoarse, I would have kept on begging until I had no voice at all. Please tell me that you forgive me, and tell me I'm not too late, that there's still reason for me to hope that you'll forgive me and give me the honor of claiming you, one day, as my wife, even though I've acted so badly and don't deserve you."

Overwhelmed, she could scarcely contain the joy that washed over her heart. But she couldn't resist asking, "Even if it takes months or even years for me to find another midwife for Trinity before we marry?"

"I'll be right here, waiting for you. I might be down on my knees praying morning and night for the strength to wait, but that's exactly where I've been for the past few nights, until last night, when I realized that I had made a terrible mistake."

Moved by the sincerity of his words and the emotion churning in his eyes, she was stunned that God had touched his heart at almost the same time He had touched her own.

Unwilling to tease him any longer, the sound of wagon wheels caught his attention. He looked to the source and pointed beyond the others to a buggy that had just pulled up to join them. "Is that my *sister*? Y-you even asked Anne and her husband to be here?"

She did not bother to look and shrugged. "Once I told Anne that I was coming to see you today and why I was coming, she insisted on being here. Now that she's finally arrived, I suspect Eleanor and Micah aren't too far behind with little Jacob."

She barely had the words out of her mouth before his eyes opened even wider. "I don't see another buggy, but . . . but is that Reverend Welsh I see riding down the entrance path now? You actually convinced *him* to be part of this little plan of yours?" he asked and stared at her.

"Reverend Welsh doesn't know anything more than what I told him," she insisted.

He cocked a brow, but there was just a hint of a smile on his lips. "What did you tell him?"

She moistened her lips and squeezed his hand. "I explained to him that we had planned to marry but had had a disagreement over my duties as midwife. And that now that Jane Trew has taken over my responsibilities, there wasn't any reason for you not to give me another chance, other than the fact that you were too stubborn, a quality that's not always as endearing as you claim it to be."

She paused to swallow the lump in her throat and repeated almost the same exact words he had once spoken to her. "And I told him that you challenge me, Thomas, and you always have. That you have a clear and honest view of the world and your place in it as a godly man, and that you're more worried about other people most of the time than you are for yourself. That you're unlike any man I've ever known, and that I love you with all that I am or hope to be. And that I was going to come and stand right here until you talked with me and agreed to give me another chance. To give us another chance. And since I had every hope that you would, I asked him to come and marry us."

He took her other hand. "Today?"

"Right now. Then I'll give my friends the order they're expecting to hear."

He nearly choked. "To do what? Since I have every intention of accepting your proposal and having Reverend Welsh marry us right now, there's no need for any of your friends to use those ridiculous weapons on me."

Before letting him think she was completely daft, she pressed a quick kiss to his lips. "The weapons aren't for you. They're for our cabin. I suspect this little army of mine might need to tidy things up a bit before they set out the wedding feast we brought with us."

He pulled her into his arms and kissed her back. Then he kissed her one more time until she was breathless. "Is there anything else we need to talk about or do before I ask Reverend Welsh to marry us?"

"I can't think of a thing, other than maybe enjoying one more kiss. Can you?" she offered with a grin and wondered if the minister would consider marrying them just as they stood, holding each other as if they might never let go.

He answered her question with another very sweet and passionate kiss. And then just one more.

Imagine that.

Delia Parr is the author of seventeen historical and inspirational historical romance novels, including *The Midwife's Tale*, *Hearts Awakening*, *Love's First Bloom*, and *Hidden Affections*. The mother of three grown children, she was a longtime high school teacher in southern New Jersey before retiring to Florida's sunny west coast. In between visits to her grandchildren in several different states, she spends her time writing and volunteering alongside other women who share a bond of sisterhood as sisters of faith.

More Historical Fiction

You May Also Enjoy . . .

Still reeling from her father's death, Lucinda Pennyworth arrives in Buttermilk Falls, New York, seeking a home with her mother's family—and a fresh start. As she begins to establish a new life for herself, she dares to hope that a handsome West Point cadet may have a role in her future.

Flirtation Walk by Siri Mitchell
sirimitchell.com

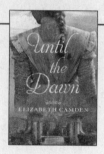

National Weather Bureau volunteer Sophie van Riijn has used the abandoned mansion Dierenpark as a resource and a refuge for years. But now the Vandermark heir has returned to put an end to the rumors about the place. When old secrets come to light, will tragedy triumph or can hope and love prevail?

Until the Dawn by Elizabeth Camden
elizabethcamden.com

◊ BETHANYHOUSE